Praise
Confessions of Super Mom

"Overflows with laugh-out-loud and read-out-loud moments."
—*The State* (Columbia, SC)

"Melanie Lynne Hauser's quirky characters sparkle as brightly as a newly Swiffered floor, and her writing shines like freshly polished glass."

—Meg Cabot, author of *The Princess Diaries* and *Queen of Babble*

"At the heart of this story is a narrative about a lonely, wronged woman who just wants to do right by her children and stand up to an uncontrollable world. Hauser slips in soliloquies on motherhood and womanhood that, though brief, are moving, showing us Birdie Lee's heart and, in that, the wishes and dreams of Super Moms everywhere." —*Publishers Weekly*

"Forget the speeding bullets, locomotives, and tall buildings—with wit, humor, and some sage motherly advice, Melanie Lynne Hauser's Super Mom finally gives readers a true hero for our time."
—Jennifer O'Connell, author of *Off the Record* and *Dress Rehearsal*

"Never has there been a more appealingly down-to-earth heroine or a superhero with more enviable powers. Moms everywhere will wish they could be like the Super Mom of Melanie Lynne Hauser's charming, funny, and heartfelt novel . . . and will ultimately realize they already are."
—Pamela Redmond Satran, author of *Babes in Captivity*

CONFESSIONS OF

MELANIE LYNNE HAUSER

 NEW AMERICAN LIBRARY

New American Library
Published by New American Library, a division of
Penguin Group (USA) Inc., 375 Hudson Street,
New York, New York 10014, USA
Penguin Group (Canada), 90 Eglinton Avenue East, Suite 700, Toronto,
Ontario M4P 2Y3, Canada (a division of Pearson Penguin Canada Inc.)
Penguin Books Ltd., 80 Strand, London WC2R 0RL, England
Penguin Ireland, 25 St. Stephen's Green, Dublin 2,
Ireland (a division of Penguin Books Ltd.)
Penguin Group (Australia), 250 Camberwell Road, Camberwell, Victoria 3124,
Australia (a division of Pearson Australia Group Pty. Ltd.)
Penguin Books India Pvt. Ltd., 11 Community Centre, Panchsheel Park,
New Delhi – 110 017, India
Penguin Group (NZ), cnr Airborne and Rosedale Roads, Albany,
Auckland 1310, New Zealand (a division of Pearson New Zealand Ltd.)
Penguin Books (South Africa) (Pty.) Ltd., 24 Sturdee Avenue,
Rosebank, Johannesburg 2196, South Africa

Penguin Books Ltd., Registered Offices:
80 Strand, London WC2R 0RL, England

Published by New American Library, a division of Penguin Group (USA) Inc.
Previously published in a Dutton edition.

First New American Library Printing, August 2006
10 9 8 7 6 5 4 3 2 1

⬛ REGISTERED TRADEMARK—MARCA REGISTRADA

New American Library Trade Paperback ISBN: 0-451-21856-6

The Library of Congress has cataloged the hardcover edition of this title as follows:
Hauser, Melanie Lynne.
Confessions of Super Mom/by Melanie Lynne Hauser.
p.   cm.
ISBN 0-525-94910-0
1. Motherhood—Humor. 2. Mothers—Humor. 3. Parenting—Humor. I. Title.
PN6231.M68H38 2005
813'.6—dc22   2005002099

Set in New Baskerville

Printed in the United States of America

To Dennis, Alec, and Ben, who taught me to fly

CHAPTER 1

Every superhero has an origin.

That's what Martin says, and since he's thirteen, short for his age, and somewhat of a geek, I'm tempted to believe him.

OK, so here goes—for the first time I am about to reveal . . .

The Origin of Super Mom. (That's me.)

To tell the truth, it's a little embarrassing. I wasn't put into a rocket and sent to Earth by my parents just as my home planet exploded. I wasn't given a special ring by visiting aliens. I wasn't bitten by a radioactive spider.

No, it wasn't anything nearly so glamorous; my beginnings are quite humble. I was merely the innocent victim of a Horrible Swiffer Accident.

It all began on a bright, sunny Tuesday morning. Right away you can tell that this doesn't fit in with other superhero origins, or so Martin says. Most origin stories take place at night, usually in a laboratory or a dark alley. And nearly all are accompanied by really dramatic thunderstorms.

But no. My story, my origin, began on a weekday morning during a commercial break for the *Today* show. On the floor. Of my bathroom.

It was a typical school day. Kelly and Martin were shuffling through the kitchen like zombies while I nipped at their heels, making peanut-butter sandwiches, signing permission slips, and shepherding them out the door just in time for the bus. Then I collapsed on the sofa with my second cup of coffee and caught a few minutes of Katie and Matt.

Now, this is my favorite time of day. The only time when I have a few moments to myself, the only time I can just relax and let my mind take me places no one else wants to visit with me anymore. Sometimes I allow myself a glimpse into the future, but more and more these days, as my children are growing up and away, I find myself in the past—when my children were small and soft and perfect, when my hand reached down, not up, to smooth a lock of hair.

So on this morning of my origin, I settled in on the couch and sipped my coffee and turned on the TV. And there was Katie Couric interviewing Adam West for some cheesy Batman reunion movie. I giggled at all the old film clips—you know, Adam West never really looked that good in tights, even back in the sixties. He had a serious case of man boobs.

But then the next thing I knew, I was following my memory down a sidewalk full of cracks and pits—the sidewalk in front of our old house. I was running after Martin, who was running after Kelly. And he was in his Batman "costume"—a cape I made out of an old pillowcase. He used to wear that thing all the time; he would have slept in it if I hadn't been convinced he would choke to death. He was so cute in that cape, all brave and serious.

So in my mind I was chasing Kelly and Martin down this sidewalk. But where were we all running? To the ice-cream man? Away from some horrible monster? Were we late?

Early? Or just having fun? Even as I was following them in my memory, so real I could see the faded checks on the pillowcase, smell the fresh asphalt on the road, I was wishing I could remember. Sometimes it seems so sad, the parts of their childhood I've forgotten. Sometimes I look at them now—big and sullen, hiding behind the awkward mask of adolescence—and I can't remember what they looked like when they were my babies.

But I shook the cobwebs from my brain, took another sip of coffee, and concentrated on the television, chuckling at a very old, very paunchy Adam West trying to wedge himself into the Batmobile. I think he got stuck because right away they cut to a commercial. Then the phone rang and it was a telemarketer and I had some fun with her, sobbing that my husband had just died and I was getting ready to go to his funeral so it wasn't the best time to talk about lowering my interest rates. And all of a sudden my favorite time of the day was over. Just as fleeting, just as fragile, as childhood itself.

And so to work. I put my coffee cup in the dishwasher, gave the counters a final wipe, and headed upstairs to the bathroom. Where I was confronted by a Stain of Unusual Origin.

It was in the middle of the floor, half on, half off the bath mat. It was purplish brown. It was disgusting.

I dropped down on all fours, my nose to the ground, sniffing like a bird dog.

"Hmmm," I said, tasting it, smacking my lips like the professional I was. "Not ammonia. Or salt. Maybe carbon-based, with a little red dye number two? Definitely not Preparation H."

Which left a variety of options, since this is the only bathroom in the house and we all have to share. I ticked off the usual suspects: lip gloss, Vaseline, hair dye, nail polish, mouthwash, soda, chocolate milk, foundation, eyeliner, model paint, melted crayons, exploded pen, petrified candy bar, blood. Finally I grabbed a sponge and tried to remove it with plain old water. Optimistic, I know. But you have to try.

Nothing. So I took the bath mat downstairs and threw it into the washer, then grabbed my trusty Swiffer and went back for the linoleum.

Now, I consider Swiffer the greatest invention in modern housecleaning history, right up there with treated dust cloths and flushable toilet-bowl wipes. I have a special closet stocked with all of my favorite tools, and the Swiffer has the place of honor, next to my lightweight foldable stepladder.

I studied the stain from all angles, positioned my trusty Swiffer, pulled the lever back, and released one quick stream of cleaning fluid. It hit right in the middle of the stain and then I Swiffered, gently yet vigorously. I stepped back to survey my handiwork.

The stain was still there.

I frowned. I released three long streams of fluid, Swiffered less gently, more vigorously, then looked again.

The stain was still there. It hadn't even faded. It had, in fact, darkened and spread.

I dropped to my knees again, sniffing, analyzing. Definitely not makeup or soda or crayons. Paint would have faded. Blood . . . it didn't look like blood to me. But just in case . . .

I ran to get a bottle of bleach, sponging some on the stain. No improvement at all.

By now I was on a mission. No stain had ever defeated me before. And I wasn't about to let this one get away.

I trotted to my closet and grabbed every cleaner I owned: Pine-Sol, Industrial Strength Windex, that new orange cleaner I bought from an infomercial, as well as old-fashioned Borox and Clorox and even Lava Soap. I sprayed and scrubbed and wiped and dabbed; the stain didn't budge. And soon it was obvious that the stain was stronger than any one individual cleaner. It was also obvious that if I didn't hurry up and get going, I would be late for work.

It was not obvious, at least to me, that I'd forgotten to turn on the exhaust fan.

I had one last chance to eradicate this vile, dastardly stain. I was angry, hot, light-headed, and late. So I did something I'd never done before. Something I'd only heard whispered about at PTA meetings or in secluded aisles at the grocery store—one of those Suburban Legends.

Little did I know I was about to become the stuff of legend too. For what happened next is It. How I came to be. The origin of my superheroness.

I poured everything—all the bleach and Pine-Sol and Borox and Clorox and even the Lava Soap—into the Swiffer reservoir. Then I aimed, pulled the trigger, and fired an unknown number of rounds at the stain. I kept firing, my finger growing numb as the stain finally weakened, gasped, yet still clung to life. I Swiffered and Swiffered until my arms took on a life of their own, until my head spun and the room blurred and all of a sudden the flowers on the wallpaper came to life. They leaped off the wall, grabbed petals, and started singing "Ring Around the Rosy" as they circled me. I screamed and dropped my Swiffer, inhaling a swift, sharp

plume of the most powerful cleaning formula heretofore unknown to man . . .

And then I passed out.

I don't know how long I lay there, although I do remember thinking I'd better clean the bottom of the toilet with a
toothbrush, as from my perspective—flat on my back—things
were looking a little dingy.

But I couldn't move, couldn't get my body to work right.
For a moment or two I tried. I sent determined messages to
my legs, arms, head, urging them to move. But they refused,
pinned to the floor by unseen chains.

And I continued to hallucinate. I fell into a deep well of
images and thoughts: The daisies from the wallpaper were
there, still dancing and singing; Adam West and his man
boobs were roaring past in the Batmobile—he laughed, then
paused to give me a knowing wink; even the stain, which now
looked like a huge jellyfish floating in the sky, danced and
wiggled its hips. The air was so thick with chemicals—pine
and orange and bleach and ammonia—that I gasped and
wheezed until I gave up and let the fumes invade my lungs.

Then the flowers changed their tune, their Munchkin-
esque voices starting in on "The Daring Young Man on the
Flying Trapeze"—the song I used to sing to Martin and Kelly
when they were babies. *"He flies through the air, with the greatest
of ease, the daring young man on the flying trapeze . . ."* and I was
flying—flying down a familiar sidewalk, chasing after Martin
and Kelly, Martin's cape billowing out behind him, Kelly's
pigtails doing the same. The sidewalk was endless and grew
wider as we ran, the children giggling while I shouted for
them to watch out, look both ways before you cross that
street! Hold hands if you're going to the park! Doesn't any-

one have to go to the bathroom? And all the while they kept laughing and running as I chased them, my arms outstretched, waiting to catch them if they fell. Then they grew bigger and bigger and stopped laughing; they just kept running away until Martin's cape flew off and hit me square in the face so I couldn't see them anymore. I couldn't see if they were all right. I couldn't see where they were going, and I was falling, falling—falling off the trapeze. The daring young man's hands reached out to me. I tried to grab them, only he turned into Martin and Kelly. We all reached out to each other and . . . and . . .

"Mom?"

I landed hard on the bathroom floor. I tried to sit up but hit my head on the toilet bowl and fell back down again.

"God! Mom? Are you all right? Mom?"

I opened my eyes and blinked. Kelly's face was looming over me, so pale that the tiny freckles on her nose stood out like flecks from a copper penny. Her eyes were enormous; she looked like she was about to cry.

"Honey? Honey—oh, ohhhh . . ." I tried to sit up again, but my head was throbbing.

"Martin! She's OK! Martin!" Kelly shouted in my ear.

"Sshhhh," I whispered, managing a brave smile. "Just help me up, all right?"

She put her arm under me and helped me to my feet, so gently I had to stop for a minute and stare, wondering who she was and what she had done to my fifteen-year-old daughter.

"Mom?" Martin ran up. He rubbed his eyes with his sleeve and looked so young and frightened, I wanted to hug him. But I couldn't; my body ached and throbbed and felt alien to me. There was a moment when I wasn't sure if I remembered how to use my legs.

"What time is it, sweetie? Why are you back so early? Why aren't you at school?"

"It's four thirty," Kelly replied.

"What?" My legs scrambled beneath me. "Four thirty? Son of a—! But I missed work! I missed the whole day! What happened?"

"When we came home from school you were passed out."

"Yeah. You were covered by all sorts of towels and empty bottles and stuff. What happened, Mom? Been on a little cleaning binge?" Martin tried to laugh but his eyes looked scared.

"I don't know . . . I just . . . wait . . . the stain! Is the stain still there?" I tried to turn around, but Kelly and Martin kept steering me toward my bedroom.

"Mom, you need to lie down," Kelly insisted. "Should we call a doctor?"

"I don't need to lie down. Apparently I've been lying down all day. Oh, jeez. I need to call work. They'll kill me— Hand me the phone."

"Just wait a few minutes. The fumes were pretty strong in there. Are you sure you're all right?"

"Yeah, you know, those chemicals can really alter your brain waves. Were you trippin'?" Martin looked a little too interested.

"Was I what?"

"You know. Trippin'. I mean, you inhaled a ton of chemicals, you know. So what did you see? Talking pigs? Rainbows? Bugs?"

"Dancing flowers," I replied, easing into bed.

"Dancing flowers? Cool! What else?"

"Adam West in the Batmobile. You wearing that old cape you had when you were little, remember? And Kelly had pig-tails. Oh, and a big jellyfish."

"Wow! This is so great! Batman? Really? Did the jellyfish talk?"

"Martin"—Kelly folded her arms across her chest and shook her head—"Martin, she's obviously sustained major head trauma. I'm going to call Dad."

"No!" I almost fell out of bed. "No. Kelly, honey? I don't think we need to call your father. I'm fine, really I am. I just got a little dizzy from all the fumes and I must have passed out. But I'm fine now. Really I am. Fine." I plastered a big, comforting Mom smile on my face and nodded. But I wasn't fine. My limbs and joints felt stiff and heavy, my head was pounding, my eardrums hurt. And it seemed like my blood was boiling inside my veins, I felt so hot beneath my skin.

But the last thing I needed was a visit from my ex, Doctor Dan. I would take a vision of Adam West in ill-fitting Spandex over that, any old day.

"I think we can manage just fine, honey. But could you make me some tea? Maybe some toast?"

My daughter hesitated at the door, her face still pale and young, and I had a quick glimpse of her as a child, always so serious, her face pinched and solemn, her gray eyes wide and wary.

"I'm all right, sweetie. Really I am. A little tea and toast and I'll be myself again. Don't worry."

"OK," she finally said, turning to leave. "Martin, don't bother her."

"What a wench." Martin scratched his nose.

"She's just concerned. You know how she gets when she's scared."

"Yeah. Bossy and mean. Just like she is when she's not scared. Do you want another pillow?" He shoved an extra one behind my back, propping me up so that my spine was all twisted, which didn't help my headache in the least. But you know what? I didn't mind at all.

It's such bliss to be cared for. And when you're a mother—a single mother—that doesn't happen very often. I just wanted to fall back and surrender myself to my children's attention, let them kill me with their kindness. Literally— Martin shoved another pillow behind my back, cracking my skull against the headboard.

"Oof! Thanks, sweetie. Hey, could you bring me a couple of aspirin and a glass of water?" I closed my eyes and imagined lolling in bed all evening, my dinner brought to me on a silver tray, my children dabbing at my lips with a linen napkin.

"OK, Mom!" Martin bounced off the bed, scattering the pillows, wrenching my back again. But I smiled anyway, knowing that at least for this moment my children remembered me. Loved me.

I snuggled down under the covers and waited for my tea and toast and aspirin. I waited, and waited, and waited . . . Noises in the kitchen. Radio blaring, microwave beeping, dishes and pans clattering. Now the phone was ringing, my children were shouting—

"Miss Know-It-All, I do so know how to microwave brownie mix!"

"Yeah, but you're supposed to put it in a bowl first, imbecile."

"Well, duh!"

"Nice vocabulary, Einstein!"

I sighed. I threw off my blanket and stumbled down the hall, stopping at the top of the stairs. "I'll be right down," I croaked. "Eat something nutritious!" But no one answered.

"Never mind about me," I said with a sniff as I shuffled off to the bathroom, "up here, all alone, weak from toxic fumes. I might fall and hit my head and have a brain hemorrhage, but that's OK. Just put my body out with the garbage if I don't make it through the night. . . ." I opened up the medicine cabinet and grabbed some aspirin; then I stared in the mirror. My eyes were bloodshot, my face was pale, and there were deep, purple crescents under my eyes. "God." I shivered, turning away from the apparition in the mirror. A forty-one-year-old woman does not look her best after a day spent sprawled on the bathroom floor.

Suddenly I tripped over an empty bottle: that new orange cleaner from the infomercial. I bent down to pick it up and read the label: CAUTION! HEAVILY CONCENTRATED. DILUTE WITH WATER FIRST. DO NOT MIX WITH OTHER CLEANERS, ESPECIALLY BLEACH.

"Too late for that," I mumbled. Then something else caught my eye.

The stain. The vile, dastardly stain. It was still there. Grinning at me. Mocking me.

I couldn't help myself; I sank to my knees and reached for an empty can of Borox.

But before I could grasp it, my right hand burned. It went rigid and pointed right at the stain, something wet and hot and gritty shot out from my fingertips, and then my right hand was upon it, palm down, scrubbing and scrubbing so fast it was just a blur. I tried to stop myself—my left hand grabbed my arm, but still it kept scrubbing and scrubbing, liquid shooting out in measured spurts. I thought I must be bleeding or something; I tried to cry out but no sound came—

And then all of a sudden it stopped. My right arm hung limp by my side. I shook it and it felt all right; I flexed my fingers but saw no blood.

But there was something else I didn't see. The stain. It was gone. In fact, the entire floor was polished so bright it hurt my eyes.

Somehow I pulled myself up. I looked at the floor. I looked at my hand. I raised my fingertips to my nose and sniffed. They were slightly damp and smelled of orange and bleach and ammonia . . . and Swiffer fluid.

I shook my hand one more time and a droplet, a clear blue tear of fluid, glistened on my index finger. When I wiped it on my T-shirt, the material suddenly brightened and stiffened like new.

"Kids?" I managed to whisper, my lips dry and cracked. "Anybody?"

No one answered. Only the bathroom floor seemed to hear. It raised its shiny face to me and smiled.

I stumbled down the hall, afraid to look back, then crawled into bed and pulled the covers up over my head. Hours later, when Martin and Kelly finally remembered to check in on me, I grunted and pretended I was asleep. But I wasn't. I was studying the palms of my hands. They were rough, with tiny little bumps and crevasses, abrasive yet gentle.

Just like the bottom of my Swiffer.

"So you hit your head on the toilet? Tell me again, how did you end up on the floor in the first place?" Carrie leaned on her register.

"I didn't have the exhaust fan on, so I guess I passed out from the fumes." I rubbed more moisturizer on my palms.

"What's wrong with you? You've used half a bottle of that stuff since you got here, Birdie!"

(OK, now is the part where I have to reveal my secret identity. In real life I am known as Birdie Lee, mild-mannered cashier at Marvel Food and Fine Beverages. It's short for Lady Bird Lee. My mother, unlike every other young woman in the early 1960s, couldn't stand Jackie Kennedy. "She's so snobby," Mom would say with a sniff. "So stuck-up with her designer dresses. Now, that Lady Bird Johnson. She's a real person. Someone you could have over for coffee and a Danish." So, unlike the rest of the female population born in 1962, I was named after plain, dumpy Lady Bird, not tall, glamorous Jacqueline. It has proven to be depressingly prophetic.)

"I don't know." I frowned at my textured hands. "I think I have a rash or something. Maybe from the chemicals?"

"You should have gone to a doctor right away." Carrie turned to greet a customer. "Those chemicals can really mess with your brain." She started to scan groceries; I went over to bag for her.

"Yeah, I know. I've been informed by my son." I didn't tell her about the part where my arm turned into a scrubbing machine. I decided I must have dreamed that; it must have been part of the whole "trippin'."

Carrie scanned, I bagged; we have a good rhythm together, and we make a good team. (Although we refuse to let Monty, our boss, enter us in those lame bagging contests you read about in the local paper. We have our dignity, after all.)

"Oh, boy. More Patriot Pops." I reached down into a box.

"Don't forget your free toy. Do you want Teddy Rough Rider or George Washington Carve 'Em Up?"

"Don't you have any Abe Lincolnators?" Mrs. Banks, the customer—a tidy, round woman who always insisted on paper bags instead of plastic—stuck her head over the conveyor belt. "That's my son's favorite character."

I shook my head. "He's everyone's favorite. We ran out of him last week."

"Well . . ." Mrs. Banks surveyed the box, full of plush toy figures from the newest video game sweeping Astro Park, American Justice. "He plays that game all the time. And he just loves those Patriot Pops."

"One hundred percent processed sugar, shaped like mini American flags. God bless America." Carrie sighed. "Chrissie loves 'em too."

"But they're made by New Cosmos," Mrs. Banks pointed out. And in unison we all three looked out the window. There, across the street, sat the biggest jewel in the Astro Park, Kansas, corporate crown: New Cosmos Industries. Once the site of a small sugar-processing plant, it had seemingly morphed, overnight, into a shining symbol of American can-do ingenuity. A huge campus of sparkling buildings, meticulous landscaping, ribbons of walking paths, all for the legions of happy Astro Park citizens newly employed in the manufacturing of patriotic junk food. Liberty Lemonade ice pops, chocolate and vanilla Democracy Drops, Betsy Ross-a-Roni in a cup, Old Glory Gummi Flags, to name just a few. And the ubiquitous Patriot Pops, which was currently running a product tie-in promotion with the American Justice video game.

"I'm just so proud to support a local business." Mrs. Banks beamed. "And my Frank is so happy to be one of the Brethren."

"Brethren?" Carrie raised an eyebrow.

"You know. That's what they're calling the employees now," I told her.

"Because 'employee' is so cold and corporate. But New Cosmos is just one big happy family!" Mrs. Banks nodded.

I looked over at the main building. Seven stories of gleaming glass under friendly arched roofs and gables. In the daylight it looked like a crayon drawing of Cinderella's castle. But at night . . . I shuddered. Whenever I left work at night, there were always two seventh-floor lights on. They reminded me of eyes, and I could swear they followed me all the way home. Even now, thinking of them, the hairs on the back of my neck stood up. I shuddered again. Then I double-bagged some hamburger.

"Um, Carrie? Those carrots scanned wrong."

"Huh?"

"Those carrots came up wrong, on the scanner. They're on special, forty-nine cents a pound. They came up seventy-five cents."

"How do you know what they came up? My scanner screen isn't working." Carrie stared at me. So did Mrs. Banks.

"I don't know. I just . . . well, I just knew. The scanner didn't sound right." I stopped bagging and frowned at the scanner. It had sounded wrong, only I couldn't begin to explain just how.

"The scanner didn't sound right? How does it sound? It always makes that same beep. Are you all right?"

"Yes, I'm all right. Never mind. I don't know what I was talking about."

"Well, that's a funny thing." Carrie rescanned the carrots and checked her register tape. "You were right. They did come up wrong."

I shrugged and kept bagging. Carrie resumed her scanning.

"Those bananas are twenty-nine cents each. You keyed in organic, but they aren't." I hoisted a bag of kitty litter into the cart.

"I did not key in organic and, anyway, how would you know?"

"Check," said Mrs. Banks. Carrie glared at me, but she looked at the receipt.

"Oh, God. I'm sorry." She started tugging on her bangs like she always does when she's nervous. "Birdie, how did you know I keyed it in wrong?"

"I told you—it just sounded wrong." I shook my head a little, trying to clear my ears of a funny, urgent buzz that I hadn't noticed before. Then I went back to my register and rubbed more moisturizer on my palms before I picked up the latest issue of the *National Enquirer*. (Which I only occasionally read because it's stocked right by my cash register and sometimes I get bored, OK?)

Carrie didn't say anything as she finished up with Mrs. Banks. Then she switched her light off and joined me.

"Hey, get this!" I pointed to a headline. " 'Carolina Fisherman Finds Real-Life Baby Moses.' Look! That sure looks like a baby in a basket, doesn't it?"

"It's a doll."

"Nuh-uh. That's a real baby—although the beard does look kind of fake. . . ."

"So what's going on with you? How could you tell the scanner was wrong? Are you sure you're feeling all right?"

"Yes, I'm just fine. Jeez! I just had a little accident yesterday, and so what? Oh—look! 'Superman Really Does Exist! "He rents the apartment above my garage," says Edna Mortar of Gainesville, Florida. "Pervert! Him and his X-ray vision," sputtered the grandmother of two.' Look Carrie! Look at that picture—"

"Birdie!" Carrie snatched the paper out of my hands. "Stop! Your palms look like scrubbing pads. You have a goose egg the size of New Hampshire on your forehead. You're hearing things in the scanner! You need to go home. Now. I'm making you."

"Carrie, I can't. I can't afford to take two days off."

"I don't care. I'm telling you now—"

"Lady?"

A little boy was picking through the candy bars in my aisle. He had a runny nose.

"What?"

"Lady, where are the super-king-size Hershey bars?"

"Have you eaten your lunch yet today?"

"Huh?" He looked up and wiped his nose with his sleeve.

"Don't do that. Use a tissue." His hand dropped to his side. "Did you eat your lunch today?"

"Y-yes . . ."

"You did?" I leaned toward him, drawn by a flicker of hesitation behind his eyes.

"Yes?" His lower lip started to tremble.

"You. Are. Lying, young man," I boomed in a voice that shook my cash register. "You haven't had your lunch yet, and your mother did not say it was OK for you to have a super-king-size Hershey bar. Now, go get an apple from produce and find your mother. She's in the cereal aisle, and she's looking for you. You should be ashamed of yourself, worrying her like that!"

He burst into tears and fled.

Carrie tugged her bangs, then reached over and switched

my light off. "O-o-o-kay." She took me by the arm, gently, as if she were afraid I might break. "You're going home now. I don't know what just happened, but you scared a little boy to death, and we'll probably get sued. So you need to go home."

"But, Carrie— C'mon, you knew he was lying, didn't you? What child needs a super-king-size Hershey bar at ten thirty in the morning?"

"Maybe he was lying, maybe not. But you put the fear of God in him somehow, and that's probably his mother I see marching toward us. So go. Get out of here. I'll handle it."

"But someone needed to tell him he was going to spoil his lunch—"

"Go!" Carrie pushed me and I tottered away on legs that were stiff, like they hadn't been broken in yet. Everything about me felt fragile and tender—like I was trying out a new body. The lights were too bright for my raw eyes, the sounds—of cans clunking against metal shopping carts, of heels *click-click-click*ing on tile—too sharp for my sensitive ears.

Then it happened. I was walking by the juice aisle and I saw it all happen: A little girl reached for the apple juice, the bottle tilted from the shelf, then slipped from her grasp as it fell right toward her. Then I saw myself. I was scooping her up and handing her to her mother before the bottle hit her. But not before it hit the floor. It shattered, splashes of juice and shards of glass coating the floor and the shelves.

And before anyone could move, before anyone could blink, the mess was gone. The little girl and her mother looked at me. I looked at my right hand, still sticky with apple juice and that funky cleaning fluid from the night before. The muscles in my right arm ached. But the floor was sparkling, shiny and new.

"Is she OK?" I asked the mother. She nodded, her mouth gaping, her eyes blinking. "Good." I was shaking with adrenaline, ready—eager—to clean something else. I reached over to the little girl and with my trembling index finger erased a dark red stain—cherry Popsicle, I believe—from her *Blue's Clues* T-shirt.

We studied each other, the little girl and I. I gazed into her eyes, into her soul, and saw—everything. Everything about her. I saw the map of her life—the day she fell off a step stool in the kitchen and chipped her front baby tooth; the raggedy old baby blanket she still slept with, the corner worn down where she clutched it every night. "Don't do that again," I said. Her eyes, big and blue and terrified, did not waver from mine. "Remember the cookie jar you broke last week? You need to stop grabbing things. Ask your mother for help. And stop flushing your brother's LEGOs down the toilet." She nodded, and for a moment I was satisfied that she would do as I said; for a moment I felt like the most powerful mother in the universe and this was my child. They were all my children.

But then I saw myself through the mother's eyes: this crazed cashier with stuff spurting out of her hands babbling on about LEGOs and toilets. I backed away as the mother gathered the girl close; then I ran, speeding past Carrie and Monty and the angry mother with her crying boy who was stuffing pieces of Hershey bar in his mouth between sobs. But when I reached the door I stopped and looked back. I couldn't help it. I started giggling, bubbling over with fear and exhilaration—and power.

"I just— I just— Well, for heaven's sake!"

"What? Birdie, what is it?" Carrie clawed at her bangs.

"Well, you'll never believe it, but . . ." I looked at my strange hands—strange and terrifying and powerful; my skin pricked and burned with a quick flush of adrenaline. The zesty scent of orange, bleach, ammonia, and Swiffer clung to me, invading my pores. Then I looked at my friend, who couldn't do what I had just done. And I didn't know which one of us to feel sorry for.

"But, Carrie? Carrie?" Tears sprang to my eyes, sobs mixed with giggles punctuated by hiccups.

I turned and fled, my white sneakers a blur, my tingling arms outstretched as if to catch a current that would spirit me away. "I think I just did one hell of a cleanup on Aisle Four!"

Then I drove away in my dented minivan. And as I did, I could swear I felt those eyes from New Cosmos following me, all the way home.

Now, of course I've since edited my infamous remark to "Cleanup on Aisle Four," and made it my catchphrase. Martin pointed out that every superhero has a catchphrase— "Shazam!" (Captain Marvel). "Up, Up, and Away!" (Superman). "To the Batcave!" (Batman). "Great Hera!" (Wonder Woman).

So my catchphrase is part of my legend, which is what comes after the origin. Some people call it a "saga," I think. I'm not sure. I get a little confused, now that I'm the stuff of . . . well, legend. Thank goodness I have Martin to sort it all out for me.

But at the time I wasn't thinking about posterity and my place in the pantheon of superheroes. All I knew, as I sped away from work, was that I had to get home and call the doctor because something was very wrong with me. Which I started to do—I mean, I really did pick up the phone and dial the number, but while I was on hold I chickened out. What was I going to say? That I could terrorize small children with just a glance? That I was oozing fluids? That I could clean things up really well?

I'd been doing all these things, in one form or another, for years. Hadn't I? All of a sudden I couldn't remember what was normal and what was not. And I was afraid to have some-one else make that decision for me.

So I didn't call the doctor. I drank a glass of wine instead. Then I took a nap and when the kids came home I smiled a lot, I talked at them in a bright, shiny voice, and they shut their eyes and ears against my brilliance. In other words, it was a typical evening. Then I went to a PTA meeting. Life, as they say, goes on. Even when you're recuperating from a Hor-rible Swiffer Accident.

"What are you doing here?" Carrie blinked at me from be-hind her glasses as we met in the main hallway of Jerome Siegel Junior High and High School.

"What do you think?" I patted her on the top of her head. I love doing that, because Carrie is the only person in the world who can make me—dumpy little Birdie—feel tall. Car-rie is truly petite, with tiny bones and delicate features like a bird; I'm merely short.

"What do I think?" She slapped my hand away. "I think you should be home in bed."

"Can't. I'm secretary, remember?"

"So? So no one records the minutes for a change. Who cares?"

"Madame President cares, that's who—"

"Hello, ladies."

We turned around and beheld our fearless leader, Per-petual PTA President Patty Osborne. She was dressed in a business suit, her face a perfect mask of matte makeup. And as usual, when confronted by her obvious perfection, I tugged on my oversize shirt, pulled at the waist of my jeans, and felt my nose grow shiny with perspiration.

"Hello, Patty," I mumbled as I scuffed my dirty tennis shoes on the floor.

"Now, Birdie, do you have your tape recorder? And copies of last month's minutes?"

"Yes, Patty. Of course I do. I always do."

"Well, one has to ask, doesn't one? Especially in your case, dear. And besides, one can never be too prepared!" Suddenly she was joined by her equally resplendent husband, Lex. The two of them presented such an image of parental perfection I felt my stomach heave. Lex put a practiced arm around Patty as if they were posing for one of their many publicity pictures (rumor had it they employed a clipping service): Mr. and Mrs. PTA under the mistletoe at the annual Christmas party; Mr. and Mrs. New Cosmos handing out turkeys to poor people at Thanksgiving. For Lex and Patty had somehow turned a passion for baking flag-shaped cookies into a multimillion-dollar corporation that had just been named to the Fortune 500 list. (Something I never understood, since no one ever bought their cookies before. Even Marge Miller's Kasha-and-Curry Jumbles outsold them at PTA bake sales.) Now this failed baker was CEO of New Cosmos Industries, a fine, upstanding citizen, president of the chamber of commerce, devoted PTA parent—and father of my daughter's new boyfriend.

"Well, hello, Birdie. And how is that charming daughter of yours? It's been a whole day since she's been over to see Harry." Lex chuckled and gave me a playful punch to the shoulder.

"Hee-hee. That's a good one." I rubbed my shoulder; the punch didn't feel all that playful to me. "I hope she isn't being too much of a pest."

"Why, of course not. We're just crazy about that girl, you know. So polite and sweet, such a good influence on Harry."

"It's amazing how wonderful she's turned out, under the circumstances, isn't it?" Patty smiled, her lips tightly pressed together.

"What does that mean?" Carrie bristled.

"Nothing. Nothing at all. Come, dear, we need to set up the chairs." Patty beckoned to Lex as she took off down the hall, her high heels clipping along on the polished floor.

"Who wears Chanel to a PTA meeting? Puh-leeze. And why do you let her treat you like that, Birdie?"

"Like what?"

"Like—like that! Like you always do. Ever since, well, you know."

"Yeah, I know."

"Birdie, I've told you and told you. It wasn't your fault your son's entire second-grade class was traumatized and they had to call in special counselors the next day. You were the victim. Your esteemed louse of an ex-husband, Doctor Dan, was to blame." Carrie's little legs whirred along, faster and faster as she got angrier and angrier.

"Well, I know that," I panted, trying to keep up. "But some people still seem to hold me responsible."

"That's because you let them." Carrie nodded, pleased with her diagnosis; she was going back to school for her psychology degree, although Howard, her husband, kept threatening to move out until she got some real patients. The beer and tacos she made him eat right before bedtime so he could have wild dreams for her to analyze were giving him an ulcer.

"I do not let them!"

"Yes, you do, Birdie. You suffer from low self-esteem. Plus a major martyr complex. Some people treat you like a doormat, and you just let them."

"Some people are total morons," a warm, wry male voice informed us. Carrie and I both jumped.

"Hi, Carl," Carrie said in that singsong way she uses whenever the two of us happen to meet: Carl Sayers, lone single father in the Hawthorne School District Parent/Teacher Association; Birdie Lee, lone single mother, ditto.

Carrie looked at him, then looked at me; an elfin grin crossed her face as she looked at her watch. "Oh, my," she said, her face a cartoon of surprise. "I need to run ahead. I have things to do. Meet you two in there!" And she scurried down the hall.

"Carrie, wait—" I took a step after her, then stopped. I smiled at Carl, who smiled back. "Um . . . hi. Nice night."

"Yes, nice night. May I carry that for you?" He pointed to my Jolly Green Giant tote bag.

"Oh, no. Thanks, though. I've got it." I slung it across my shoulder and started toward the cafeteria.

"So, what's on the agenda tonight?" Carl fell into step beside me. I tried not to think about how easily our strides matched.

"Oh, the usual. Bake sale, banned library books. Patty's 'Top Ten Tips for Teen Parenting.' "

"Wonderful," Carl said, and groaned. "Listen. Do you think it's too late to sneak out and go have a drink instead?"

"Ha-ha. That's funny! Sneak out! As if!" My face burned hot, but my stomach turned cold, and my brain began to hurt as I tried to figure out if I had just been flirted with or not.

"I guess you're right." Carl shoved his hands in his pockets and started whistling. I peered at his face but couldn't see anything beyond his usual friendly expression; forehead wrinkled but the ends of his mouth tilted up in a bemused smile. He always looked like he was trying to figure out the punch line of a joke.

"So, um, how's work? In the lab?" I asked.

"Oh, you know. Same old thing. Isopropyl and calcium carbonate and beta tests, with a few lab mice thrown in."

"Right . . . mice . . ."

"What, you don't care about the effect of ultraviolet rays on the chemical elements of pigment dyes?" Carl stopped and frowned, although his brown eyes were twinkling.

"Well, I—I was never any good in chemistry."

"That's OK, neither was I. Which is why I'm just one of many developmental scientists in a pharmaceutical company. Hey, did you see Martin's latest?"

"His latest?"

"Cartoon? For the school newspaper? It's pretty good; you should read it." Carl was the sponsor of the cartooning club, of which Martin was a member, along with Carl's own son, Greg, and assorted other short, uncoordinated boys. Martin was deep into the adventures of Rapsta Gangsta, a crime-fighting rapper whose sworn enemy was the principal of a certain junior high school who wouldn't permit his songs to be played at social events.

"Oh. No, I haven't seen it yet. Always the last to know, aren't we?" I shrugged and a tote strap slipped off my shoulder.

"Always!" Carl smiled and reached out to tug the strap back up; his hand, warm and strong and very masculine, lingered on my shoulder for just a fraction of a moment longer than was necessary. Or so it seemed to me as I stood still, afraid to move, afraid to look up or down or anywhere other than at the patch of floor in front of me: industrial blue linoleum with little flecks of gold and silver. And in that fraction of a moment I was only conscious of that. Linoleum. And the warm, steady presence of a man's hand on my shoulder, his warm breath, his solid muscles.

"Hey! Come back here! Gimme that!" Two boys came tearing down the hall toward us, the one in front holding a backpack high above his head. "Dickwad," panted the smaller boy in the rear. "I need that! I have a test tomorrow!"

"Tough shit," crowed the big one in front. "What are you gonna do about it, go crying to the principal again?"

A hot, angry flush came over me. I felt my eyes narrow, my nostrils flare . . . and my right hand go rigid. All of a sudden the boy in front slipped, skated around for a second, tossed the backpack in the air, and fell hard on his butt. "What the hell?" Tears came to his eyes, as he sat on the floor in a pool of—

Cleaning fluid. I stared at my hand, droplets of liquid still clinging to my fingertips. The floor was covered in slick, antibacterial cleaning fluid. The scent of orange and Clorox and Swiffer filled the air. "Ohhhh—ohhh—are you all right?" I stammered.

The boys didn't answer me. The small one picked up his bag. I started to back away. "Uh-oh, I have to go now!"

"What?" Carl bent down to pull the boy up from the floor.

"I . . . uh . . . oh, dear!"

"Birdie, are you all right?"

"Yes, I'm fine, I just have to . . . I'm so sorry . . . I have to . . . bye!" Carl started to say something, but I couldn't wait to hear; I turned and ran down the hall, cleaning fluid trailing behind me. I ran down hallways and dead ends and staircases, trying every door, but they were all locked. I finally found a restroom and hurled myself inside—only to encounter more filth and grime and cigarette butts than I'd ever seen. My burning arm shot out and waves and waves of cleaning fluid streamed from my fingertips and it felt good—oh-so-good. I scrubbed and cleaned and collapsed on the floor, sated, exhausted. Terrified.

What the hell was happening to me? What had I done back there? I shut my eyes against the fluorescent lights and felt the room spin. I shook and shook my right hand so hard that it felt like it might break off, but at that moment I would have welcomed it. Better to have one hand than this freakish, sputtering thing that had attached itself to my body and wouldn't let go.

"Get off me!" I shook my arm and slammed it against the floor; I held it under the faucet and tried to wash it away with hot water, even though I knew my skin would scald. But it didn't. I poked and poked at my spongy hand, but I couldn't feel it. I couldn't feel anything. And so I burst into tears.

After a minute I rubbed my eyes with my right hand—only to sob as if a searing hot poker had stabbed at them. I stumbled to the sink and splashed cold water on my itching, oozing eyes until they felt like ice cubes. Then I sank to the floor, too exhausted, too frightened to move. I didn't know what would set my hand off again, and the next time it happened, I just might die.

And then I did want to die. Just melt away and expire, a wasted, quivering mess of funky fluid. Because, I realized with a sick jolt to my stomach, I had just leaked in front of Carl Sayers. I pulled my knees to my chest. I felt so naked and exposed, like when I was breast-feeding and my milk would come in when I wasn't expecting it. I was leaky all the time then, uncontrollable, raw. Just like now.

"This is great," I whispered to myself. "Just great. I'm a walking soap dispenser. Although that bully did deserve to fall on his butt." I sat on the bathroom floor for a long time, wondering if I could remain there all night—my kids might not notice. Carrie might not either. Carl—

I wondered if he would notice.

"So I said to him, look, mister, if you think you can get away with that . . ." A woman's voice echoed in the hallway outside.

Someone was coming toward the bathroom. I unfolded myself and looked in the mirror; there were black smudges under my runny brown eyes and perspiration had curled my bangs, darkening them beyond the usual mousy brown. I tried to fix myself up but as I tugged at the collar of my tan corduroy shirt, I realized there was no way on earth that Carl Sayers had been flirting with big brown, blobby, leaky me.

I sighed and adjusted my tote bag. On my way out I brushed against two women on their way in. "Oh—will you look at this?" I heard one of them say. "Just look at how clean this restroom is!"

"Must be the new janitor," the other one replied. "Do you smell Swiffer?"

Holding my breath, I tiptoed toward the cafeteria. Carl and the boys were gone. I found a seat next to Carrie and turned on my tape recorder. Patty was just about to slam her gavel.

"Birdie?" Carrie whispered.

"What?"

"Are you all right? You look a little pale."

"I'm fine."

"How'd it go?"

"How'd what go?"

"Carl. You. You know he has a crush on you, Birdie. He has for the longest time."

"Yeah. Right. Well, I doubt that he does anymore—if he did in the first place. Which I also doubt." I twisted around to see where Carl was sitting; he was at a table at the other end of the room.

"Birdie. How long has it been?"

"Since when?"

"Since . . . you know."

"Since the incident? The year the entire second grade had to seek therapy? Since my divorce?"

"Yes. Since then."

"I don't know. A while. A couple of years."

"Four years," Carrie corrected me.

"Six years, six months, two weeks and three days," I corrected her. "Now, shhhh. Patty's looking at us."

"Uptight bitch." Carrie made a face. I giggled, relieved to be with my friend, relieved to be able to laugh at someone as silly as Patty Osborne. I almost felt normal again. But I sat on my freakish right hand, just in case.

"Now"—Patty rapped the table with her gavel—"if we've exhausted the topic of natural-light makeup mirrors in the girls' bathrooms—and I'm sorry to say this just isn't in the budget this year—on to a special piece of new business: video games."

"Oh, Jesus," Carrie said, groaning.

"Now, one might not feel that this is under the umbrella of PTA business. Per se. However, one must do what one can, and given all the terrible, morally bankrupt video games out there, when one finds a fine, upstanding, patriotic game one must act. So I would like to discuss endorsing American Justice as the official video game of the Hawthorne School District Parent/Teacher Association."

"What?" Carrie almost jumped out of her seat.

"Something similar to the Good Housekeeping Seal of Approval. I know we've discussed banning certain games before—"

"Which is fascist and unconstitutional," Carrie piped up.

"Well, yes. Unfortunately." Patty frowned. "So instead of a ban, why not an endorsement? The game is very educational."

"You've got to be kidding!" Carrie started to twitch.

"The heroes are based on actual historical figures. And they fight terrorists at different American landmarks, teaching children a great deal about our heritage. Not to mention geography. So I would like to introduce a motion concerning a PTA endorsement."

"Plus with every game you get a free coupon for Patriot Pops," Mary Denton, who was seated next to Carl, chimed in. "I agree with Madame President. We should support our local industries. And besides, all the kids are playing it anyway, aren't they? I know my Jeffrey just loves it."

"Jordan, too," Marge Miller piped up. "Ever since he got it he can't stop playing it."

"Same with Miranda!" Terry Glass joined in. Every parent in the room was nodding and whispering. Except for Carl. He stared into space, his brow furrowed.

"Well, of course, if any of you would read my brochure, 'A Self-Made Millionaire's Top Ten Tips for Teen Parenting,' you'd know that tip number four stresses the importance of screening all television shows and video games." Patty smiled her perky smile that allowed those of us in the first three rows a glimpse of her wisdom teeth. "This is a perfect example, allowing our teens the freedom to play such games, yet using our influence—"

"Bulls forty-eight, Phoenix thirty-six at the half!" A muffled, staccato voice cried out. I turned around to see who was talking, but everyone was watching Patty.

"But it's just wrong," Carrie said. "Have you ever played this game, Patty—I mean, Madame President? It's extremely violent."

"I disagree. It's a fine game that embodies patriotic values—defending our homeland, fighting terrorism. Values, I might add, shared by all of us at New Cosmos Industries— love of mother, love of father, and above all else, love of country."

"Truth, justice, and the American way," Carrie whispered.

"That's Superman," I whispered back.

"We'll run down the Eastern Conference highlights in a minute. But first, a word from our sponsors—" I turned around again. Someone was listening to a radio.

"Did you hear—?" I nudged Carrie.

"Shhh, this is important, Birdie."

"So, do we have a second?" Patty turned her gaze to Mary, whose husband was in line for a promotion to New Cosmos Family Counselor (formerly Human Resources Director). Mary immediately seconded the motion.

"Thank you, Mary. All in favor of officially endorsing American Justice, say 'aye.' "

Everyone said aye. Except for Carrie, who shouted nay. As for me, I dropped my tape recorder and ducked under the table to retrieve it during the vote, a useful technique I had perfected over the years.

"Motion carried." Patty banged her gavel down. "The Hawthorne School District Parent/Teacher Association officially endorses American Justice—"

"Pacers one-oh-one, Milwaukee ninety-four. New Jersey ninety-eight, Orlando eighty-eight . . ."

"What the heck?" I stood up and looked around the room. Carrie pulled me back down.

"And now I want to remind everyone to attend the grand opening of New Cosmos Patriot Park on Saturday. I'd like to thank the CEO of New Cosmos for allowing the PTA to set up a membership table at the entrance." She winked at Lex, who winked back, and everyone laughed except Carrie, who made a gagging motion with her finger. "Now, let's adjourn by saying the Pledge of Allegiance." Patty raised her hands; everyone but Carrie and I stood in one swift motion. Even Carl shook himself out of his trance and rose, a bit befuddled.

The staccato voice was abruptly shut off. I shook my head.

"I must have water in my ear," I muttered to Carrie as I stood and placed my hand over my heart. Carrie rolled her eyes and did the same, although she sighed heavily after "And liberty and justice for all."

"And we're back. Getting ready for the jump ball are Darren Jameson and LaQuante Jones . . ."

"Carrie!"

"What?"

"Don't you hear that?"

"Hear what?"

"That voice. A radio or something. I think it's a basketball game."

"What are you talking about? We're in the cafeteria. The gym's at the other end of the building, and besides, there's no basketball game tonight."

"So . . . you don't hear it?" Now the voice was settling into a play-by-play of the ball game; the Bulls had just scored a three-pointer.

"Hear what? Birdie, are you still hearing things like you were this morning?" Carrie turned to me. The meeting had broken up; lots of people were milling around Lex and Patty, shaking hands and testifying excitedly about New Cosmos. It was like a mini-revival meeting.

"Um, no, I'm not hearing things like this morning . . ." But I saw the look on Carrie's face, that sharp, penetrating look that makes you wonder why on earth she needs glasses. "OK, I am. I was hearing something—like a radio."

"There wasn't a radio on. I was here the whole time. Birdie, I'm really starting to worry about you. Won't you see a doctor?"

"I can't. I just . . . can't. I can't explain it."

"Maybe"—she hesitated, tugging her bangs—"I hate even to suggest this, but maybe . . . Doctor Dan? Could you talk to him about it?"

"Carrie." I shoved the tape recorder in my tote bag and got up, knocking over my chair. "I can't believe you just said that."

"Sorry. Sorry, Birdie, really I am. It's just . . . I've never seen you like this. You seem so different to me—"

"How?" I froze in midflight, one leg up in the air like a flamingo. "How am I different? Can you tell? What can you tell? Do you see—"

" 'Night, Birdie. Carrie." Carl was standing between us. "I was wondering, are you chaperoning the Junior/Senior Harvest Dance this year, Birdie? Oh, and are you, Carrie?"

"I, um, well, I—"

"Yes, she is," Carrie said. "Aren't you, Birdie?"

I nodded.

"Me too. See you then."

"OK," I said, and gulped. Carl turned to leave, and Carrie grabbed all of our things and shoved me after him. We didn't catch up, but we did spend a nice minute or so watching him walk down the hall. And I had to admit he had a nice rear end for a middle-aged man. He didn't have one of those flat butts like some men get. His was nicely rounded, just filling out his back pockets, from which a little cord was hanging . . . a little black plastic cord, attached to an earphone, attached to a . . .

"Radio," I whispered, gripping Carrie's arm.

"What?"

"Look!" I pointed at Carl's butt.

"Well, yes, Birdie, it's very nice, but don't you think you're getting a little ahead of yourself?"

"No! Look—a radio! With a little earphone!"

"That devil!" Carrie laughed. "Well, I have to hand it to him. I wish I'd have thought of that. No wonder he always seems so calm and collected after these meetings. He's not hearing a word of them!"

"No! Remember I told you I was hearing things?"

"Yeah? So?"

"I bet you it was . . . never mind. Never mind, never mind, never mind!" I hit myself on the side of the head. "I'm being silly. Of course not. It couldn't have been. Of course not."

"Birdie, go home. Go get a good night's sleep. Take tomorrow off if you need to." Carrie tucked her arm in mine as we walked to our cars. "Because, frankly, I'm a little worried about you. You're exhibiting paranoid tendencies, and that, coupled with your already low self-esteem, could lead to—"

"Carrie." I smiled at my friend, who was blinking like a

mole in the parking lot lights. "Go home yourself. Feed Howard a taco or two and have a good time analyzing his dreams.
And stop worrying about me."

"You know, I could help you out, if only you—"

" 'Night, Carrie." I stopped at my minivan.

"Well, I would say sweet dreams. But it would be wasted."

"Sorry." I shrugged. I never dream. Carrie hates that about
me; she takes it personally. But I just never did, even when I
was a girl. I can't remember a single dream I've had, ever.
Not even nightmares. Which is a good thing, if you ask me.

I stood with my car door open, watching her drive away. I
waved at a couple of other people; then I raised my face to the
stars, feeling the cool night air blow a kiss across my face. There
were too many stars to count but that was all right; the sky
was comforting and soothing. Like a blanket or a painting—
something I could just lose myself in and no one would ever
find me.

A yellow Mustang screeched around a corner, windows
open, radio blaring, tearing through the quiet night like a
jagged knife. Something inside me quivered; I felt a reso-
nance, a vibration, a warning—

And before I knew what I was doing I had jumped into my
dented minivan and was roaring after the car. It stopped at a
stop sign. I honked my horn and leaped out, running up to
the driver's open window. Inside were five teens. Not one of
them was wearing a seat belt.

"You!" I shook my finger at the driver, a lanky boy with
pink hair and a nose ring. "You! Slow down! And wear your
seat belts. Now."

"What the fuck?" He turned around and laughed at his
friends. "Who's the granny on steroids?" He turned around
again and smirked. "Go fuck yourself."

"YOUNG MAN!" The vibration within my chest thundered, rumbled in my rib cage, and forced its way out of my throat. I pointed my finger at the tip of his nose. "You will buckle your seat belts. RIGHT. NOW. And you will slow down and go the speed limit. Or else."

"Or else what?" The smirk was fading from his face; his eyes grew pale and honest with fear.

"Or else I will take away your car keys and ground you for a week. And that goes for all of you!" I stuck my head in the car window, held each trembling teen in my Merciless Gaze, and nodded—just once—for emphasis.

And they did. They all buckled their seat belts. In unison. "Y-yes, ma'am," the driver sputtered, not meeting my eyes.

"That's better." I stepped back and folded my arms across my chest. "You may go now."

"Yes, ma'am," he repeated. Then the car inched slowly through the intersection and proceeded up the street at a crawl.

An unexpected wind rustled the trees and shot through my still-quivering body. My face was drawn to the stars again, eerily incandescent in the inky sky. I raised my right hand, studying its outline, like a map of some mysterious island with jutting peninsulas and narrow coves, black against the stars. I drew strength from their bright energy and felt myself glow right here on earth, vibrant, shimmering—

Powerful.

Then . . .

"I'm losing my mind," I mumbled as something strong broke inside me. The wind died down, the stars dimmed and a car honked at me to get out of the street. "I'm totally losing my mind." I dragged myself back into my minivan and started for home. Once I pulled up next to the yellow Mustang at a stoplight. The driver saw me, blanched, then looked away. When the light turned green, he waited for me to go first before he continued, precisely one mile under the speed limit.

I sat in my car for a long while after I got home, staring at my house with the peeling paint on the shutters, the one porch light hanging crooked. I didn't want to go inside. I didn't want to become Kelly and Martin's mom again, nagging them about their homework and messy rooms and lost allowances. I wanted to remain that person who had drawn strength from the stars, who had found, in the outline of her hand against the luminous night sky, a mystical land of enchantment. So I cracked open the car window, pushed my seat back, and closed my eyes for a moment, breathing in the smoky, musty night air—one of the neighbors must have been using the fireplace. It was almost that time of year.

I shifted in my seat and accidentally hit the On button on the tape recorder. Suddenly Patty was banging her gavel, Carrie was heaving her great sighs, we were whispering about Carl. But there was more. A lot more.

I heard things. Things I'd never noticed before: clicks and cadences that sounded like heartbeats, breathing, the squeak of a tennis shoe against a linoleum floor. I heard people talking in the background—not just the usual murmur, but actual conversations. *"You take a package of frozen noodles,"* Marge was saying, *"and add a can of green beans . . ."*

"But what about Friday night?" Terry was asking someone. *"Can't they do it on Friday night?"*

"Bulls forty-eight, Phoenix thirty-six at the half . . ." There! That's what I'd been hearing—a radio announcer. And on the tape, Carl Sayers grunted and whispered, *"Go, Bulls!"*

So I had heard it. I had heard his radio, even though I was

sitting all the way across the room, even though he'd been us-ing earphones. And somehow my tape recorder had picked it up; had picked up the voices and sounds and sighs and scrap-ings of everyone and everything in the room. Or maybe—

"Birdie. Doesn't Birdie look nice tonight?" I jumped at the sound of my name. *"She always looks so nice and neat."* It was Carl's voice.

"Yes, she does," Mary replied.

"Hmmmm," Carl continued. He sounded thoughtful. He sounded puzzled. He sounded . . . interested.

I shut the tape recorder off.

How long had it been? I sat in my car and tried to remember.

How long had it been since anything new and exciting had happened to me? How long had it been since I'd felt the way I was feeling now—different, better, changed in some signifi-cant way I couldn't understand? I couldn't remember; had I ever felt this way before?

And how long had it been since a man's voice had made me jump out of my skin, made me wonder how it might feel if I jumped out of my clothes and into his arms? How long since I had touched a man, kissed a man, been held and stroked and loved by a man?

Too long. So long, I thought I'd forgotten how. How a man's voice could stir up so much longing—coals of warmth and wonder stirring in my womb, prompting me to think of someone other than myself. And Kelly. And Martin.

I rewound the tape recorder and played it again. *"Doesn't Birdie look nice tonight?"* Carl's voice asked, soft and warm as a summer breeze tickling my neck. *"She always looks so nice and neat."* I shut the tape recorder off right there; I didn't need to hear any more.

When I finally went to sleep that night (I'd zapped the kitchen clean before I could stop myself), I sat cross-legged on my bed eating an orange Popsicle, listening to that part of the tape over and over. *"Doesn't Birdie look nice tonight? She always looks so nice and neat—"* Pause, rewind, play again. When I licked the last gooey drop from the stick, I allowed myself to wonder about the next time we might meet, Carl and I.

I threw away the Popsicle stick and went to bed with sticky fingers, a whisper of orange around my mouth. I could have zapped them clean in an instant. But I didn't want to.

I wanted to fall asleep with the memory of something sweet upon my lips.

CHAPTER
3

And so the first couple of days passed after my Horrible Swiffer Accident. Life became a little complicated; I dribbled all the time (something I hadn't anticipated happening until I was at least sixty-five). But given the state of modern housekeeping, I couldn't walk into any public place without starting to spurt. So I took to wearing a plastic bread bag over my right hand and when anybody asked why, I told them I had a rash. Which wasn't a lie, since my hand remained spongy and grippy despite the gallons of hand lotion I'd used. And earmuffs—I wore those, too. I put on an old pair of earmuffs (Tigger earmuffs, to be exact) whenever the constant humming and whispering in my ears got to be too much for me.

Now you can imagine how my children reacted to the sight of their mother wearing a Wonder Bread wrapper on her arm and Tigger earmuffs on her head. Kelly refused to let me come within two miles of school (she actually mapped it out for me in red ink); Martin pretended he didn't know me, even when it was just the two of us alone in the house.

But on the bright side, our house was really clean. I zapped that mysterious Christmas tree–shaped stain that had been on the family room ceiling ever since we'd moved in; I eradicated the orange stains on all of my old Tupperware; I bleached the kitchen curtains so bright and snowy, they were like angels' wings. Soon our house sparkled like a new toy. And no one noticed but me.

And once in a while I got that taut, vibrating feeling. It reminded me of how sometimes I knew a bad thing was going to happen in the split second before it did. You know . . . you watch your child stand up on a chair to reach for a glass above the sink and you say to yourself, mesmerized, "Now he's going to lose his balance and fall and hit his chin on the counter and we'll have to go get stitches." And next thing you know, you're sitting in the emergency room.

That's the feeling I sometimes had. And what's really weird—

Each time I had that feeling, I looked around me and saw someone in danger. A toddler who was about to fall out of a grocery cart. The little girl down the street who was riding her bike without a helmet. The posse of teenagers who were so absorbed in conversation that they almost walked through the crossing gate at the train tracks near school. And so I straightened the toddler in the cart, walked the little girl back home and made her put on her helmet, shouted at the teens to stop before the train came roaring by.

And all was right with the world, or at least with my small corner of it. As long as I was around.

Then the following Saturday morning I tripped over something outside my bedroom door.

"Who left this?" I picked up a comic book. Spider-Man was

on the front, swinging through the air. "Martin? Is this one of yours?" I dropped it outside his bedroom. Then I heard voices again. This time they were coming from inside Kelly's room; faint, monotone, staccato. Just like the voice I'd heard at the meeting:

'Sup?

Nothin'

See you later?

Yep.

Kewl, babe. Love You.

Me too. Then I heard a happy little *ding*, like a tiny bell.

"Kelly?" I knocked on her door. Silence. Then—*BRB.*

"What, Mother?"

"Honey, who are you talking to in there?"

"Nobody."

"Kelly. I heard someone. Who's in there?"

"Nobody!" She opened her door an inch. One gray eye peeked out from behind a curtain of sandy blond hair.

"Kelly, I know what I heard!"

"Mom. You're losing it. Go bug Martin." She shut the door.

"But . . . Kelly—"

'Sup? The whispery, monotone voices continued.

Nothin'. Mom. You know.

Tragic.

"Kelly!" I rapped on the door again.

"What?!" She opened the door an inch and a half. I was treated to two gray eyes peeking out from behind a curtain of sandy blond hair.

"Who are you talking to in there?" I stuck my foot in the door before she could shut it. She sighed deeply, meaningfully, then let me in.

"No one. See? God. What is your problem? You've been acting so pathetic lately. Did you lose your earmuffs or something?" Kelly scowled, sitting down at her desk. But then she raised her head and gazed at me, chewing a fingernail; her face grew a little pale. "But you're all right, aren't you? I mean, after the accident the other day, you're not still, um, tripping, are you, Mom?"

"Honey, I'm fine. Really I am. I just thought I heard . . . well, you weren't talking to anyone or anything, were you?"

"No, I'm just IMing Harry."

"Oh! Harry! Well, isn't that nice!"

"What?"

"I mean, well, how are things? In school, and . . . with Harry . . . and . . . how are things?" Are you having sex? Are you being careful when you have sex? Is he good to you? Do you love him? But I couldn't ask these questions; I was too afraid of the answers. The bravest act I could manage was to tuck a strand of hair behind her ear; she stiffened and pulled away.

"They're fine. He's fine. I'm fine. I have to get dressed now."

"I'm sorry. I'll leave you be." And I dared to plant a kiss on top of her head before I shut the door, so quick I was spared the sight of her face. But outside her room, the door shut tight, I heard the voices again:

Your mom again?

Yep.

What's the 4-1-1?

Nothin'. Mom stuff. I can't wait for next weekend with my dad!

Your dad is kewl. My dad says so.

Yeah. He is.

But your mom . . .

Yeah. I know.

I shut my eyes for a moment. I wished I could march back in there and tell Kelly—everything. Everything she didn't know about me, about her father—things a child shouldn't know. Sometimes it was too hard to keep on this way, carrying the burden of her happiness on my back until I almost couldn't stand up straight. Finally I went downstairs, storing what just happened—the voices, what they'd said—away in my mind, like a squirrel with a nut. I was hoarding clues lately, all these strange things that had happened—were still happening—ever since the Horrible Swiffer Accident. But so far I hadn't had the time—or the courage—to add them all up.

The kitchen was a mess from breakfast, and so I zapped it clean without thinking. It was becoming second nature to me, this amazing ability to clean with the power of ten thousand Swiffers. I was even experimenting with new techniques. My favorite was a funky little underarm zap accompanied by a crossover with my left hand.

"Mom?"

"Martin?" I turned around, hiding my dripping hand underneath my armpit. Damn, that fluid was cold!

"Mom, did you just—"

"Make you a snack? Why, are you hungry? How about a sandwich? Peanut butter? Ham? Bologna? Peanut butter and bologna on ham?" I ran to the pantry and grabbed the bread.

"I just ate breakfast. Mom?"

"Hmmm?" I ran a sponge across the counter, just for show. I didn't look up.

"Mom— Nothing. Well, I guess I'd better—"

"Oh! Guess what!" I spun around and clapped my hands.

"What?"

"I was talking to Mr. Sayers the other night. About your comics. He said your latest one was pretty good! Way to go, buddy!"

"Mom!" Martin's eyes narrowed into little slits while his eyebrows drew together into one squiggly line above them. "Why were you talking to Mr. Sayers?"

"Why not? We were at the PTA meeting and he mentioned you and—"

"But why were you talking to him? About me? I hate it when you do that. It isn't any of your business; it's just a stupid cartoon and I don't know why you were talking to anyone about it. You're always doing stuff like this, talking to my teachers, asking what's going on with me . . . Mom, I just need my privacy!"

"I'm your mother. I like to talk about you. I like to know what's going on with you. Remember when you were in third grade and I went on that field trip to—"

"Mom! You're not going to do that again, are you?"

"Do what?"

"Start all that 'remember when' stuff."

"Oh." I turned around and studied the counter. "Do I do that? A lot?"

"Yeah. You do." He sounded so weary of me. "Besides, Mr. Sayers? He's kinda OK, I guess, but . . . I don't know. It's just weird that you were talking to him."

"Well, parents talk to each other, you know."

"I know. But it's still weird."

Neither of us said anything for a long moment.

"Well, I'm gonna go now . . ."

I heard the hesitation in his voice, the apology.

"OK. Bye, sweetie." I turned around and smiled. "See you later? Do you need any extra money?"

"No." His face relaxed so that he had two distinct eyebrows again. "No, thanks. Oh, and . . . well, Mom? I meant to ask you . . ."

"Yes?" My right hand trembled, and I shoved it in the pocket of my jeans.

"The other night . . . did you . . . did you get some more Patriot Pops? We're out."

"Patriot Pops? I'll get some today, sweetie! Patriot Pops! No problem!" My hand stopped trembling just in time for me to wave good-bye to my son as he loped out the kitchen door.

Then the phone rang.

"Hello?"

"Birdie?"

"Ohhhh, hi . . ." I sank into the kitchen chair, my knees suddenly weak. Kelly came rushing downstairs, coating her mouth with one last layer of lip gloss. I yanked her purse as she scurried by, almost pulling her off her feet.

"Mom!"

"Thanks," I mouthed, shaking the phone at her. "Your father." A guilty little smile played at her shiny lips and she shrugged. Then she sauntered out the door without a backward glance.

"Birdie, Kelly called me just now."

"Just now?"

"Yes. Right before my first appointment, by the way. Doesn't she know my schedule?"

"Dan, she's fifteen and your daughter, not your secretary."

"Well, anyway"—I could hear the stern disappointment in his voice. It weighed me down, pressing on my bones—"she said that you'd had some sort of accident the other day?"

"Yes . . ." I held my breath and waited for him to ask if I was all right.

"Birdie? Birdie? Are you there?"

"No, it wasn't an accident." I exhaled. "I must have inhaled some fumes, from bleach or something, while I was cleaning the bathroom—"

"Didn't you have the exhaust fan on?"

"No, I didn't have the exhaust fan on—"

"Well, why didn't you?"

"I don't know. I forgot. I was in a hurry and—"

"So, Kelly told me you're acting strange. Hearing things. Acting paranoid. She said Martin told her he saw you doing something in the kitchen, too, a couple of nights ago—"

"He—he did?" I closed my eyes. Wasn't Martin asleep when I'd zapped the kitchen? I was sure I'd checked. Although maybe I hadn't. Maybe I'd been too busy thinking about Carl Sayers's voice.

"Yes, although that part wasn't clear to me. But earmuffs, Birdie? Really? I sent the child-support check; I always do. So why are you dead set on embarrassing me?"

"I'm not embarrassing you, Doctor— Dan. It's not about you, it's about—"

"It's bad enough that you got a job as a cashier. It's bad enough that you're bagging Tater Tots for my patients. But now you're dressing like a homeless person? Birdie, honestly."

"But it's not . . . I'm not trying to—"

"Listen, I have to go, but I wanted to make sure that you weren't endangering the children in any way."

"Oh, for God's sake. Endangering the children? Yes, Dan. Yes, I am. I'm putting razor blades in their peanut butter sandwiches. I'm putting strychnine in their toothpaste!" I jumped up from the chair and started pacing the kitchen, a tightness winding itself up in my chest, fueled by a strange new flicker of fury. "I'm telling them to play in the street! I'm forbidding them to ride in the car unless their seat belts are unbuckled! I'm starching their underwear, for crying out loud!"

"Birdie. There's no need to be sarcastic—that's unlike you. Just be careful, will you?"

I thought I heard something in his voice—a softness, or a question. Something I hadn't heard in years, and it knocked my legs out from under me. "Careful? You . . . want me to be careful? Why, sure, I'll take care of my—"

"Just be careful not to do anything stupid. Just be careful not to embarrass me any further. And if I get another call from Kelly about this, I'm coming over myself. Before my scheduled weekend. Do you understand?"

"Yes." My voice dropped down to a whisper so soft it barely parted my lips. "I understand." But he'd already hung up. Doctor Dan didn't need to hear what I had to say.

I sat there with the phone in my hand and tried to remember one thing about him—about us—that was good. It's a little trick I learned a long time ago, the thing that prevents me from poisoning the children against him. But I won't do that. I'm a good mother; it's the one thing in life I know. Even Doctor Dan used to say that about me, although the way he said it—dripping with disdain—let me know he didn't think it much of an accomplishment.

So I sat in the kitchen and remembered the first time I heard my name.

"Birdie," Dan said with a smile. We were sitting on the edge of a fountain outside a lecture hall at college. I'd been waiting for him; it seemed like that's all I did back then—wait for him. I waited a long time, but I didn't mind. There was nowhere else I could think of; nowhere else I wanted to be.

Finally he sauntered down the steps of the hall and found me sitting patiently on the bench. We'd only met a couple of weeks before, and so we were each delirious at the sight of the other.

"Birdie," he said, taking my hand, cupping it in his big, capable doctor's hands. "Such a pretty little name, for such a pretty little girl. Birdie. My little brown wren."

And I giggled and hung my head and knew that until that moment I'd never really heard my name before. It had just been a thing, a label. Until that moment when Dan placed my little hand in his like it was a delicate flower and said my name, giving it meaning, giving me life.

"Birdie." I said it now, alone in my sparkling kitchen, my little hand lonesome on my lap. And then I remembered another voice saying my name, and I wondered.

Could the second time around—at hoping, at longing, at hearing my name spoken by a man—ever be as sweet and as thrilling as the first? Things matter so much more when you're young. You have to love, or else you'll die.

Now, well, I wasn't sure. I wasn't sure if middle-aged people could love like that. We're so much more . . . settled. We know that there are more important things than dying for love, than living for love, than dying to think that you'll have to live without love. Like, say, making sure you buy your daughter the right brand of jeans to wear to school so she won't hate you forever. Like coming up with just enough money to help your kids with college, but not so much as to spoil the chances for financial aid. Like trying to remember if you already have a gallon of milk at home or if you need another, because if you buy another and you already have a full one at home, chances are the new one will go bad before you can drink it all. . . .

I sighed and went upstairs to shower. I couldn't believe how foolish I was acting.

When you're in love, or hope to be in love, you don't spend your time thinking about spoiled milk.

"So, how are you today?" Carrie took my arm; the sidewalk was crowded with happy families eager to celebrate the grand opening of New Cosmos Patriot Park, giddy to take advantage of the free admission for children under twelve. Strolling costumed colonial figures passed out free samples of authentic Revolutionary-era junk food.

"I'm fine." Like a good little divorced mother who was dependent upon her ex for child support, I had left my earmuffs and bread bag at home. Which was just as well; I doubted that Patty and Lex would have let me in if I'd showed up like that. In fact, the entire crowd seemed polished and shiny; practically everyone there was associated in some way with New Cosmos, either one of the "Brethren" or related to one. Whole families were walking around with goofy smiles, mouths rimmed with red-white-and-blue sugar.

"So?"

"So what?"

"Well, what did you think of the PTA meeting the other night?"

"Patty and Lex remind me of Mr. and Mrs. Potato Head." A perky Abigail Adams with blindingly white teeth handed me a cup of Patriot Pops.

"That's not what I was talking about—"

"Seriously. Have you ever noticed? They both have enormous heads—"

"Birdie, I was talking about Carl. He made such a point of saying good-bye to you, and then he asked if you were chaperoning the Harvest Dance!" Carrie's eyes were sparkling like little blue stars behind her glasses.

"He said good-bye to both of us, not just me. And he asked you if you were chaperoning too." I shrugged, hoping that Carrie wouldn't notice I'd actually curled my hair and dabbed a little perfume behind my ears, just in case . . . well, just in case.

"Oh, Birdie! You're not that stupid. You know what he meant."

"Carrie"—I bit into a raspberry flag; my teeth recoiled from the sugar—"we have nothing in common except for the fact that we're both divorced and have sons who are geeks. It's stupid. And anyway, I think you're jumping the gun a bit. All he did was walk me to the PTA meeting, offer to carry my tape recorder, and say good-bye. That's all. Yuck. Remember when they couldn't give these things away at bake sales? They taste just the same."

"Don't change the subject. And don't make such a face, Birdie! People are staring!"

"You sound just like Doctor Dan. Who, by the way, in case you were wondering, called this morning."

"Bastard. What'd he want?"

"Kelly apparently called him up and told him about my

little . . . er, accident. And she happened to mention that I've been acting a little strange—which I haven't, by the way. And so of course he proceeded to lecture me about embarrassing him and threatened to come over if I didn't behave myself. Oh, and he hinted that I might be endangering the kids."

"Endangering the kids! What an asshole!" Carrie tugged her bangs so hard I thought she would rip them off. I grinned and threw away the Patriot Pops. Once she got going on the subject of Doctor Dan I knew I was safe for a while.

"Endangering the kids," she muttered, twitching all over like she was a marionette. "Why, you're the best mother I know! No one in his right mind would ever accuse you of such a thing! Doesn't he realize what you've done with them, in spite of his best efforts to ruin your lives and turn his children into little mechanical windup toys? The nerve of that man! And after all he did to you, after that incident in second grade—"

"Hmmm, mmmm." I nodded, barely listening, happy to let Carrie fight my battles for me. "Ooh!" I pointed at the American Justice ride. Dozens of people were standing in line, waiting patiently for their chance to race a giant Liberty Bell over the Golden Gate Bridge before terrorists blew it up. A costumed Abe Lincolnator posed for pictures, his stovepipe hat (which doubled as a machine gun in the video game) perched demurely on his head. "Let's ride that one, Carrie!" I dragged her over to the end of the line.

"For which he should be strung up by his toenails," she continued without missing a beat. "Embarrassing *you* like that in front of the children—"

"You go, girl." And then I saw Kelly and Harry, standing

in line for the American Dino-Kidz ride. They made a beautiful couple, I had to admit, both tall and blond. He bent
toward her, stroking her cheek, whispering, and she nodded,
so happy, so content; almost mesmerized. And my stomach
fluttered. Because I remembered feeling that way too—
completely taken in by a man. It's terrifying—and thrilling. You couldn't stop yourself. All you could do was
hope that the man would be kind, respectful, and not take
advantage of your willingness—your need—to follow him
anywhere.

"And he has the nerve to show up at the annual PTA
Christmas party with her, as if he's such a kind, loving
parent—" Carrie was still twitching beside me.

"Right on." Kelly and Harry had vanished, swallowed up by
the crowd. I tried not to panic. She was fifteen. He was seven-
teen. He wouldn't let anything bad happen to her. Would he?
Biting my lip, in desperate need of a box of Give Me Liberty
or Give Me Death by Chocolate Cookies, I nearly mugged a
costumed Patrick Henry.

All of a sudden I got that singing feeling in the back of
my head. Something bad was about to happen. I froze, almost choking on a cookie; somehow out of all the crowd and
noise and spinning rides, my eyes picked out a toddler climbing a rail on a footbridge, about twenty-five feet above the
ground.

"He makes me so mad," I heard Carrie say before I took
off like my tennis shoes were rockets, weaving in and out of
the crowd, vaulting the stairs to the bridge just as the little
girl slipped through a tiny slit in the mesh fencing. There was
no way I could fit through it; without thinking I pointed my
right hand and sliced a Birdie-size hole in the mesh with a

forceful stream of cleaning fluid. I pushed through it and grabbed the little girl, dimly aware of the garbled laughter of the crowd all around us. . . . It was like they were in slow motion but I was on fast-forward. I scooped her up in one arm just as the portion of the fence she was clinging to ripped away from its support. My heart was beating so loud, I couldn't hear anything but its tattoo in my ears and the child's heavy breathing. I swung us back inside the mesh fencing with my other arm, aware of only one thing—the trust in her grave green eyes. For a moment it was just the two of us, locked in an embrace: intimate, intense. Then everything around us seemed to speed back up; I had only enough time to squeeze her sticky hand before her mother turned around to grab her. "Oh, thank God!" she cried, reaching out to touch me as I tried to flee. "How can I ever thank you? Who are you?"

"I—I'm—"

All of a sudden I was surrounded by people. "Did you see that?" "How'd she do that?" "Who is it?" I spun around and around, cornered by the voices, the stares, the hungry look of the crowd. Somebody grabbed my arm. Somebody else pulled on my shirt.

"I'm nobody. It's not important," I gasped as I tried to push my way through the crowd. "Leave me alone! Go . . . eat some Patriot Pops or something!"

"But wait," I heard the mother call after me. "I want to know who saved my little girl!"

"It was Superman," somebody said. The crowd started to laugh.

I stopped. I turned around, narrowed my eyes, and gazed mercilessly at the giggling mob. They stopped giggling, as of one accord. "No, it wasn't," I declared. "It was me. Just a . . . just a mom. But we can be pretty super too, you know." Then I turned and trotted back to the American Justice ride.

"Where'd you go?" Carrie turned to me and blinked. "And what happened to your shirt? Did you tear it?"

I glanced down at my shirtsleeve, which was ripped from elbow to wrist. I hid my arm behind my back. "Oh, I just had to, um, go to the bathroom. Must have gotten my arm caught on something. Hey!" I grabbed the empty box from her. "You ate all my cookies!"

"Sorry." She grinned, backing away from me—and right into Lex Osborne, accompanied by an enormous security guard with a scar above his left eye. Lex's thick white hair, so shocking on someone his age, streamed behind him; his handsomely tanned face was dark with concern.

"Did you see what happened? I heard there was an incident—a little girl?"

"We didn't see anything, did we, Birdie?" Carrie looked at me. I shrugged.

"I had a report of something happening, some mystery person grabbing a child. We can't have that kind of thing happening here."

"Oh, no! It wasn't like that!" I shook my head. "I mean, I may have seen something, but it looked like the child was in danger. Like maybe the fencing was bad."

Lex narrowed his eyes at me.

"Well, it sounds like I need to conduct a full investigation. C'mon, Lars." He turned on his heel, whipped out a cell phone, and whispered something. Only I heard it: *"Buy the brat off with a year's supply of Patriot Pops. That'll teach her,"* Lex hissed as he pushed his way through the crowd, followed by the massive security guard. *"But I want to find whoever else was there. . . . Don't give me excuses! Find him. Now!"*

I swallowed hard. Then I grabbed Carrie and started to run in the other direction.

"C'mon. I think I should go. I just remembered, I left a roast in the oven!"

"But it's one o'clock in the afternoon!" Carrie panted behind me. "Birdie! Wait up! Where are you going? What's wrong? Don't you want to see what happens next?"

But still I ran, on trembling but powerful legs, adrenaline pumping through my veins, propelling me through the crowd. My eyes searched the park, scanning for—danger. For trouble. For children in need.

For Lex and his hulking sidekick.

I saw Martin at a concession stand, loading up on Liberty Lemonade ice pops. I raced over to him.

"Hey, Mom. Aunt Carrie. Did you hear about the hero? Who saved that little girl?"

"Mr. Osborne was looking for him . . ." Carrie said.

"Jeez. Why does everyone assume it was a man?" I muttered. "Martin, have you seen Kelly?"

"She's with Harry. She said she'd get a ride home with him."

"Well, you're coming with me now."

"Mom!"

"Wait, what happened to you, Birdie?" Carrie was staring at me. "I didn't notice but your jeans are ripped too. Why, you look like you—"

"Climbed a fence," Martin said, pointing at my legs. I looked down. My jeans were torn; my legs were covered in scratches and dried blood. All of a sudden I was aware of the pain; I felt like I'd been dragged through a field of thorns.

"Oh. Ow. Ew . . ." I dabbed at an open cut on my knee. "And I left my purse at home. . . ."

Carrie and Martin just gaped at me.

"Well, I have Band-Aids in my purse," I informed them, blinking away frustrated tears. "And antibacterial hand wipes. So I need to go home. Please? Now? Won't somebody please take me home?"

Martin didn't say anything. He looked long and hard at my cuts and scrapes. Then he took my arm and led me through the crowd.

When we got home, I went upstairs to change clothes, bandage my cuts, and search the medicine cabinet for morphine. Unfortunately we were fresh out, but we did have an old bottle of baby aspirin. So I chewed about fifty, chasing them down with a glass of wine. And then I tripped over another stack of comic books outside the bathroom door. It was the last straw on my aching camel's back.

"Martin!" I screamed at the top of my lungs.

No answer.

"Martin Stanley Lee, what is it with you and these comic books?"

No answer.

"Well that's it, buddy, no allowance this week. Next week either. If you think I'm going to keep picking up after you day in and day out . . ." I scooped them up and opened the door to his room. I was about to toss them onto his bed when I noticed the one on top. It had been outside my door this very morning—*The Amazing Spider-Man,* Number 301. I picked it up and in spite of myself, I had to smile; proof that my thirteen-year-old with the floppy hair and rock music was still a little boy at heart. He still loved his superheroes—like Spider-Man, pictured here flying through the air, his hand extended, some kind of fluid shooting out of it . . .

Some kind of fluid. Shooting out of his hand. I studied the picture. Then I raised my right hand, flipped it into the exact same pose, and lo and behold. Fluid shot out of it.

I put the books down, picked up the next one in the stack—the one that had mysteriously appeared outside my bedroom yesterday. *The Amazing Spider-Man,* Number 46. "Beware the Rage of a Desperate Man!" And there was Spider-Man grappling with some evil guy, his hand extended behind his back, fluid spurting out.

Ooh. I hadn't tried that before—the behind-the-back flip. I imitated the pose on the comic book—and voilà! Fluid shot out of my hand. Just like—

Spider-Man.

I stood in my son's room and looked around at the posters on his walls. The Fantastic Four posed in a group next to his closet; Superman flew overhead, tacked to the ceiling above his bed; Wonder Woman and her Amazonian breasts stood at attention directly above his dresser.

And hanging above his computer was Spider-Man, swinging through the air, one arm around a blond girl, his other arm extended, fluid shooting . . . well, you know.

A spiderweb glistened in a far corner of the window. I crouched down, flung my arm up like in the poster, and spun my cleaning fluid, watching it soar in a high arc across the room, catching beads of sunlight before destroying the web. I felt, again, the weight of the toddler in my arms as I carried her to safety on the footbridge, the two of us alone in our own little world of peril. Something bad had almost happened. And I alone had possessed the power to prevent it.

I gathered up the stack of comic books. I shuffled down the hall to my bedroom and shut the door.

And I began to read.

Through my study of the average superhero, helpfully chronicled in a series of comic books (mostly reproductions) dating from the 1930s to the present, I have learned the following:

A superhero generally has a bunch of cool toys and weapons to help him/her out. (Although I have to question Wonder Woman's golden girdle. I doubt that its only function is to supply her with Amazonian strength. It's a *girdle*. And nobody has a waist that tiny!)

Those superheroes who are not born with their powers or descended from mythology often discover them through some fluke of science, often accompanied by that ubiquitous lightning. Radioactivity sometimes plays a part, particularly if this superhero was born after 1945.

A superhero always has an archnemesis. Someone whose sole purpose in life is to kill the superhero so thoroughly that nothing is left but tiny bits of former-superhero DNA. I admit that it was this last discovery that gave me pause.

Because I realized that afternoon, after reading about The

Flash and his Horrible Chemical Accident; Clark Kent's struggle to keep his powers a secret from his adoptive parents; and Peter Parker's fear the first time he had to rescue Mary Jane from some terrible fate . . .

That I was a superhero. Me. Little ol' Birdie Lee from Astro Park, Kansas.

"Well, hell." I put the last comic book down, drained the rest of my wine, and sat there a moment, letting the full realization of what had happened during that Horrible Swiffer Accident wash over me like ice water. I shivered, wondering if I'd ever find a warm, safe place again. Then I ran to the windows and pulled the curtains shut, afraid that evil henchmen with reptilian names were already taking aim at me.

"Well, hell," I repeated. "So, now what?" I picked up a Wonder Woman comic, studied it for a minute, then ran to my full-length mirror. I took a big breath, planted my fists on my hips and spread my legs apart. I sucked in my stomach. I pushed out my breasts.

"Shazam," I said. "To infinity and beyond!"

Then I let my breath out and everything (hips, legs, stomach, and breasts) returned to its normal, doughy, distinctly nonsuperhero state.

"Spandex," I told my reflection, which nodded thoughtfully in return.

Just then I heard a noise in the kitchen.

"Martin?"

"Mom?"

I picked up that one issue—*The Amazing Spider-Man,* Number 301. It had been outside my door this morning. Someone had put it there. Someone had put the others outside the bathroom door. And it occurred to me—

That *someone* was downstairs stuffing Oreos in his face.

"Martin?"

"Hmmmm?"

"Can you come here a minute?"

"Mmmfwweum oormmemmwrrk . . ."

"Don't talk with your mouth full!"

"Mmfffsssorry!"

"Come here, please."

Big sigh. Feet stomping up the stairs. Finally he pushed open my door, sandy hair flopping over his eyes, shoulders hunched over in his green army jacket.

"Huh?" Black crumbs lined his mouth. My hand quivered but I shoved it in my back pocket.

"I noticed that someone's been leaving comic books outside my door lately."

"Yeah?"

"Was that someone you?"

"Maybe." He scuffed his shoes on the floor and they left a big greasy black mark. My hand ached and burned and the seat of my jeans felt wet and I just longed so much to let loose, be myself, be who I was now and zap up the mark and tell someone my secret. Someone who wouldn't tell me to go to the doctor or call my ex-husband, someone who would believe me. Someone who read comic books and drew comic books and communicated through comic books, hidden under his dresser, left outside my bedroom door for me to discover—myself.

"Well, were you trying to tell me something? Sweetie?"

He shrugged.

"Something, maybe, about something you'd seen me do?"

"I dunno."

"With my hand, like cleaning stuff up?"

He shrugged again.

"Martin." I sat down on my bed. "Come here."

He shuffled over, his eyes trained on the ground. He sat down primly, like a little old man on a park bench.

"I couldn't help but notice that you'd left these Spider-Man comics, like you were trying to tell me something. And the thing is, I think I have something to tell you, too. And it's about . . . this." I picked up the comic with the picture of Spider-Man flying in the air, his hand extended. "Does this look familiar? Like maybe something you've seen me do . . . oh, never mind. It's stupid. It is, isn't it? It's too stupid to even think about. I don't know what I'm doing. Maybe Kelly's right. Maybe your dad's right. Maybe—"

"No!" Martin startled me into silence. He stared at me with those wide eyes, young, hopeful—wanting to believe. "No," he continued, his voice barely a whisper. "I mean, what do you think? What were you going to tell me, Mom? Because whatever it is, I might understand."

I looked at my son. Once he thought I had the power to change night into day. I was the last person he saw before he went to bed and the first person he saw when he woke up. I hung the moon, conjured up the sun. I was his hero. And then he grew up.

It was his hands, I thought. It was his hands that got to me. Big hands with prominent knuckles, hard, sinewy. I remembered his baby hands, so soft and plump with the dimples on the back, small enough that I could enfold his fist in my own palm, as tenderly as I would a baby chick, and keep it safe, forever. Now his hands were bigger than mine. They would enfold my tiny, gnarled hands one day, sooner than either of us could imagine. There's not much time—that's what I was thinking at that moment. Not much time left to be his hero.

"OK, then." I took a breath, stood up. "Go get a glass of milk."

Martin didn't question me. He just ran downstairs and returned, panting, with a glass of milk.

"Set it on the dresser."

He did.

"Now knock it over."

He hesitated for a minute—after all, he'd spent his entire life listening to me tell him not to spill things. But his eyes, blue and trusting, never wavered from mine as he pushed the glass off the dresser. Then he stood back and watched . . .

As I felt a surge of pride run through my body, through my spine and chest and arms until it spurted out in a glistening arc, from my right hand came a steady stream of fluid that caught the falling glass and pushed it back up on the dresser before it could fall to the ground and shatter. And the few milky drops that splashed to the floor were taken care of by my grippy, spongy right hand, which went to work in a perfect, poetic movement of scrubbing and swirling, ending with a dramatic flourish that kind of took me by surprise. Then it was my turn to stand back. And watch.

"Holy shit," said my son, my baby, his face flushed with excitement and disbelief and something else I couldn't put my finger on.

"Well, yes, dear. What you said. Neat though, isn't it?"

"Fuckin' awesome!"

"Martin!"

"It's like you're this superhuman machine," Martin burst out. "I knew it! I saw you the other night and I wasn't sure.

Then today at the park—you saved that little girl, didn't you?"

"Yes." I hung my head modestly.

"Wow! When did this happen? How? Why?"

"I don't know." I grinned, because I had just figured out what I saw in his eyes: admiration. "I think it started after that accident in the bathroom—"

"Yeah, the fumes, that must have been it." Martin shook his floppy hair and started to pace. "Some sort of chemical accident. Like Barry Allen."

"Barry Allen?"

"The Flash."

"Oh, right."

"So what else can you do?"

"Well, I'm not exactly sure. I can sort of sense things, like when people are in trouble. Mainly kids, like today. It's like something shivers along my spine and then I turn around and see something bad about to happen. And so I stop it. Oh, and apparently I have the ability to terrorize young children by knowing what's in their hearts."

"Super Spider Sense." Martin nodded, as if this was exactly what he'd expected.

"Huh?"

"Super Spider Sense. Like Spider-Man. He developed Super Spider Sense after—"

"He was bitten by the radioactive spider!" I snapped my fingers. Martin nodded approvingly.

"So, it's like you have Super Mom Sense, isn't it? I mean, moms clean things, they know when kids are in trouble, they know when kids are lying—"

"Super Mom Sense." I nodded. "Cool!"

"Anything else?"

"Well, voices. I hear these voices. And I'm not sure what they are."

"Voices? Really? You have superhearing, like Superman has X-ray vision?"

"No, not exactly. I can't really hear people talking, unless— well, it sounds silly."

"What?" Martin sat down next to me and folded his arms. He looked just like Doctor Dan right then, right down to the dimple.

"Well, I can hear people on the tape recorder, but I couldn't hear them at the meeting. Except I did hear Carl—Mr. Say-ers's radio, though. . . ."

"What?"

"Wait a minute." I grabbed the tape recorder from my bed-side stand and pressed Play. "Listen to this. What do you hear?"

"I hear some lady talking about PTA stuff. I hear Aunt Car-rie calling her a bitch. I hear—"

"But do you hear the other voices?" It was right at the part where Marge was talking about the frozen noodles.

"Nope."

"Huh." I scratched my head. *Doesn't Birdie look nice to-night?* "Oops!" I blushed and switched the tape recorder off.

"Oops what?"

"You really didn't hear anything?"

He shook his head.

"Good."

"Do it again," Martin urged, a sly, boyish look on his face.

"Do what?"

"Do that Spider-Man web-flinging thing."

"But there's nothing to clean up."

"Well, you're good at cleaning. I'm not so bad at making messes!"

"That's true." I smiled at my son, who rose, took my hand, and led me out into the world again—where we spent an unforgettable hour together. Martin spilled things and I cleaned them up. It was as simple as that. And I couldn't remember when I'd had a better time.

"So tell me," I said after eradicating a spectacular combination of hair gel, potting soil, and peanut butter, "now what?"

"Huh?" Martin was setting up a pyramid of model paints, all with their tops off. He grabbed a baseball, took careful aim, and fired.

"What do I do now?" I flung my cleaning fluid to all corners of his bedroom, catching the rainbow of color before it hit the ground.

"What do you mean? I guess you clean things. Save little kids." Martin shrugged and took a hefty swig of Coke. Then he crushed the half-empty can with his hand, sending streams of Coke flying all over the place.

"But how?" I zapped it all up with a casual flick of my hand. "Do I roam the earth, like that guy in *Kung Fu*, just searching for messes? Or do I just go on like usual?"

"Well, that seems like kind of a waste, doesn't it?"

"That's what I was thinking. And how about this other stuff? Hearing things, seeing things, making little children cry?"

"With great power comes great responsibility," Martin droned, in a perfect imitation of Doctor Dan. Which I had the good sense not to point out.

"I know, I know. Stupid Peter Parker." I flopped down in his beanbag chair.

"Hey!"

"Hey what?"

"Can you fly?"

"Huh?"

"Well, according to most of the Marvel comics and all of the DC ones, you should be able to fly. Do you think you could fly me to school sometime? That dickwad on the bus, Jamie Flugal? The total asswipe who always picks on me? He would so piss his pants if he saw that!"

"Martin, watch your language. Fly?" I hadn't thought of that. Could I fly? Me? Birdie? Once upon a time I was somebody's little brown wren. Maybe it had been an omen. "I don't know." I looked at Martin, who was pale with excitement. This was obviously a much bigger deal than shooting cleaning fluid out of my hands. "Maybe I should try it out?"

"Yeah! Let's go!" And Martin ran to his window and opened it.

"What are you doing?"

"Here! Go! Just leap out the window and fly. C'mon, Mom!"

"Whoa. Wait. Hold on a minute." I walked over to the window and looked down at the ground—several hundred feet below, or so it appeared to my doubtful eyes. And hard. Martin's bedroom is above the patio. Which is made of flagstone. Plus there was patio furniture. And a plant stand. With pointy, rusty edges. Which would probably hurt, should I somehow become impaled on them.

"Maybe we should try something less . . . high," I suggested.

"Why? Are you scared?" Martin looked truly astonished,

his jaw slack and his eyebrows arched as high as they could go. I believe at that moment he had forgotten that I was still his mother, the woman who was terrified of spiders and water bugs and caterpillars, the woman who still slept with a night-light in her bedroom.

"No, no, not scared. Exactly. Just . . . cautious. Yes. Cautious! We don't want to tip the neighbors off, do we? What would happen if Mr. Shoemaker looked out his window and saw me flying over his house?"

"Right, right." Martin nodded, thinking.

"How about"—I searched the backyard—"the top of the back stoop?"

"Mom. Please."

"OK. How about the top of the garden shed?"

"That should work!" And Martin was running down the stairs and outside faster than—The Flash.

But I followed, my eagerness to discover another new superpower overcoming my eagerness to continue my perfect record of unbroken bones. And to tell the truth, I couldn't wait to do it—fly. I couldn't wait to feel light and lithe and—and—feathery; I couldn't wait to float above my little corner of the world and look down on everyone and feel pity for them. But mostly, I couldn't wait to feel young. Because doesn't flying bestow, if not exactly immortality, then something close to eternal youth? You just never imagine old people flying, do you? It's always the young—tiny Russian gymnasts, Peter Pan, that daring young man on the flying trapeze—who you picture dancing through the air with no worries or fears to hold them down.

And right then, looking up at an empty, cloudless sky with room for all the dreams I'd been afraid to reach for, all my life before, I wanted to fly.

"OK, Mom!" Martin waved from the top of the garden shed. "C'mon up!"

"Uh, how?"

"The ladder around the back!"

"OK . . ." I approached the ladder. I made sure it was resting solidly against the shed. I took a step up. I wondered how long it had been since I'd climbed a ladder. I figured, conservatively, about fourteen years.

But my son was up there waiting for me. And I wanted to fly.

"Hi, honey." I groaned as I hauled myself over the top rung.

"Isn't it cool up here?" We surveyed the backyard—the vegetable garden, tangled with weeds; the back of the garage where we take all our old appliances to die—I could see the old coffeemaker and a sewing machine my mother gave me one Christmas; the back of the house, a patchwork of mismatched curtains, a climbing trellis of ivy, the patio set with its faded striped cushions.

And it all looked very comforting. Cozy. Like a home.

"Do you come up here a lot?" I joined him, careful not to look down, on the roof ridge.

"Yep," he said with a contented little snort. "Tons. I like it."

"What do you do up here, all by yourself?"

"Just think. About stuff. Sometimes a man needs his own personal time, Mom."

"Oh." My mouth twitched, but I sucked my cheeks in and prevented a smile from escaping. "I didn't realize."

"Well, yeah. I mean, with you and Kelly . . . I kind of need a place where I can just be manly. I guess."

"I guess." I frowned as he turned his face away. My son. He wasn't much of a talker; except for tennis shoes and hamburgers he never seemed to need much from anyone. But there I was wrong. There was one important thing—or person—he did need. And nothing I could do, not even now that I was a superhero, could give him that.

"So. Are you gonna just jump off?"

"Well, sure . . ." I stood up, wobbling a bit. Then I looked down.

It wasn't really that far. If I happened to fall. Just five feet or so. Maybe ten. No more than that. Ten feet. That was all. And the grass was nice and lush in this part of the yard . . . which reminded me that Martin forgot to mow it this week. But I wasn't about to bring it up right then.

"Why don't you go down there, just in case?"

"Just in case what?"

"Just in case—you know. I don't make it?"

"But, Mom. You will. You're a superhero now." And there was such understated confidence in his voice. Such assurance—there was no question. I could fly. I could almost believe it myself.

"Well, anyway. I'd feel better. OK?"

"OK." He scrambled down the ladder. "OK, Mom. Here I am!" He waved from the safety of solid ground. "Go ahead!"

"Yeah. Go ahead," I whispered. "OK!" I waved. I put my hands over my head. I bent my knees. I pushed myself forward.

I fell to the ground.

"You OK?" Martin stood rooted to the same spot, apparently too surprised to move.

"Ye-es . . ." I picked myself up. There were enormous grass stains on the knees of my jeans, which I took care of with a flick of my fingers.

"You didn't fly."

"Yes. I know."

"How come?"

"Beats me." I tested my legs and arms, shaking them, walking about. Nothing seemed broken, although everything ached.

"Well, maybe you didn't do it right."

"Well, tell me how to do it right. I'd like to know."

"Jeez, Mom, don't get mad at me. It's not my fault."

"Sorry. Sorry, sweetie. I know. It's just that . . . well, what should we do now?"

"Try again? Duh?" Martin shook his head.

"Oh. Right." I climbed back up the ladder. Martin stood below, pacing like an expectant father.

"OK, Mom. Think. What do you do before your cleaning fluid shoots out? What do you say, what do you think?"

"Nothing. I don't know. I see a mess and then I just point to it and know that it'll go away. I see it gone, all clean and new."

"Good. This is great! So, just see yourself flying. Point to the sky and see yourself flying, and then fly!"

"That might work." I stood up straight, pointed to the sky, saw myself floating above the trees . . .

Saw myself falling to the ground. In slow motion. I had time to count the buttons on Martin's jacket—seven.

"Wow." Martin gave a low froggy whistle. "That must have hurt."

"Yes. Yes, it did." I pushed myself up again and zapped the grass stains from my tennis shoes. "Did it ever occur to you that I might not be able to fly?"

"Well, sure. I mean, Batman can't fly."

"Batman can't fly? Well, why didn't you tell me? Thanks, Martin. So not every superhero can fly or swing or jump?"

"No, not everyone. It all depends on their powers. And

technically, Batman doesn't have real powers. He just has really cool gadgets, plus he trained in martial arts, plus he has a butler named Alfred."

"Well, that explains a lot—a butler? How do you get one of those?"

"I think you need to be born to wealthy parents and witness their cold-blooded murder and then inherit everything."

"Oh." We sat down together in the tall grass. I looked up to the sky and was filled with longing and sadness for a dream I'd never even known I'd had. Until now. "Maybe—maybe I'll discover I can fly later? Does that ever happen?"

"Well, I guess. Sometimes a superhero becomes stronger."

"Good," I whispered.

"You know." Martin shook his head, his hair flopping into his eyes. "Of all the people I know, I can't believe you're the one who gets superhero powers. I mean, come on."

"What do you mean?"

"I mean, you're Mom. You don't really do that much. You just clean and stuff. You're not that strong—you can't even change the lightbulb in the porch light; you always make me—"

"You think that's because I can't do it?" I narrowed my eyes.

"Well, I mean, you can do it. Probably." He lifted his chin, and for a minute it looked strong and chiseled—just like his father's. Just like a man's.

"There's no probably about it, buddy. And don't you forget it. But that still means it's your chore, not mine."

He picked a blade of grass and stuck it between his two front teeth. "So how will you get around?"

"Huh?"

"How will you get to the scene of the crime? How will you chase the bad guys?"

"What bad guys?"

"The ones you'll need to catch. You're a superhero now, Mom. Remember what I said? 'With Great Power Comes Great Responsibility'?"

"Stupid Spider-Man."

"So how will you get around?"

"Honey, I don't know. I guess I'll just have to drive that." And I pointed to my minivan. Which was new. Once. But now it was rusty, hard to drive on ice, and had about 85,000 miles on it.

"That?" Martin squeaked. "Oh, no. That'll never do. You need something like the Batmobile."

"Well, I don't have a butler, remember? Nor did I inherit millions. This is what we have. We'll have to deal with it."

"Oh, boy. I can just picture you putt-putting after bad guys in that thing."

"I don't like this talk of bad guys. It's making me a little nervous." I squirmed in the grass.

"But you'll have to have an archnemesis."

I thought of Lex and his hulking sidekick, and felt a little nauseated. Although it may have just been the baby aspirin and wine. "Well, let's just not think about that right now. We'll worry about it when the time comes."

"OK. How about your costume, then? What kind of costume are you going to—"

"Mom? Martin?" We heard Kelly slam a door in the house, back from the park.

"Kel? Hey, Kelly, out here—"

I clamped my hand over Martin's mouth.

"Wait a minute," I said. "Think about it. You're my trusty sidekick, right?"

He nodded, a shy, pleased look flickering across his face.

"So I can trust you. But I have to maintain my secret identity, right? Like everybody else. Peter Parker doesn't tell Aunt May that he's Spider-Man, does he?"

Martin shook his head.

"OK. Soooo, let's not tell Kelly, shall we? We can't have everyone knowing. And Kelly, well, she might not understand this like you do. She might—"

"You mean she might tell Dad?"

"Right." I sighed. "So let's just keep this our secret for now, OK?" I dared to put my arm around my son. But he didn't move away.

"OK, Mom. I mean . . . Super Mom."

"Oh, I don't know about that." But I grinned from ear to ear. Super Mom. Did you hear that? That was me. My son had just said so.

"This was a nice day, wasn't it?" Martin started walking to the house and I followed more slowly, my legs still stiff and bent from hitting the ground so hard.

"Yes, it was."

"Can you maybe get me out of school sometime? For a secret mission or something? Or maybe there'll be a big chemical spill and you'll need help. Or maybe you can put Jamie Flugal, that total asswipe, in a Super Time Out! Cool! Can you do that? A Super Time Out?"

"I don't know. I've never tried it. There are a lot of things I haven't tried yet." The day was fading away. Kelly had turned on the light in the kitchen, a beacon to guide us home. Martin was scampering ahead of me, disappearing into the dusk, but I could still hear him.

"What else do you do . . . oh, I know! Nagging! You nag all

the time, even before this. Do you think you'll do some kind of Super Nagging? I wonder what that would be like. You could try it on me, you know. I wouldn't mind. I can be like your test villain if you want. That'd be cool! Oh—Super Spanking! That would be awesome! Only maybe you'd want to try that out on someone else. . . ."

"Maybe." I could see Kelly inside grabbing plates and silverware, getting ready for dinner. She was smiling to herself, and I wondered what secret she was nurturing. I hoped it was a good one, a tender one. One to place under her pillow tonight, to help shape her dreams.

"And Super Grounding! Wow! That could be so tremendous! Definitely don't try that one out on me, though, if you don't mind, OK, Mom? Super Grounding! That's sweet. . . ."

"Uh-huh." I smiled at my son in the darkness. But he didn't see.

CHAPTER 5

GIRL SAVED BY MYSTERY MOM screamed the headline.

The grand opening of New Cosmos Patriot Park was marred by a near-fatal accident. Fortunately the day was saved when a woman—known only as some sort of super mom—vaulted over protective fencing and saved a little girl from falling to certain death. "Thank goodness for this hero," said Lex Osborne, self-made millionaire CEO of New Cosmos. "We only wish she would come forward so we could thank her properly. The safety and sanctity of family is the number one priority for New Cosmos, and this selfless act of mother love deserves to be rewarded."

The little girl, three-year-old Hannah Hayes, is doing fine. As to how she made her way through the protective fencing, no one knows. The incident is under investigation.

BATHROOM AT BUS STATION GETS OVERNIGHT MAKEOVER declared another headline a few days later.

Baffled transit officials are wondering just how or why someone entered the building late last night and scrubbed the bathroom until it was like new. "Even the faucets were polished. And the men's urinals—good golly! I had no idea the porcelain was white," enthused a grateful Dean Kimball, head of maintenance.

MYSTERY WOMAN BREAKS UP TEEN SEX PARTY trumpeted the headline a couple of days after that.

"Dude, we were up at the junkyard parking, you know?" stated Darren Sorkin, a high school senior. "And anyway this crazy lady comes driving up in this minivan, honking her horn. She started knocking on all the cars there—Dude! You know, if this car's a-rockin', don't come a-knockin'. But she did anyway. And she kept screaming, 'I know what you're doing in there! You're too young for this kind of behavior! Think of the diseases, you young people. Think of AIDS!' And we were like, whoa, little dudette, chill. But she hauled us all out and said she'd tell our parents if we didn't break it up right then. And I don't know, man, but something about the way she looked at us—man. I haven't felt that guilty since I was six and I stole my mom's bus money."

When asked what this mystery health advocate looked like, Mr. Sorkin replied, "Weird, man. I mean, she had all these Ziploc bags full of stuff—Wet Wipes, dental floss, Band-Aids. She wore this weird cape made out of a pillowcase. Oh, and a paper bag over her head with the eyes cut out."

"I have got to get a better costume," I muttered, folding the paper.

"What?" Carrie looked up from her battered copy of *The Interpretation of Dreams*.

"Nothing!" I hid my copy of the *Astro Daily World* within the folds of this week's *National Enquirer*. "Just this article—check it out!"

"Birdie." Carrie heaved a great sigh and went back to her book.

GIANT GLOBS OF BIRD POOP MENACE NEIGHBORHOOD— MISCHIEVOUS SUPERHERO TO BLAME? According to Mrs. Elmore Duffey of Shakerville, Kentucky, the sudden appearance of football-sized dollops of aviary excrement is no mystery to her. "It's that Birdman, that lives over in them apartments," the tiny grandmother of twelve reported. "He thinks he can get away with it, but he don't know I got me a telescope from the Wal-Mart the other day. I know what he's up to, that's for darn sure. He drinks a fifth of Jack Daniel's and then he goes flyin' all over the place, gigglin' like the devil he is. Then—splat! I have to say, he's gettin' better with his aim, though. The other day I saw him make a bull's-eye on the Portillos' cat. Poor Fifi! Got it right on top of her head, she did. Drunken superhero bastard."

I giggled. "Hey, Carrie, listen to this—" But then I stopped giggling. I studied the photo of a blurred man with wings standing behind a half-closed door, his hand up to the camera, waving it off. Then I quietly folded the paper and tucked it away.

"Good afternoon," I said as a customer unloaded her cart. I turned the conveyor belt on and started to scan. Then I stopped, holding a bag of peanuts. I bent my head toward the scanner. I smiled.

"These will be on sale Friday, two for a dollar," I whispered.

"Ohhh! Birdie, thank you. I'll just . . . could you please put those back for me?"

"My pleasure!"

"Birdie, why do you always have such a long line of customers lately? Hey, folks, I'm open here!" Carrie waved her arms, all alone at her register.

The six regulars who were lined up for me just smiled. No one moved.

"I couldn't say," I replied, scanning a carton of ice cream. The scanner beeped; a little voice told me a secret that only I could hear. "Next week this brand is fifty cents off," I whispered.

"Birdie, you're an angel!" Mrs. Townsend, who I knew for a fact was on food stamps, leaned over and clasped my hand. "Bless you!"

"Don't mention it," I said as I kept scanning. "It's all in a day's work!"

"OK, so what do you have?"

"Well, I've been doodling during cartooning club," Martin said, clutching his notebook to his chest. We were in the garage, our secret hideout; Kelly never plunked a pedicured foot in there with all the rusty tools and cobwebs and one lone lightbulb hanging by a cord from the rafters.

"Yeah? Well, show me, show me!"

"Hold on, Mom." Martin grinned, milking the suspense for all it was worth. "I want to point a few things out first. For one thing, I know you wanted to look cute, but let's face it. You're not exactly Wonder Woman. Or Supergirl. Or Batgirl. Or . . ."

"OK, OK." I held up my hand. "I get it. I'm still a forty-one-year-old mother of two. So, no short cheerleader skirt? No jewel-encrusted halter top?"

"Mom! Ewwww!"

"Sorry. . . . Next?"

"Well, next thing is, a superhero's costume is very impor-tant. It has to be easy to draw for the comic book, but practi-cal enough to stand up in fights and stuff. And it should tie into the whole origin—like Superman's cape is the blanket he was wrapped up in when his parents put him on the rocket that took him away from Krypton right before it blew up and they all were toast. So I tried to keep that in mind."

"Let me see! Let me see!" I reached toward the notebook, but he slapped my hand away.

"The last thing: Secrecy is important. I mean, Superman looks exactly like Clark Kent except for the glasses and the way his hair curls down on his forehead. The people in Me-tropolis have to be pretty dumb not to know he's Superman, if you ask me. I think Astro Park is smarter than that, so we have to be careful. And then, well, there's Dad. He can't find out, for sure. So I had to think about that a lot."

"Martin! Let me see! The suspense is killing me!"

"Well, OK." Martin started to flip over his notebook, but then he hesitated. "Remember, I'm only thirteen," he said, suddenly shy.

"But you're a very talented thirteen." I smiled and ruffled his hair.

"Mom!" He smoothed his hair back down. "OK. Here you are!" And he presented me with the first artist's rendition of—me. Super Mom. In all her maternal glory.

Clad in a green, full-skirted housedress the color of a Swif-fer WetJet, with a giant apron with huge pockets tied about her waist, the cartoon me had a single strand of pearls around her neck, earrings, and high-heeled pumps. On her remarkably flat chest (a slight artistic liberty upon which I didn't comment) was a big orange "S". Her eyes were hidden behind a plain black mask, like the Lone Ranger's, only the ends turned up slightly like those cat's-eye glasses that old ladies wear. A tiny little dish towel cape, the tacky kind with fringe, completed the ensemble, held in place by two giant clothespins.

"I look like June Cleaver on steroids," I said, my heart sinking. I could just imagine what Wonder Woman would say about this costume. Hers was so glamorous! (Even with the girdle.)

"Exactly! She's probably the most famous mom in the world, and since your powers are exactly like hers, only about ten million times more powerful, I thought that would be a good idea. I mean—look at it! Anyone with half a brain would know that it's Super Mom! And that's really important, you know. Your image has to be recognizable."

"But how am I supposed to fight crime in high heels?"

"Oh, I thought of that. Dr. Scholl's foot cushions!"

"Oh. What's with the pearls, though? How will I get them on in time? That seems like a lot of accessorizing to me."

"Don't you like it?" Martin hunched down and shoved his hands in the pockets of his army jacket.

"Oh, sweetie, yes! Of course I do! I love it! I really like the clothespins—that's a nice touch. Just the right amount of humor!"

"Well, Mr. Sayers kind of helped me with that part."

"He did?" Carl had seen this? Had helped design this? For me? But of course, he didn't know it was for me. He thought it was just another cartoon Martin was working on. But still. A little thrill tickled my spine, to think of his hand in this, the creation of my new identity.

"Oh, honey." I reached out to my son and gave him a quick hug. "I love it. Really I do. So now what?"

"Well." He squirmed out of my arms. "I guess you make it."

"Hmmm." I held the drawing up to the lightbulb. "What kind of material did you have in mind?"

"Well, something industrial, like a cleaning cloth or something."

"Like a treated dustcloth?"

"Yeah—something like that! That would be cool, wouldn't it? All this dirt would just kind of stick to you, like you were Magneto!"

"Who?"

"From the X-Men. He's an evil mutant."

"Oh. Well, I'll see what I can do." I started to hand the drawing back, but then stopped. "Is this mine? Can I keep it?"

"Sure."

"Would you . . . wait a minute." I opened up the toolbox and rummaged around. "There!" I held up a grease pencil. "Would you sign it? For me? It's a first edition, you know."

"Sure." Martin hung his head but I could see his quick grin. Then he signed his name, Martin Stanley Lee, in that tiny scrawl he has, all the letters scrunched together so that it looked like a smushed bug on the bottom of the page.

"Thanks, trusty sidekick." I tugged the chain to turn the lightbulb off.

"Mom!" Martin pulled the garage door down behind us.

"Where have you two been?" Kelly asked as Martin and I entered the kitchen, blinking our eyes at the sudden brightness.

"Oh, um, out in the garage. I had to show Martin something I wanted him to do."

"Well, you two certainly have been spending a lot of time out there."

"No, not really, sweetheart. We haven't. Have we, Martin?"

"Nope." Martin headed down to the basement. I heard the TV switch on, followed by the familiar anthem of American Justice.

"Don't spend too much time on that game!"

"Mom, can you bring me down some Patriot Pops?"

"What's that?" Kelly reached for the drawing.

"Nothing." I tucked it in my pocket. "He was just showing me one of his cartoons."

"Hmmmph," she snorted. "Really, Mother, you shouldn't let him spend so much time doodling. Or playing video games. Or reading comic books. It's unhealthy, all that fantasy. He needs to open his eyes and live in the real world for a change, the real world without superheroes and villains and battles."

"Oh, honey." I tried not to smile; she looked so serious. She always looked so serious. Was there ever a time when she just laughed to be silly, giggled like other girls over nothing at all? "Don't you ever want to go off on adventures? Don't you ever think about it sometimes?"

"But they're not real." She chewed on her fingernail. "People aren't heroes, you know. They're just people. It's silly to wish for things that aren't real."

"I guess . . ." And I almost told her, right then and there. I almost told her that there were shifts in the landscape that you couldn't see, fault lines and sinkholes, things that could alter your surroundings so subtly that you never noticed them until you put your foot down and found yourself just slightly off-balance. Or that sometimes the changes were more seismic—great tumblings of rock or earth falling about you, shaking your senses, turning you upside down on your heels until you didn't know what was real anymore.

I almost told her my secret.

But I didn't. And by not doing so, it seemed to me that I created another fault line, right there in my kitchen, just the same as if I'd drawn a line in the linoleum: Kelly and her father versus Martin and me.

"Well, anyway"—I looked at my daughter, weighed down by one more thing I couldn't tell her—"do you need any help with your homework?"

"No. I finished already." She turned to go upstairs.

"Kelly—wait—did Harry ask you to the Harvest Dance?"

"Yeah." She was halfway up the stairs by now.

"Oh. Well, isn't that nice. But—are you sure that's what you want? Is he? What you want? Kelly, is he good to you?"

Her door slammed. She didn't tell me. And it was only what I deserved, after all.

I sighed, got a box of Patriot Pops, and went down to the basement. My trusty sidekick was sitting in a beanbag chair, engaged in a battle: Teddy Rough Rider and George Washington Carve 'Em Up were kickboxing the bad guys—in black, with dark skin and hair, a couple in turbans—on the lawn of the White House.

"Martin, get your feet off the coffee table. How many times do I have to tell—" And then I stopped dead in my tracks. Because the television was talking to me, underneath the cartoon video game sounds of grunts and *pows* and explosions. There was an undercurrent, a buzz: more voices. Just like all the others I'd heard since my Horrible Swiffer Accident. But as I drew nearer, my blood ran cold. These were not like the others, not at all.

"Eat Patriot Pops," they whispered excitedly. *"Patriot Pops are what you want. Mmmmm. Crispy, sugary. What you crave. Eat Patriot Pops."*

"Mom, I want those Patriot Pops," Martin whined. "Hand 'em to me."

"Ask your parents to buy more Patriot Pops," the voices sang. *"Patriot Pops are good for you! They have Calcium and Vitamin D! Eat Patriot Pops!"*

"Did you know they have Calcium?" Martin asked. "And Vitamin D?"

I ignored him, the box clutched in my suddenly trembling hands, and turned the video game off right in the middle of a spectacular battle on top of the Capitol building.

"Mom!" Martin dropped the controller in amazement. "Why'd you do that?"

I turned the video game back on. Martin fast-forwarded through the titles and started over again.

"Eat Patriot Pops," the voices teased. *"Patriot Pops are what you want!"*

"Do you hear that?" I asked Martin. He shook his head. "You don't?"

"Hear what?"

"That—those voices." I stared at the television. Abe Lincolnator was running across Thomas Jefferson's nose on Mount Rushmore, his stovepipe hat shooting fire bullets. *"Patriot Pops, eat Patriot Pops,"* the voices buzzed. I turned the game off again, then turned it back on.

"Patriot Pops are what you want."

I studied Martin, who was hunched over the controller, his tongue sticking out of his mouth. Did I detect a paunch around his waist? "How long have you been playing this game?"

"About five minutes."

"No. I mean, when did you buy this game?"

"There was a coupon for it in a box of Patriot Pops."

"I thought there was a coupon for Patriot Pops in the video game."

Martin shrugged. "Which came first, the chicken or the egg?"

"Which, indeed?" I tapped my nose, thinking.

"Mmmmm. Crispy. Sugary. Patriot Pops. What you crave."

"So can I have the Patriot Pops?"

"No," I told him. "As a matter of fact you can't. And turn off that game."

"But—"

"No buts about it. And don't push it, or I'll put you in a Super Time Out."

"Man"—Martin threw down the controller—"it kind of sucks having a superhero for a mother."

"Yeah, well, try looking at it from my point of view." I marched upstairs, prepared to toss all the boxes of Pops and Drops in the trash, but instead I collapsed into a kitchen chair. Because I'd just realized something.

In all this superhero business, I'd only concentrated on other people's children. It had never occurred to me that my own would need the protection of Super Mom. But now I realized that danger lurked everywhere—in the eyes of handsome young men, in the comfort of our own family room—and not even a superhero could protect them from it, not completely. There was just too much. I'd liked it better when I couldn't see it all, couldn't hear it all. When I'd been a mere mortal mother, worried only about the things everyone else was worried about: sex, drugs, interest rates. But I couldn't go back; my worries had increased exponentially along with my powers.

And that, to quote my trusty sidekick, kind of sucked.

Oh, the magic of a perfect autumn night! Crisp leaves, bracing air, the promise of desire in the stars, a first dance, a first kiss. A first night.

"You look so nice, sweetheart! Doesn't she, Martin?"

"Yeah." Martin didn't look up from his comic book, which I'd bought to make up for the fact that American Justice was now in a shoe box on the top shelf of my closet. "Nice."

"Martin!"

"I said she looks nice! Jeez."

"Thanks." Kelly tried her best to frown, but even she couldn't keep it up tonight. And my heart just ached at the sight of her loveliness. Her glossy hair was pulled back from her face, except for a few loose strands; her pure young shoulders, perfectly balanced, held her spaghetti-strap dress with grace and poise.

"I wish he'd hurry up!"

"Who, honey? Harry?"

"No, Daddy. He said he'd come by and take pictures, remember?"

"Yes, I remember."

"Is that what you're wearing?" Her anxious eyes flickered over me.

"Y-e-e-s, what's wrong with it?" I tugged at my suede skirt, smoothed my new cashmere sweater.

"Nothing. That's really weird, Mom. You look nice for a change. It's just kind of weird."

"Yeah. And what's that on your lips?" Martin raised one eye over the top of his comic book.

"Just a little lipstick."

"And on your eyes?"

"Just a little eye shadow."

"Weird." Both Kelly and Martin said it at the same time.

"Not really." I turned away and smiled at my new secret identity: Glamour Mom.

The doorbell rang.

"I'll get it!" Kelly danced to the door. "Daddy!" She squealed like the little girl she never was, and jumped into his arms. Which weren't quite ready for an embrace, I couldn't help but notice.

"Sweetie," Doctor Dan murmured, looking over her shoulder at the living room, the hallway, checking to see if there was anything new that shouldn't be there, or anything missing that should be.

"Hey, Dad." Martin didn't look up from his comic book. Dan gently pushed Kelly away.

"Hey, sport," he said in that hollow, hearty way he'd adopted ever since—well, ever since Martin was in second grade and witnessed—well, ever since.

"Hello, Dan," I said. And then I smoothed my sweater again, just because.

"Hello, Birdie," he replied, raising his eyebrows. "Well. You're not . . . you're not going on a . . . I mean, are you going out?" He pushed his ash-blond hair back from his forehead, where it had a tendency to flop, just like Martin's.

"I'm chaperoning the dance." And I couldn't hide a tiny smile, pleased that he'd wondered if I was going out on a date, and that the thought seemed to push him just a little off-balance.

"Well, well, that's why you look different. Nice, that is. Doesn't she, sport?"

"Yeah." Still Martin didn't look up from his comic book.

"Well, let's get this show on the road." Doctor Dan rubbed his hands, preparing to take charge, act the patriarch, get the Kodak moment over with so he could scoot back to his big new house on the other side of town.

"Where's Dixie? Didn't she want to see Kelly?" I asked.

"She had a council meeting tonight. She works so late, you know. She's so busy with her career."

"Well, it's a shame she had to miss tonight."

"Some things are more important than missing a little high school dance, Birdie. Things like taxes and roads, things that a woman like Dixie is naturally very interested in—"

"I'm sure the city of Astro Park just can't run without her!" I kept a pleasant smile on my face, for the children.

"No, it can't, Birdie. Just as I'm sure the Marvel Food and Fine Beverages would tumble to the ground without your highly valued ability to fold paper bags."

Martin hid his face in his comic book. Kelly started to chew her fingernail.

"Oh, Kelly! Honey! Don't." I started over to her. "You just put nail polish on! Why don't you take her picture, Dan?"

"That's a good idea," Dan said, forcing another hearty smile. "Smile for the camera, all right, Kel?"

"OK, Daddy." She stood in front of the fireplace, blinked her eyes and smiled; Dan clicked the camera. And there he had it, another perfect picture to put on his desk at work, for his patients to cluck over—"Oh, Dr. Lee! You have such a beautiful family. You must love them so!" And he does. Especially when they're frozen in time in a tiny silver frame, to be displayed at his discretion.

The doorbell rang again. Doctor Dan made a big show of answering it and giving Harry a stern, fatherly look. "Don't keep her out too late, son. She's my little girl." A speech, by the way, which would have caused Kelly to spontaneously combust if I had made it. But she didn't bat an eyelash; she even giggled, pleased to bask in the attention. I couldn't blame her for that. She was fifteen, pretty, and more than a little selfish. And I was glad for her.

"Nice to see you, Dr. Lee. And you look very lovely tonight, Mrs. Lee."

I scowled at Harry. He was handsome, polite, poised. And that's exactly why I didn't trust him. Most boys his age were too embarrassed to breathe properly, let alone converse with an adult. But Harry was smooth, practiced—just like his father, Lex Osborne. Just like Doctor Dan, for that matter.

No wonder I didn't trust this boy.

Doctor Dan took another picture of the two of them, Harry's arm possessively around Kelly's waist, a perfect smile on his face. Then it was time to leave. Dan departed with another hale "See ya, sport!" for Martin, a cool, appraising look for me, and a stiff hug for Kelly. Harry guided Kelly to the door. I ran after them.

"Kelly?"

"What, Mom?" She turned to me, her whole face lit up, her eyes incandescent silver stars. Harry kept his arm firmly around her waist.

"Just—have fun tonight, sweetheart." I kissed her, careful not to smudge her makeup. "And . . . just be good." I looked Harry in the eye; he met my gaze with breezy arrogance.

"Don't you worry about a thing, Mrs. Lee," he purred. "I wouldn't let anything happen to my Kelly." Then he pulled her out of my house, into the night.

I watched them drive off, wishing, just for a minute, that I could ride with them. And it wasn't only because his car was nicer than mine. Then I ran upstairs to the bathroom. A visit from Doctor Dan always did this to me, sent me scurrying upstairs to fix my hair or change my clothes, cursing the betrayal of my mirror, certain that the reflection I saw in his eyes was the true one and so my memory of myself was not to be trusted.

But for once the mirror reflected back to me the person I'd been before he'd arrived: a confident woman, with sparkling brown eyes and rosy cheeks, hair curling around her shoulders just right, almost like a 1940s movie star. Lips half-parted, breathless with anticipation. I blew a kiss at my movie-star self, giggling at my foolishness.

When I came downstairs, Martin was waiting. He pointed at the paper bag I was clutching.

"Is that it?" He still wouldn't look at my face; I'd no idea that makeup was such a powerful child repellent. "You didn't forget anything, did you, Mom?"

"I don't think so." I rolled the top of the bag down, tight, so no one could see inside.

"Are you ready?"

"No," I admitted, thinking of all the things that could happen tonight. "Not at all."

"That's OK, Mom." My son patted me on the arm and smiled. "Just do your best."

Have you ever chaperoned a high school dance?

Well, it's hell. It's everything you think it's going to be, only worse.

Sex. Sex. And more sex. Thoughts of sex, smells of sex, murmurs and shudders and whispers of sex. And drugs. And drinking. And hearts being broken, crushed under big clunky Steve Madden shoes, shredded against prickly razor stubble.

Bad things happening. Bad things to happen later. Bad things that just happened in the parking lot.

And for me, with all my senses aquiver—spilled punch over there; boys with half-empty silver flasks in that corner; a couple contemplating having unprotected sex in the locker room—well, all I can say is I felt like I was going to explode the minute I walked into the gym. Every nerve ending sang; I thought I was going to jump out of my skin.

"Hello, Birdie."

I whooped and jumped; fortunately my skin stayed in place.

"Oh! Hi, Carl."

"You look nice tonight." *Doesn't Birdie look nice tonight? She always looks so nice and neat.*

"You too—thanks, I mean. Thank you."

"What's in the bag?"

"Oh, nothing." I clutched the paper bag to my chest. "Just something for Kelly."

"Well, welcome to the New Cosmos Harvest Dance." Carl pointed to a huge banner hanging from the scoreboard: NEW COSMOS INDUSTRIES IS PROUD TO SPONSOR THE JEROME SIEGEL JUNIOR HIGH AND HIGH SCHOOL ANNUAL JUNIOR/SENIOR HARVEST DANCE. "And guess what's for refreshments?"

"Patriot Pops and Democracy Drops?"

"How'd you know?"

"Just a lucky guess."

Carl turned and surveyed the dance floor; I pretended to do the same. Although I was really checking him out. And then I giggled at the thought—me, at my age, checking a guy out!

"Did you say something?"

"Nope!" I giggled again. He was so cute! I mean—ahem—he was so handsome. His eyes were kind, so brown and sweet and kind, and he had these two deep creases on either side of his mouth that made me long to trace them with my finger. He was wearing a nice suede shirt and Dockers, and his hair was parted, which made me smile, even if he did look a little dorky. But I'd never seen him with his hair parted before. Which made me think that he'd made a special effort tonight. Which made my heart skip a beat as I wondered what—or whom—he'd been thinking about when he'd dipped his comb in the water and made a careful straight line through his thick black hair.

"Nice hair," I blurted.

"Thanks." Carl looked sheepish; then he messed it up just like a little boy. I had to smile.

A goofy kid wearing a tuxedo T-shirt walked by, carrying a glass of punch. "Hey, Mr. Sayers," he said, obviously happy to see someone who would talk to him. "Cartooning club was awesome today."

"Hey, Stevie. Yeah, it rocked," Carl replied. The boy raised his punch glass in a toast, and some big burly guy bumped into him from behind.

"Hey, dweebus! Mr. Osborne has a room set up for losers like you to play American Justice. Since no one's gonna dance with you anyway."

The dweebus hiccupped and spilled his punch all over the place.

But I stood perfectly still. My hand twitched a little but that was all. I'd been practicing, you see. I'd learned to control all my leaking—the trick was in pinching the fleshy part of my right hand, between my thumb and forefinger. At most, I looked like I was trying not to sneeze. No one would suspect I was anyone other than Birdie Lee, mild-mannered cashier at the Marvel Food and Fine Beverages and member of the Hawthorne School District Parent/Teacher Association.

And that was my plan for tonight. My other recent outings—the ones reported in the paper—were trial runs, made under cover of darkness. But tonight was my big test. Could I hack it as a superhero? Could I be Birdie Lee, mild-mannered PTA chaperone, and Super Mom, fierce protector of children everywhere? And most importantly, tonight would answer the burning question—

Could I fight crime in high heels?

"I'll go get a janitor," Carl told the boy, who sighed, apparently used to moments like this. "C'mon, Birdie."

"Oh! OK," I said, surprised. What did this mean? Were we chaperoning partners or something? Did I miss the part where he chose me, or I chose him?

But as his hand pressed against the small of my back,

sending tiny quakes rocking up my spine until they tingled my hair and shivered back down again to where his hand remained, steady, protective—I was sure. I hadn't missed that part, not at all.

"Don't play that video game," I called back to the dweebus, who didn't appear to have heard me. But Lex Osborne, who at that moment was posing for a picture for the school newspaper, did. His leonine head, with its magnificent white hair, swiveled in my direction. I could feel his eyes, oddly lit in the semidarkness of the gym, follow me all the way across the floor. It was just like those eyes of New Cosmos, following me home from work at night.

"Oh, hi, Carl, Birdie!" Carrie was patrolling the punch table, but she stepped away just in time to sidle up to us and roll her eyes until I had to stomp on her foot. "Ow!"

"Oops! Sorry, didn't see your foot there." I grinned and patted her on the head.

"Right. Howard!" She barked. Howard came trundling up, his bald head sparkling like the disco ball hanging from the ceiling. "Howard, look, here's Birdie! Doesn't she look nice tonight? Doesn't she?"

"I guess. Hi, Birdie. Hey, Carl." Howard and Carl shook hands.

"So, what are we supposed to do? Just walk around and act like we have authority?" I asked Carrie.

"Oh, so you haven't received your assignment yet?"

"Assignment? No, I—"

"Well, Birdie, I'm glad to see you've arrived. One must be punctual at all costs, mustn't one?" Patty Osborne drawled, resplendent in an evening suit with matching Ferragamo pumps. "Since you were one of the last to arrive, I've decided to give you the bathroom assignment. Report any suspicious behavior to myself or Principal Davis. Do you think you can handle that?"

"We were just going to find the janitor," Carl said, looking at me. I opened my mouth to agree, but Patty was too quick.

"Fine. Let's find him together, shall we? And then I have a special job for you, Carl!" And Patty hooked her arm through his and dragged him away. I watched him go, wishing with all my superpowers that he'd look back; I held myself so still, afraid to move, because if I did, I'd surely miss him looking. But he didn't. And all of a sudden I wasn't so sure about anything anymore.

"Oh, well." I turned and smiled at my friends; Howard clicked his tongue and handed me a glass of punch. Then he ran back to the table, where a suspicious group of boys was circling the punch bowl.

Carrie was twitching all over—I thought steam would come out of her ears. "That bitch! How dare she? Look at the way she just kidnapped poor Carl! When it was clear he wanted to be with you! And to stick you in the bathroom—good God!"

"Never mind, Carrie. We're here to chaperone, remember? Somebody has to be in the bathroom." But my shoulders sagged, and so did my panty hose; I felt as crumpled as the bag I was clutching.

"But why does it always have to be you?"

I didn't have an answer to that, so I downed my punch in one quick gulp, slammed the glass down on the table, wiped my mouth with my sleeve, and marched off to my post. And that's when I realized it was going to be a long, difficult night.

For the girls' bathroom was sin central. Not in the actual committing of it, but in the methodical planning.

"So after the dance, you guys are coming over, right? My parents are out of town and my brother said he'd buy the beer . . ."

Jennifer Brown, 255 Sequoia Street. I made a mental note. *Underage drinking.*

"Hey, let me borrow a cig, 'kay? Meet you out back?"

Karen Dudley and Mary Campbell, illegal use of tobacco on school property.

"His sister has a stash. We could cruise by there later, see if she wants to sell us a little?"

Iris Zeigler. Possible possession of cannabis. I began to wonder if I should have brought a notebook in which to keep track. Super Mom was going to be busy tonight.

But for now, all I could do was frown at the young ladies in question and endure their scornful laughter. And suddenly I knew how Clark Kent felt when he was teased by Lois Lane and Jimmy Olsen. He must have felt furious, because he knew he could kick their sorry asses anytime he wanted to, yet he had to be careful not to expose his true identity and embarrass his daughter beyond all reason . . . Oh. Right. That was me. For the first time it occurred to me that there was probably a reason most superheroes were childless.

"Pssst."

I looked around. The gaggle of girls had left; I checked in all the stalls but they were empty.

"Pssst."

"What? Who—"

"Birdie?"

"Yes?"

"Come out and play!"

"Carl?" I stuck my head outside the door. Carl was standing there, his back against the wall.

"Pssst. Come on out; the coast is clear. Patty had to run home because somebody spilled punch all over her Dolce and Gabbana suit. What's a Dolce and Gabbana?"

"It's a designer," I said and laughed, joining him. "Or, they're a designer, two of them. Dolce. And—"

"Gabbana."

"Right."

"How do you know this stuff?"

"I have a daughter."

"Ohhhh."

"Thanks."

"For what?"

"For springing me. For . . . remembering me."

"How could I ever forget you?" Carl turned to me. It wasn't just a line. He looked honestly perplexed. How could I forget the sky? The moon? The stars? How, indeed?

And that was the moment I stopped thinking about spoiled milk.

"Well . . ." Our hands touched and my heart fell—I fell—into his eyes, which reflected back to me my truest self of all. "I, I, uh . . ." My lips felt numb—too dumb to form words.

"Birdie, I—I—uh . . ." He bent toward me; I held my breath and knew. I'd been waiting for this moment for a long, long time. I'd just needed him to remind me.

"Carl, I . . ."

"Yes? I mean, yes?" He bent over me, shielding me from the crowd. We were in our own little protective cocoon in which we could only look at each other, stammer, and grin.

"Oops! Sorry, Mrs. Lee." Suddenly a posse of teens ran toward the bathrooms; the music had stopped and Lex Osborne was tapping the microphone, preparing to make a speech. "Sorry, sorry!" Laughing young people rushed past us, swooping us up in their energy and light. Carl and I laughed too, swatting at them like fireflies.

"Oops!" Someone knocked against me and jostled my bag. It ripped open and—and—

Stuff poured out. My stuff. A black mask, pearls, a pair of lacy underwear, the color of Swiffer green. One high-heeled pump landed right on top of Carl's left shoe.

"Birdie—" Carl looked down. And frowned. Then he looked at me, the most interesting expression on his face. "Birdie . . . this is . . . you said it was for Kelly?"

"No! No!" I dropped to my knees and started scooping things up. My face burned so red I could hardly see. "God, no! Not Kelly! Why would you think . . . No! It's mine!"

"Yours?" Carl had bent to help me, but all of a sudden he sat down, hard, as if his legs had given out. "This is . . . yours?"

"Oh! Yes. I mean, no . . . I mean . . . oh dear!" I felt sick to my stomach. "No, yes, it's my costu— I mean, I won't need it until later tonight. I mean . . . oh dear!" I snatched at the pair of underwear, which seemed to have a life of its own, dancing just away from my reach. "You never know when you might need a clean pair!"

Carl let out a strange sound, something between a gasp and a guffaw. I blushed again.

"Well, whatever your plans for tonight are . . ." He slowly stood up. "Good luck."

"Well." I tried to laugh, but it came out more like a gurgle. "I bet you don't see that every day, do you?"

Carl whistled and shook his head, his brown eyes dancing. "Remember, I'm a scientist? We don't get out much."

"That's a shame." I lowered my voice to what I prayed was a sexy growl. "You know, I was a Girl Scout. 'Be prepared!' was our motto."

Carl's mouth twitched, his eyes danced some more, and he suddenly turned toward the dance floor. I could see his shoulders shake, and he made that strange guffaw/gasping sound again.

"I see a—situation out there," he said in a garbled voice. "I'd better go check it out. Oh, and Birdie?"

"Hmmm?"

"I made Eagle Scout. If you need any help getting a merit badge, let me know."

"Oh!" I gasped, then waved as he walked away—until I realized I was waving the panties. I dropped my arm, sidled back into the bathroom, and shut myself into an empty stall, where I gave way to a few strangled hiccups.

Be prepared?! Why did I say that? What must he have thought of me? What kind of woman runs around with a paper bag containing what could best be described as a homemade S&M costume? Only a lunatic, a sexed-up soccer mom—a ditzy superhero who just had to have matching panties for her new costume. And I decided right then that I didn't want to do this. It was hard enough being me, Birdie Lee, divorced mother, PTA lackey, former Girl Scout. It was hard enough navigating this life without adding superhero to the mix. Didn't I have enough opportunity to embarrass myself daily? And no one was making me do this, were they? No. No one at all. So no one would know if I decided it was too much. No one except—

Martin. But I made myself forget the way he'd looked at me lately, the way he'd been proud to be seen with me, talk to me, laugh with me. He was a big boy. He'd get over it. And so, eventually, would I.

I remained in the stall for a long time, perched on a toilet, clutching my paper bag. Not caring at all if Patty got mad at me for not being at my post. I also didn't care if some stupid teen smoked a cigarette behind the scoreboard, or planted a stink bomb in the ventilation system, or decided to urinate in the potted plants in the foyer. I didn't care about anything at all—except Carl. And what, exactly, he had meant by "merit badge."

"I told you not to call me here." Lex's voice, right outside my stall door, made me jump so high I hit my head on a pipe.

"Sorry," another male voice answered. *"But you said you wanted an update. Operation Pied Piper is right on schedule."*

"Cobblepot, you're a genius," Lex crowed.

I peered under the stall. There was only one pair of wingtip shoes. I lowered myself until I was almost flat on the floor and saw Lex pacing the empty girls' bathroom, talking on a cell phone. But I could hear both sides of the conversation. And I wasn't at all surprised by this. I was too numb, for one thing. And for another, it made sense: the scanner, the tape recorder, Kelly's IMing. So I could hear both sides of a cell phone conversation? So what else was new?

"What about you? Free plush toys—brilliant," continued the voice. *"Oh, by the way, you don't happen to have any more Abe Lincolnator dolls, do you?"*

"Sorry."

"Damn, he's my nephew's favorite. Oh well. Keep up the good work—it appears to be succeeding."

"God bless the little dears." Lex flipped his cell phone shut, stopped by the mirror to fuss with his hair, then strolled out of the bathroom.

Well, damn. No, no, no. I was not going to do this. I didn't have to do this. Just because I happened to be in the wrong place at the wrong time. Just because I happened to hear . . . something. I wasn't sure just what, but it couldn't be good because my chest was quivering. And I wasn't cold anymore. I was burning hot with outrage and worry and fear for children—all the children I'd never seen in my life. Something bad was going to happen. Something bad was always going to happen—drinking, sex, drugs, evil. And they were all just babies, every one of them—somebody's babies. Somebody who didn't know what dangers they faced, what trouble they could get themselves into. What evil people there were in the world. But—

But I did. I knew. Because—

I was Super Mom.

"Well, hell." I frowned. I opened up my crumpled bag. And then I started to change.

Well, let me just say this. You cannot fight crime in high heels. The pearls were kind of a drag too. But the apron was brilliant.

So I changed clothes in a tiny stall in the girls' bathroom. It brought back a lot of memories. Most of them unpleasant. I shimmied into the June Cleaver dress I'd made from treated and dyed-green dustcloths, tied the apron around my waist, and stuffed my huge pockets with all my supplies.

OK, here is the official description of Super Mom's Apron of Anticipation—which Martin wanted to call the Apron of Anal-retention, but I retained the power of veto: antibacterial hand wipes (but I can't list the brand until I get the endorsement deal straightened out, which should happen any day now), Band-Aids, dental floss, tampons, scissors, Pull-Ups, animal crackers, saltines, apple juice, junior ibuprofen, assorted ointments, crayons, safety pins, Kleenex, and clean underwear.

I staggered a little once everything was in place, and the apple juice tended to slosh, and I stuck myself with the scissors more than once. So there were a few kinks to work out. But all in all I was pleased. The clothespins did an excellent job of holding the dish towel cape in place, and the mask fit perfectly. But I couldn't figure out the clasp for the pearls, so I had to leave them behind. Then I bravely tottered out in my high heels, trolling for teenagers in trouble.

It didn't take me long to find them. I ran out of the gym toward the parking lot, my ears buzzing, the hair on my head quivering. My Super Mom Sense led me to a bush near the Dumpster, where I could hear someone retching.

"Are you all right?" I parted the branches and saw a young man bent over, puking his guts out.

"Huh?" He swung his head toward me and wiped his mouth with the back of his hand.

"Don't do that. Use this!" I reached into a pocket and handed him an antibacterial hand wipe. "What is it, too much beer?"

He nodded, his eyes wide, his mouth hanging open.

"Well, eat these." I handed him some saltines. "And drink this." I tossed him the apple juice. "Now, where did you get the beer?"

He bent over and puked again.

"That's all right, I'll wait." I folded my arms and looked up at the sky. I hummed the tune from *Jeopardy*. And when he was through vomiting, I asked him again.

"I'm not telling," he replied. Then he sat down and nibbled on a cracker. "Who are you, anyway? It's not Halloween yet, you know."

"I'm . . . I'm—" I stopped. I hadn't said it out loud before. This was my big moment. "I'm Super—oh gee, I can't believe I'm saying this, really, if you knew me at all you'd never believe me, but—well, I'm Super Mom!" And then I giggled.

He snorted.

"Super Mom? You? What's with the cape? Can you fly, Super Mom?"

"No. At least not yet. But someday, I hope—hey! Wait a minute! Tell me about the beer. Where did you get it?"

"Why should I tell you?"

"Because," I suddenly thundered, drawing myself up to my full five feet, three inches. "Because. I am Super Mom. I am all mothers. I am the embodiment of nurturing. I am the seeker of truth by and for all children, including minors under twenty-one years of age, which means you, buddy. I have the power and the authority of all mothers to protect children from harm. To teach them right from wrong, to punish if necessary with a swift but gentle hand. Wow!" I paused to take a breath. "I have no idea where that came from! Oh, I can also clean with the power of ten thousand Swiffers."

"Lady, you need to work on your speech. It's a little wordy. Superman's is way better: Defender of Truth, Justice, and the American Way. That's a lot catchier."

"Well, this is my first time. . . ."

"No duh."

"Now, listen to me, young man," I thundered again. This time he didn't sneer. "Where did you get the beer?"

"I'm not telling."

"Yes, you are."

"No, I'm not."

"Yes, you are."

"No, I'm not."

"OK, that's it." I bent down and peered into his eyes with my Merciless Gaze. "Lose the attitude, young man. You will tell me, right now, or else."

"Or else . . . what?" He tried to look away but I grabbed his chin and held firm.

"Or else I will take away your driving privileges for a week. You have a date on Friday, don't you? That cute girl in World History? We'll see how much fun you'll have without a car."

"How can you—" Sweat broke out on his brow.

"Never mind. I can. Now. Are you going to tell me?"

"No . . ."

"All right. Hand me your keys. Right now."

He didn't move.

"I SAID, NOW!!"

"OK, OK! Just, just, stop that, OK?"

"Stop what?"

"That thing you're doing—just like my mom does. She looks all sad and disappointed in me and I can't stand it.

Don't look at me that way, OK? Please?" By now he was whimpering, chewing on his fingernail. Tears rushed to his eyes. "I'll be good now. I promise."

"I know you will, son," I murmured. Then I wiped his forehead and gave him a hug.

"I'm sorry," he whispered.

"Me too," I whispered back. "Now tell me where you got the beer."

"Sid Cummings." The boy wiped his runny nose with his sleeve. I rolled my eyes and handed him a Kleenex. "He's across the street with a bunch of kids. They're having this other party."

"All right. I'll take care of it. Now go inside and splash some cold water on your face. I'll give you back your keys tomorrow—there's no way I'm letting you drive now. Remember, don't drink and drive. The life you save may be your own!"

"OK." He nodded. I gave him another hug and an animal cracker. Then I left, running across the school parking lot, where I got one of my heels caught in a manhole cover and said a very un–Super Mom–like bad word. "Son of a—"

"Hey, look at that!"

"Who is it? What is it?"

"I'm Super Mom," I informed the gathering crowd.

"It's a Peeping Tom!"

"No, I'm not." I started to hobble away.

"It's a drunk!"

"No, I'm Super Mom. Defender of—of children everywhere, embodiment of all mothers, with the power and authority . . . oh, never mind. I really need to work on that part." I wobbled across the street, ducking behind parked cars until the crowd finally went away.

"Hand me another, will you?"

"Sure." I heard the unmistakable *pop* of a beer can opening.

"Dude, this is so fly. Those dorks at the dance don't know what they're missing." A loud belch.

"Dude!" Guffaws, hiccups, followed by another belch.

I crouched behind a PT Cruiser, inching closer and closer toward an orange station wagon, which—I poked my head up to see—was surrounded by kids.

"Hey, guys, got any more?" A new voice, a masculine voice, vaguely familiar to me. The top of my head sang; my Super Mom Sense was kicking into a higher level than I'd ever experienced.

"More what? Booze or pot?"

"What do you think? I'm looking to score a little weed."

Admiring murmurs from the kids.

I scurried alongside the PT Cruiser like a spider, bobbing up now and then to look through the windows. Two boys in T-shirts and jeans were lounging on the tailgate, a red cooler between them. They were surrounded by a group of kids from the dance, the girls shivering in filmy dresses, the boys trying to look like James Bond in their suits. I couldn't make out their faces, though.

"So. How much?" That smooth, male voice again.

"Well, that depends." One of the stoners leaned back and scratched his stomach. "What kind you want?"

"Only the best. Why settle for less?" And my stomach dropped down to my shoes, as I recognized that voice as Harry's. Harry Osborne. My daughter's boyfriend.

The stoners started to laugh, but then one of them reached back into the station wagon. He drew out a plastic bag . . .

"OK, that's it!" I popped up, my fists upon my hips just like Wonder Woman. (I'd practiced at home, in the mirror.) "Halt! I'm Super Mo—ooof!"

Someone had just tackled me from behind.

"Get off," I hissed, kicking with my high heels. "Get your hands off of me, you, you—"

"Birdie?"

I stopped kicking. I twisted around to see who had his arms around my super legs.

"Carl?"

He gazed at me, mouth open, brown eyes blinking. His arms were still clasped around my legs. "Birdie? Birdie? Birdie?"

"Yes, Carl, let go!" Finally I kicked so hard that he had to let go. He fell backward, spraying gravel all over the place.

"I—that is, Patty said—the kids said—there was some Peeping Tom, or a pervert, lurking around. So Patty sent some of us out to see and I saw this weird—that is, I saw . . . you? Over here?"

"Uh-huh." I remained facedown on the gravel, tar and dust in my nose and mouth. I couldn't look at him; I could never look at him. Never, ever.

"Um, Birdie, I'm . . . maybe I'm a little confused. But, can I ask you why you're sneaking around in a dress . . . and an apron . . . and a mask . . ."

"Don't forget the high heels," I mumbled.

"And high heels . . . Hey!" He sat up. "This looks like Martin's cartoon!"

"I know. It's kind of a funny story." I groaned and rolled over. Should I tell him? Could I trust him? And . . . would he think I was nuts and call the authorities and tell Patty and the rest of the PTA to banish me from all future bake sales and book fairs?

But his eyes. His warm, kind eyes. Trusting, like a child's. They gave me hope.

"You see, I'm a—"

"There! Over there! I saw something over there!" Lots of voices now, coming this way like a pack of dogs. Voices of authority—Patty's and Lex's and some deep male voice I'd never heard before. Someone must have called the police.

Carl and I looked at each other. I couldn't think, couldn't figure out what to do. . . .

"C'mon," he said before I could speak. He grabbed my hand and pulled me to my feet.

"Stop! In the name of the PTA!" Patty called out. But we started running.

I saw the crowd around the station wagon break up; the stoners scurried around to the front seat and slammed the doors, peeling away. For a minute I was afraid they would run down the kids from the dance, but the kids scattered like frightened mice and ran toward the school. Carl held my hand, tight. There was no chance he would leave me behind, and we kept running and running—to where, I had no idea. All I could do was trust him to keep me safe. And somehow I knew I could.

But just before he pulled me down a narrow driveway, out of sight, I saw something that made my heart drop to my stomach. One of the faces in the crowd of teenagers running toward the school, one of the faces that I had seen gathered, I realized with a sick taste in my mouth, around that station wagon, one of the faces that now turned pale in the dark night, so pale it was like a beacon of light, pure, beautiful, and innocent—

Was Kelly's.

CHAPTER 7

"So I'm ditching the high heels," I told Carl. "And the pearls. But I really like the cape with the clothespins." Then I looked at my lap and blushed.

He didn't speak. He didn't move. He sat in a leather recliner, his hands gripping his knees. Gripping, ungripping, gripping—this was the only movement he'd made since I'd begun to tell him my tale, beginning at the beginning, with the Horrible Swiffer Accident.

"So, um, well, that's it, then. OK. I'll just leave now. . . ." I started to get up from my leather recliner, the companion to his. We were sitting in his family room—his very spare, masculine family room outfitted with the two recliners, an entertainment system, and a battered coffee table. And a bright blue wooden step stool decorated with cutout hearts, which I found unaccountably adorable.

"You liked the clothespins?" He finally looked up at me, his forehead wrinkled like a sleepy puppy's. But he was smiling.

"Yes."

"That was my idea."

"I know." I sat back down and stared at the step stool.

"Although, when Martin was drawing the cartoon, I had no idea that, well, you know. . . ."

"I know. Look. I know this is ridiculous and there's no way you'll believe me, and I'm sorry. I'm sorry for the under-wear. . . ." I blushed again, but made myself continue. "I'm sorry for scaring everyone tonight. I'm sorry for—that—you and I, back in the gym . . . oh, I'm just sorry. But like Peter Parker says, 'With Great Power Comes Great Responsibility.' Stupid Peter Parker."

"Actually, Uncle Ben was the one who said it."

"Really? I thought it was Peter Parker."

"No, it was Uncle Ben. *Amazing Fantasy.* Number fifteen. August, Nineteen Sixty-Two."

"Wow." Now it was my turn to stare. "You really know your stuff."

"I was a boy once, you know. A skinny boy who couldn't throw a football. What else was I supposed to do?"

"So, well, does this mean . . . you believe me?"

"I don't know," he said. But his eyes were twinkling. "Let's see you in action."

"What?"

"Super Mom. Let's see you do something Super Mom–like. Show me one of your powers."

"Oh! OK." I stood up. "See that cobweb over there?" I pointed to a far corner. "Now you see it, now you don't!" And I zapped it, using my new behind-the-back move. (I was show-ing off a little, OK?)

"Great Caesar's Ghost!" Carl jumped up and grabbed my hand. A droplet was glistening on my index finger; he touched his finger to mine and I closed my eyes, unable to see, wanting only to feel his touch. He turned my palm over and traced the spongy ridges and pads with his finger, tickling, teasing, until every nerve ending in my body was on edge, wanting to be tickled, teased—and more.

Finally he stopped, and I found a way to breathe again.

"Birdie," he said. Then he touched my chin, lifting it toward him. I opened my eyes. "Come with me."

"I, well, um, that is . . ." I couldn't move. I was terrified. This was too soon, too fast. And I needed to lose about ten pounds first. . . .

"Come with me." He led me toward—his basement. I followed him wordlessly, down rickety wooden stairs that led to a shadowy room that was taken up by an enormous pool table. And on that pool table was a chemistry set. A huge chemistry set with test tubes and Bunsen burners and vials of mysterious powders and liquids, litmus paper, tweezers, a microscope, and more.

"Here," he said, and sat me down on an old bar stool. Then he took a microscope slide and pressed my index finger down on it. "Tell me again, what cleaners did you use that day?"

"Cleaners?" I shook my head to clear my foggy, lustful thoughts. "Cleaners. Well, let's see. Swiffer, Borox, Clorox, Industrial Strength Windex, Pine-Sol, some orange cleaner I got off an infomercial, Lava Soap . . ."

"Did any of these have bleach or ammonia?"

"Yes."

"Which one?"

"Both."

"You mixed bleach and ammonia?" He put the slide down and looked at me.

"I guess . . ."

"And you didn't have the exhaust fan on?"

"No, I didn't have the exhaust fan on."

"You could have died. Seriously, Birdie."

"Yeah, I've been told."

"Well, I'm glad you didn't." He turned away and started fiddling with some eyedroppers and vials.

"You are?"

"Yes, I am."

I couldn't stop myself from grinning.

"You see"—he started to lecture, just like the scientist he was—"mixing bleach and ammonia creates chlorine gas. That's toxic, Birdie. If you inhale it, you can die. And given the quantities you described, I'm amazed that you didn't. Instead, it seems to have taken over, filled you with these powers. Just like Barry Allen when he was working in his lab during that thunderstorm. . . . Was there a thunderstorm when this happened to you?"

"Nope."

"Hmmm." He put the slide under the microscope. "That's unusual." He fiddled with that twisty doohickey on the side as he studied my fluids, the thought of which made me shiver and cross my legs. Then I looked around the basement, hoping to learn something about the man who had rescued me.

Despite the pool table, I could see no pool sticks. There was a dartboard. But no darts. A poster of the St. Pauli Girl, serving up two brimming . . . er, steins of beer. And an old braided rug on the floor, so faded it was impossible to tell what the original colors had been.

And there were no boxes. No shoeboxes or old baby formula boxes marked on the outside with names, dates. Our

basement was filled with these—MARTIN, ARTWORK, KINDER-
GARTEN THROUGH THIRD GRADE, GRANDMA'S OLD PHOTOS, KELLY'S
BROWNIE BADGES. Carrie's basement is the same. So is my
mother's.

Carl's basement was bare of anything that could help me
understand him, understand his past, because I really didn't
know much about it. He was divorced and his ex-wife lived in
a different state. He was raising his son alone. He had dreamy
eyes, a tender way about him; he had strong hands and sharp
bones, although his shoulders were surprisingly wide. He was
a scientist for a pharmaceutical company. He had loved
comics when he was a boy. And he believed me.

And when I thought about it that way, I realized, what
more did I need to know?

"Well, this is interesting," he said, squeezing a couple of
drops of blue liquid onto the microscope slide with an eye-
dropper.

"What?"

"Hmmm." He squeezed two drops of clear liquid onto the
slide, then adjusted the microscope some more.

"What? Carl, what?"

"This is amazing cell division. Just amazing. This fluid—
which appears to be a mixture of monochloramine, hydro-
gen chloride, sodium hydrochlorite, and citric acid, plus a lot
of other things I can't name right now—is a living thing, not
like normal cleansers. That must be what gives it its strength.
Look at this."

I put my eye to the microscope. Carl bent over me.

"Look! See the way the cells are constantly dividing?"

"Uh-huh," I whispered, shivering at his warm breath in my
ear. I had to grip the sides of the pool table to keep my balance. Then I remembered to look in the microscope. There

were little blobs of stuff on the slide, like a black-and-white cartoon—little amorphous shapes that kept dividing into smaller shapes that kept dividing into smaller shapes. Whatever was on this slide was alive and bubbling, and I realized with a jolt that this stuff was in me, in my veins somehow, giving me strength, giving me power.

"Isn't that amazing?" Carl's voice was hushed.

I looked up from the microscope, right into his face, which was so close to mine I could smell his spicy, smoky scent, his essence, his skin. I nodded.

"You're . . . amazing," he said, bending so close that I knew he could smell me, too.

I nodded.

"Birdie . . ." He lifted my chin, coming close, so close; close enough to kiss me if he wanted—

"Wait," he said, those vertical dimples deepening. "I've never kissed a superhero before."

"Great," I murmured, unable to take my gaze off his lips. "No pressure at all, thanks."

"You're welcome," he whispered. And then he kissed me.

A man's lips on mine. That's all I could think about at first. A man's lips—so soft, so insisting—on mine. Warm, moist, open—on mine. Then I forgot how to think, forgot how to breathe; the only thing I knew how to do was kiss back, and so I did.

And then his arms, big and strong, enveloped me, bringing me to him so that there wasn't anything between us, not an inch of air. We touched in places I didn't know we could. And still all I could think of was kissing him, kissing him until I could no longer draw breath and so would have to rest, forever, in his arms . . .

Then suddenly a thump above our heads jolted us apart,

hearts racing, afraid to look at each other. "Greg," Carl said in a strangled voice. And then all I could think about were my children, Martin and Kelly. Martin would be worried, wondering what had happened to me. He might need to drink a glass of milk to calm down, and did we have enough? He hated 2-percent. He would only drink whole milk. And Kelly. Where was she?

Kelly. Her face, pure in the darkness, running away, away from me. Away from danger. But she had run toward it too. She still was. And danger was a tall blond boy with cool blue eyes and a seductive smile. And what on earth was I going to do about it?

"But I can't tell her I saw her," I whispered.

Carl looked at me, his face a jumble of emotion: worry, fear, joy, hope.

"Huh?"

"Kelly. I saw her. Tonight, with the stoners—she was part of the group of kids from the dance. But I can't tell her I saw her, because she doesn't know."

"About your superpowers?"

I shook my head. "No, I can't tell her, because—"

"But Martin knows."

I nodded.

"Well, I . . . never mind. It's none of my business, is it? Birdie?"

I looked at him, this man whom I had just kissed. I could still feel him on my lips, feel the warmth upon my back where he'd held me. But—

"No." I smiled, apologizing. "It's not."

He nodded. His shoulders sagged a little.

"At least, not yet," I added.

He looked at me, touched my cheek, just for a moment, so quick I wasn't sure if I could believe it. Then he smiled.

"So, what are your plans, Super Mom?" We started up the stairs.

"Oh, the usual. Fight crime—or at least underage drinking and drug use among local teenagers. Save the world—or at least my own neighborhood. Wipe up drool, make sure car seats are being used. And clean. You know. The usual."

"Super Mom Sense." I could see the back of his head—his hair just a little bit thin—nod. "How about an evil archnemesis? Do you have one? Other than Patty, I mean."

"Ha-ha. Very funny."

At the top of the stairs, just before he opened the door, he stopped, turned around, and took my hand as if he had the right to. "So, do you need a trusty sidekick?"

"Sorry." I left my hand in his, where it felt safe and warm. "I've already got one of those."

"Well then, how about a nerdy scientist love inter— Er, friend?"

"That, I need. That, I could definitely use."

"Good." He pulled me up the final step, out into the hall, then dropped my hand as if it had stung him. Greg was sitting in the family room playing a video game. He was as short as Martin, wore the same kind of clothes as Martin, had floppy hair like Martin, only his was black. But he didn't like Martin, and Martin didn't like him. There had always been some mutual suspicion between them, a wariness, a distrust. I never knew why.

"So, then, Mr. Sayers," I said in my best chipper PTA parent's voice. "Tell me again, what do you do at work?"

"Well, Mrs. Lee," Carl answered in the same fake voice, as if we were just two PTA parents who had happened to meet each other at the grocery store, "I'm working on a new project for Moulton Pharmaceuticals. We've started working in code names, for some reason. I'm on Project Pied Piper."

"Well, that's nice—the hell you say?" I stopped so suddenly that he ran into me.

"Birdie!" He glanced at Greg, who was still immersed in his game.

Patriot Pops. Eat Patriot Pops. Mmmm. Crispy. Sugary. What you crave.

"Turn that thing off!" I shouted, running across the room and ripping the game from the console. Greg and Carl gaped at me. "Pied Piper? What's Pied Piper?"

"I—I—but, Birdie, Greg's game . . ." Carl pointed at the television.

"Yeah," Greg whined. I looked at him again. He looked a little chubbier since the last time I'd seen him. A little softer, a little rounder.

"What the hell is Pied Piper, Carl?"

"I don't know. We're all assigned to different sectors. I'm just working on isolating genes right now. They don't tell us why."

"Do you know anyone named Cobblepot?"

Carl shook his head.

"Do you know why Lex would have anything to do with this Project Pied Piper?"

"Lex? Lex Osborne? Self-made millionaire?"

"The one and only."

"Not a clue."

"Dad," Greg interrupted, quite calmly, "we're out of Patriot Pops and I really want some. Can you get more tomorrow?"

"Don't do it," I told Carl, holding the video game up in the air like a prize. "I don't care if it is a local product. There's something rotten in the state of Kansas, and I think its name happens to be Osborne. I believe I've found my archnemesis, after all."

Carl's face turned pale. He took a step toward me, then stopped.

"But, Dad," Greg whined, throwing the controller to the ground, "what about the Patriot Pops?"

CHAPTER
8

Contrary to popular belief (Kelly's and Martin's, that is), I did not come out of the womb brandishing antibacterial disposable hand wipes (which are, after Swiffer, the single greatest invention known to man).

I was, in fact, a little reckless when I was a teen. Once I had both beer and wine—just one glass each, but still—at a party. And my senior year I refused to cover my books with those horrible sticky book covers; when I turned it in before graduation my science book had been decorated with a smiley face drawn in permanent marker. The dean said I had to replace the book before I graduated. But I didn't.

So you can see I have a rebellious side too.

The worst, though, was my junior year, when I dated a punk. That's what we called bad boys at my high school—punks. You could tell a punk by his perpetual sneer, no matter what kind of mood he was in. Kevin Stanton sneered his way into my heart and sneered his way back out. And between sneers, he led me down a dark and dangerous path. One time he burned the inside of my wrist with his cigarette, just because. And even though it hurt and my stomach flipped over in a sick, shameful way, I told myself I didn't mind. I told myself I liked it. Because when I didn't say anything, he pulled me to him and traced the curve of my neck with his tongue, whispering that he'd never known a woman like me before. And it was the first time anyone had ever called me a woman. So what could I do but giggle and grab his butt—and forget about the red, throbbing circle on my wrist where he had branded me, just because?

Soon after that he drove me home from a party, too fast down a country road with his lights off. Just because. And I was terrified. So terrified that the only thing I could think to do was grab his thigh, and then he reached over and placed my hand on his bulging crotch, and the combination of the speed, his hot, heavy penis, and the dark unknown shot a jolt of liquid thrill through my body that turned me into an animal. He pulled over and stopped the car; I didn't even pause to notice that we had cheated death. I grabbed his head and kissed him so hard I thought I might swallow him; then I let him do what he'd wanted to do, and what I'd wanted him to do, ever since he first sneered at me in Biology.

But when it was over all I could think about was how messy it had been. That was the first time it occurred to me that antibacterial hand wipes might come in handy. Then I thought about how messy it could get in the future: I could have a baby with a sneering punk who liked to burn me with cigarettes. My stomach rebelled at the thought, and I ran away from the car and threw up in a bunch of weeds. We drove home in silence and when we said good night I realized how ugly his sneer was, how pimply his face; after my period came I danced a jig in my bedroom and started going out with that nice Jimmy Henderson from down the street.

And when, years later, I had a little girl—a beautiful little girl, I could see from the start; the kind of girl who would attract all kinds of men, good and bad—I vowed that I would protect her from the Kevin Stantons of the world.

I thought of that vow as I sped home in my little dented minivan, my costume wadded up in the paper bag because for all I knew, Patty Osborne had issued a PTA-endorsed all points bulletin for a lunatic wearing high heels and a cape.

"Where's your sister?" I stormed into the kitchen. Martin shoved a bag of Patriot Pops behind his back; I gave him a muted Merciless Gaze. He sighed and handed them over.

"I don't know. How'd it go tonight?"

"Tonight? What—oh, that." I turned away and dumped the Patriot Pops down the garbage disposal, trying to figure out what I could safely tell him. The underwear spilling all over the floor—no, couldn't tell him that. The mob chasing me through the parking lot—uh, no. The part where Carl kissed me—definitely not, not today, not ever. The part about Kelly—

Meanwhile, a car—a sleek rich-boy's car—pulled up in our driveway, its smug headlights shining through the kitchen window.

"My high heels broke," I said, looking out the window. Kelly got out. Harry did not. She raced around to the driver's side and stuck her head in the window for a kiss; he reached out, slapped her on the butt, then honked at her when she ran toward the house, causing her to jump. He peeled out of the driveway before she was even at the door. "We need to work on that." My fluid was starting to boil inside my veins.

"On what?"

"My high heels."

"Is that all?"

"Yes. No. I need to put this away." And I ran upstairs with my crumpled paper bag, because Kelly was almost at the door.

"But I'm your trusty sidekick," Martin yelled after me. "You can tell me!"

"Later!"

"I'm home," Kelly called out, the kitchen door slamming behind her. I shoved the bag under my bed and stalked downstairs.

"Hi, Mom," Kelly said as she opened the refrigerator. "Got anything to eat?"

"Why? Are you hungry? Really hungry? Why? Why are you really hungry?" I couldn't stop myself. I slammed the refrigerator door shut and grabbed her wrists. They looked fine.

"What are you doing?" She yanked her arms away. I shoved my face next to hers, peering up into her gray eyes. They weren't bloodshot—or were they? Was that just a little hint of pink I saw around the irises? "Mom! You're freaking me out! When did you get home? I didn't see you at the dance."

"A little while ago. I didn't see you either, except out—" I managed to bite my tongue.

"Did you see the Peeping Tom?"

"The what?"

"I heard there was this freak, this Peeping Tom spying on kids. This one guy said it jumped him from behind a bush."

"Well, I don't think so."

"Did you see it?"

"No." I narrowed my eyes at her. "Did you?"

"No." She narrowed her eyes back.

"Kelly, is there . . . did you have a nice time, honey?" She still looked so pretty in her party dress, a trace of lipstick on

her lips, her pale lashes tinted black with mascara. All my indignation drained away, and I ached to smooth her silky hair.

"Yeah. I guess. It was all right."

"Did Harry treat you right?"

"Huh?"

"Because, you know, you don't have to do anything that
makes you uncomfortable."

"I know." She wrinkled her freckled nose. "We've had this
talk before, Mom. No means no. I understand."

"Good, but—well, I didn't just mean about sex. . . ." I
found, to my horror, that I was blushing. Kelly smiled just a
little, which only made my face burn more intensely. "There
are other ways a man can hurt you. . . ."

She stiffened then. It was like a curtain had come down between us.

"Drinking, drugs, you know . . ." I forged ahead anyway.

"I don't know what you're talking about."

"You see, I know that sometimes it's hard to think straight
when you're in love."

Kelly turned away and stared out the kitchen window,
one sandy eyebrow arched. "I hardly think, Mother, that
you're the right person to lecture about the male/female
relationship."

I swallowed hard, absorbing the blow. But I forgave her for
it, because it was a magical autumn night and her dashing
young boyfriend hadn't walked her to the door and whispered how lovely she looked in the moonlight.

"We're not talking about me. We're talking about you and
Harry."

"You don't know Harry like I do. You have no idea. He
loves me."

"People who love you don't—"

"Don't what?" Her hands gripped the edge of the counter.

"Don't try to get you to do dangerous things, Kelly. I don't like that boy."

She didn't say anything; her shoulders slumped slightly as if accepting defeat. I reached toward her, ready to take her in my arms, ready to comfort her. But she brushed past me without a look.

"So . . . what? Are you forbidding me to see Harry? Is that what you're going to do?"

"Is that what you want me to do?" I followed her, studying her, trying to understand what she needed me to say next.

"No," she said, her voice flat, as if she were reciting something from memory. "No. Harry loves me. I know you're afraid he'll hurt me like Daddy hurt you, but he won't. He won't break my heart."

"Believe it or not, sweetheart, there are worse things than a broken heart."

She rolled her eyes at me. How could I possibly understand?

"But I would protect you from a broken heart," I whispered, remembering that beautiful baby in my arms, so long ago.

"Well, you can't. I don't want you to."

We looked at each other, just a normal mother and daughter after all—both of us powerless, inches apart but so far away, with an emptiness between us neither one knew how to fill. I gave up first, moving to pour myself a glass of water. She opened the refrigerator, shut it, looked around the kitchen as if she couldn't quite believe how small and shabby it was— how ordinary. And I knew she included me in her assessment, just another fixture, as functional and necessary as the extra chair at the table. Then she left the room.

I studied her as she climbed the stairs. She didn't look any different to me. She was still my daughter, the straight-A student and clarinet player, the worrier, the watchful one. And maybe I was wrong. Maybe she was stronger than I had been at her age. Maybe.

I went upstairs too, turned my light off, made my going-to-bed sounds—heavy sighs, yawns, winding my alarm clock. I tossed around in bed, pretending to go to sleep.

But my eyes stayed open, vigilant, ready.

After a few minutes I crept out of bed, careful not to make a sound. The hallway was dark; Martin's light was out. But Kelly's wasn't. Her computer whirred to life and her fingers started tapping away. I crouched down beside her door, praying my bones wouldn't creak, found a comfortable position and waited. I was going to be there a long time.

I might have felt a twinge of guilt. I really can't remember. All I knew is that it felt, at the time, as if I had no other choice . . .

No other choice but to do a little Super Eavesdropping.

CHAPTER 9

I lay low for a while. I worked out the kinks in my costume with Martin. We temporarily ditched the high heels in favor of running shoes. And I replaced the sharp scissors with blunt ones.

And then I got down to the business of cleaning up Astro Park. In between work and cooking and music lessons and laundry and PTA meetings and soccer games and yelling at the kids and reminding them to do their homework and taking them to the orthodontist and parent/teacher conferences—you know, the usual.

Super Mom. Well, really. Aren't we all?

Now, you'd think, after saving approximately six children from choking on hot dogs, five toddlers from running out into the street, countless babies from being hurtled to their deaths due to improper car seat installation, a ton of teens from buying cigarettes from that sleazy old man who runs the gas station next to the skate park, and bandaging, oh, I'd say about seventy-five skinned knees, I'd have earned a little respect from the good citizens of Astro Park. But no.

"We need to take strong measures against the Peeping Tom," Patty proclaimed from her pulpit at the next PTA meeting. "The police have instructed us to have extra parents on hand at all school events. Evidently this pervert is targeting children. And one must protect the children at all costs."

"Targeting children?" I mumbled to Carrie. "Says who?"

"Shhh." Carrie frowned. "This is serious, Birdie. I don't know where you went the other night but some of the kids were scared."

"They were not scared. They're just exaggerating. Trust me."

"Well, for once I agree with Patty. And by the way, where did you run off to the other night?"

"Something came up. Never mind."

"Again? Something's always coming up with you lately." Carrie gave me that penetrating look that made her eyeglasses redundant.

"Maybe we should set up a hotline?" Mary was suggesting. "People can call in when they see this Peeping Tom?"

"I heard it was a woman," Marge piped up. "Can you call a woman a Peeping Tom?"

"Well, then how about a Peeping Thomasina?"

Patty sighed and laid her head on the podium.

"Super Mom," a voice called out. A male voice. A voice that set my heart all aflutter.

"What?" Patty looked up.

"I hear she's called Super Mom," said Carl. I turned around. He winked. I blushed.

"Oh, yeah, didn't one of the kids—the one who was sick—mention that?" Terry nodded.

"Super Mom? Really? Well, obviously we're dealing with someone suffering from a severe mental illness." Patty shook her head. "Which is all the more reason to step up security. Birdie!"

"What?" I leaped up, my heart racing, my legs jelly. "What? It wasn't me!"

"What? Of course not. Don't be ridiculous. Pass around these sign-up sheets."

"Oh. Right." I grabbed the sheets and handed them around; when I got to Carl our hands happened to touch. And then we both grinned like idiots.

"What was that about?" Carrie hissed when I sat back down.

"Nothing."

She tugged on her bangs and scowled.

"Now, is there any old business to take care of?" Patty asked.

I gingerly raised my hand, ignoring Carrie's sharp, sudden glance.

"Yes, Birdie?"

"Remember last meeting, when we voted to endorse that video game, American Justice?"

Patty and Lex exchanged a smug little glance.

"Yes?"

"Well, I'd like to make a motion to ban it." I blurted it out as fast as I could, then slid down in my seat and tried to hide from Carrie. She started to twitch all over, like a Mexican jumping bean.

"What?!"

"I don't think I heard you right, Birdie." Patty laughed. "I thought you said you wanted to ban American Justice." Everyone else laughed too. Everyone except Lex.

"No, I *did* say that. I think we need to ban American Justice. It—it's harmful to our children."

"Well, Birdie, I believe in the past you and your friend felt that banning was unconstitutional," Patty said.

"It is!" Carrie gurgled. "Don't you people even look at your kids' homework?"

"I know." I turned to Carrie. "But I truly believe this game is harmful. Dangerous. Not good."

"Well, what video game isn't? But that's no reason to ban it."

"I know, but this is different. And, well, I think we should also boycott Patriot Pops." I hunched down, ready for the explosion.

"Boycott Patriot Pops?!" "Why, they're a local product!" "They're American-made!" "My husband works there!" "Mine too!" "I work there!" "After all that New Cosmos has done for this community—I never!" And above all, Carrie's voice, rising in volume until everyone else was just a mumble in the background: "I'm as concerned about processed sugar as you are, Birdie, but really. A boycott? What reason do you have? Do they harm the environment? Are they made by little Guatemalan children?"

I shook my head miserably, feeling the full force of Carrie's wrath upon my shoulders. I'd never been the target of her mighty righteousness before; I didn't like it one bit.

And everyone else in the PTA gradually stopped speaking and sat rapt, staring at us. Even Patty's gavel lay motionless, while Lex's eyes never blinked, just like a snake's. Nobody uttered a sound. Nobody except Carrie.

"Well, I think we need a better reason than the fact that you think it's harmful. So what? I think malted milk balls are harmful to my hips, but that doesn't give me the right to boycott them. It just means I have to exercise a little control."

"But this is different, Carrie. What if—what if I know they're bad?" I turned my head away from Lex and whispered, "What if I know something about this stuff that you don't?"

"Then tell me." Carrie refused to whisper back.

"I can't!"

"You can't tell? You with all the secrets lately? Why am I not surprised?"

"You'll just have to trust me. I found out something about that game that no one else could ever know—" Again I tried to lower my voice.

"You? You? Right." Carrie laughed—a hard, brittle sound, harsh to my ears. "Birdie, how could you possibly know something like that? What, did you read it in the *National Enquirer*? You work as a cashier in a grocery store, for heaven's sake. What could you possibly know?"

Everyone in the room gasped. Except for me. I couldn't breathe.

"Carrie, I—well, so do you!"

"That's different." Something flinty glistened behind Carrie's glasses, something I'd never seen before. "I'm going back to school for my degree. You're—you're just—"

"What? What am I just?"

"It's just different," she said, licking her lips as if some bad taste lingered there.

I felt sick. Cold, nauseated, dirty somehow.

Carrie folded her hands primly and placed them on her lap, then stared at them as if they might get away from her. Everyone else seemed stunned. Finally Lex rose, took the gavel out of Patty's hand, and chuckled paternally.

"Well, I have to thank Carrie for putting an end to this boycotting nonsense. As she rightly pointed out, Birdie is just a tad unworldly in matters of business—not to mention the legal system. But I don't doubt that her heart was in the right place, and I for one thank her for her concern for our children. At all costs, we must remember the children." Then he slammed the gavel down on the podium with such force I thought it would break in two. "Meeting adjourned!"

Everyone quietly shuffled out of the cafeteria until Carrie and I were the only two left. Then Carrie jumped up and ran to her car like it was a race. Once she turned around as if she was going to speak; I think there was something in my face that stopped her. But I don't really remember; I don't really remember a lot of what I was feeling right then.

Carl was waiting by my car.

"Do you want to go somewhere for a cup of coffee?"

I shook my head. He pulled me to him with one arm, refusing to let go.

And then I burst into tears.

"So, is this our second date, then?"

"Yeah." I blew my nose on a paper napkin. "I guess."

We were sitting on a picnic table. The sky was dark and low, gunmetal gray clouds threatening rain. But it was surprisingly warm for fall; I just had on a light jacket, and Carl wore a yellow Rocky and Bullwinkle sweatshirt.

He'd driven me to a quiet park with a couple of picnic tables, a bench, an old tetherball pole. It bordered a sweet little pond with white, regular boulders all along the edge.

I'd cried the whole way. I'd cried because I missed someone, and that someone was Carrie. My best friend. Ever since I could remember—before my divorce, even. She was the only friend I still had from my marriage. It's funny how that happens. It's funny how your whole life just splits in two after a divorce, the before and the after, and each side is completely unrecognizable from the other, right down to the people who say hello to you at your child's soccer games. But Carrie was my constant, my compass. She loved me. She respected me. I didn't realize how much I relied on this knowledge, how I carried it around with me all the time. It was something I put on every morning when I got up, just like my socks and underwear. And just as if I'd only put on one sock this morning, I felt off-balance, undone, without it.

My kids—they didn't know me. They didn't know anything about me. They just knew their lives wouldn't be right without me. But Carrie knew. She told me all about myself, even when I didn't really want her to. But now she was gone. Just like that. She'd removed herself from my life with the words she'd chosen to say.

"It's because of this stupid Super Mom stuff, isn't it?" I wondered out loud. "Isn't it?"

"Well"—Carl drained the last of his coffee, tossed the cup in a rusty trash can—"I don't know. It seemed to me this was something she'd been thinking about for a while, not just the last few days."

"I guess . . ." I didn't want to hear that. I didn't want to think about how long she'd felt this way—that I was stupid, naïve. Content with being a cashier in a grocery store because that was the best I could do, when that wasn't it at all. It was because I liked it for what it was—soothing, repetitive, pleasant in its own way. Most everyone I met there was nice. I got to see what people's lives were like by the groceries they bought. Who, for example, would load their cart up with Banquet frozen entrées and cereal bars and wrapped deli sandwiches to go, but also take the time to assemble all the ingredients necessary to make caramelized ricotta gnocchi with apples, chanterelles, and roasted squash? Well, I could tell you: the janitor at the Methodist church, that's who.

I got a kick out of reading people by what they put in their cart, hoping that sometimes they'd surprise me, like the janitor. Although most of the time, they didn't. And that was OK too. It was comforting to know that most people were predictable. Just like me.

"But she hurt you, didn't she?" Carl pulled me to him. "I hate that. I hate the idea of anyone hurting you."

"You do?" I closed my eyes, laid my head on his shoulder. It was so nice to be held, so comforting and safe—and yet not. There was also danger here: danger in being too close, danger in resting in arms that could take me so many places I wasn't sure I was ready to go. It was hard to relax knowing that somehow we'd skipped a step or two, that we'd gone from a tentative first kiss to lying in each other's arms like spent lovers. There was something very important, very explosive, that we had missed. And that knowledge made every stroke of his hand, every tensed muscle in his neck, electric and alarming.

Yet there was also comfort here. And gentleness. My body didn't know which one to long for, which one to choose—the comfort? Or the danger?

"Have you ever done this before?"

"Done what?" Carl twisted his head to look at me, and as he did I caught a whiff of his fragrance: vanilla and wood smoke.

"This. You know. This . . . us."

"About a hundred times."

"What?" I removed my head from his shoulder.

"Sure. I'd say at least a hundred."

"At least?"

"Haven't you?"

"Well, no. I mean, not that many. I mean, not even in college . . ."

"Well, that's a shame." He clicked his tongue. "Sitting on a picnic table is highly underrated. I do it every chance I get."

"Oh . . . Oh!" I laughed. "Seriously. Have you dated recently? Lately? Since, you know, your divorce?"

"Not recently. Not lately. A little since."

"Oh." I watched the ruffles of water tickling the boulders along the pond. "I haven't."

"Well, then, I guess it's all a little strange for you, isn't it?"

I nodded.

"My divorce was a long time ago," he began in a gentle voice, like he was telling me a bedtime story. "When Greg was just a toddler. We'd married young, the usual. No hard feelings. It turned out she didn't really want to be a wife or mother. I was just happy she gave me Greg. It's just been the two of us. Mostly I haven't minded that. But there are times . . . well . . . So I've gone out some, when friends have tried to fix me up. It's never become anything . . . special."

"Special?"

"Special. More than just an excuse to eat in a restaurant with linen napkins."

"Hmmmm. That would be nice. To eat in a restaurant with linen napkins." I sighed.

He laughed, his arm tightening around my shoulder.

"Well, we can do that, too, sometime. I promise."

"But . . . well, why this? Why me? No one fixed us up." I picked one particular boulder out and studied it, concentrating on the way the water nudged against it, so determined.

"No." He took my hand. My right hand. "I've always noticed

you. And I've always wondered why other people didn't; you seemed so bright somehow. You always seem to have this light about you. Within you."

I started to cry. Just to hear his words—his kind, gentle words meant only for me. They found me as I was, alone and unworthy, and assured me that no, I was not; I was good, I was necessary. I was deserving of love. And so I had to cry. Because there was no other way to prepare myself for him.

He wiped my tears; I shook my head. He kissed me until the tears mixed with something wet on his own cheeks, and then he led me to a sheltering pine tree. He took my hand, my waist, my breasts—he took my whole self within him with his arms, his lips, his quiet assurance that this was what we both needed. And he was right. I told him so, over and over until we both were so raw that we had to cry together, one perfect, broken sob that soared to the top of the tree, then fluttered and fell, coming to rest deep within my chest, pinning me forever in his arms.

He lifted my hair, kissed the sweaty nape of my neck. I blew gently on his moist brow.

"I can't believe . . ."

"How did we just do . . ."

"I didn't think we'd . . ."

"Never, in my dreams, did I . . ."

"Oh my God, I'm so . . ."

"But oh, you're so . . ."

"But you, you're, my God . . ."

"But this was so . . ."

"Good." We both sighed, rising and falling as one.

The wind turned chilly. When had it turned chilly? Sometime. We hadn't noticed just when. But now we huddled together for warmth, rolled around in our discarded clothes, pulled my jacket over us like a tarp. But the logical thing to do—get dressed and sit in the car—didn't occur to us. It was too obvious. And we were too drunk on what had just happened between us to see the obvious solution to anything just then.

"Birdie? Are you all right?"

"Yes. I am. I didn't think I'd be. I mean, I never thought I could do this again—but, well . . . You didn't really give me any time to think." I giggled.

"I love it when you do that." He smiled, and finally I was able to do what I'd wanted—trace those deep lines that gave his face such gravity.

"Do what?"

"Giggle like that. It's so cute."

"Cute?"

"I'm afraid so."

"Oh, well." I sighed, happy anyway. We lay there for a while, and I started to relive everything that had just happened from the moment he took my hand, wiped my tears with his cheek, crushed me in his arms, moved me somehow to the tree, and pulled me down with him, the way our clothes just seemed to melt away . . .

"Oh my God." I sat up, pulling my jacket around me, just in case the moon came out and illuminated my cellulite.

"What?"

"Condoms. Condoms!"

"What?"

"I can't believe this. I'm Super Mom! I can't believe we forgot condoms!"

"Oh." He tugged on his chin. "Well."

"Yes. Well!"

"Well, I . . . well, I had a vasectomy, after Greg . . ."

"You did? A vasectomy?"

He nodded.

"OK. That's good. But, oh God. Oh God! I don't know how to say this— We seem to keep doing everything out of order. I don't even know your middle name—"

"Antonio."

"Thanks. Antonio? Really? Huh."

"Birdie, I know you're right and we should have stopped, but . . . Birdie, please . . . Wasn't this perfect?"

He looked so sad, so small. And I felt terrible.

"Oh—oh, yes! Yes, Carl, it was. It was perfect. I'm sorry, I didn't mean to . . ." I made myself stop thinking about all the things that could happen—bad things, things that could wound me or kill me or even just make me have a really rotten day. I made myself stop, and simply concentrated on the fact that I was resting beneath a pine tree with a remarkable man who wanted to remember me this way—perfect. What could go wrong, with such a man as that?

"But I have a responsibility now. I'm Super Mom," I whispered, unable to lie back down. "Would you want Greg to have done something like this?"

He didn't say anything.

"That's what I thought. I keep thinking of Kelly. I'd kill her if I found out she'd done something as irresponsible as—as—"

"Making love under a pine tree with someone who cares for her very much?"

"No." I shook my head, reached for his hand. He grasped mine and held it, so tight. "Having unprotected sex with someone she hardly knows."

"You know," Carl said, clearing his throat, still clutching my hand, "you get to choose. Which way you look at it. Which one."

"I'm not so sure. We're parents. I'm not so sure we do get to choose, not anymore."

"Maybe not."

We started to get dressed, suddenly awkward, averting our eyes. Why did dressing seem much more intimate than undressing? Then we sat next to each other, our shoulders touching.

"I think it might be better," I began, glad that I couldn't see his face, "if we slowed down a little. I mean, this was— amazing. It really was." Tears sprang to my eyes, and then I was glad that he couldn't see my face. "But, Carl, I'm forty-one and I haven't dated anyone in about twenty years, and I have a daughter who is doing this too—dating—and a son who will be soon. Maybe. And I'm also going through quite a big *change* here, you know. . . . Anyway, what I'm trying to say is, we're doing it all backward. Maybe we should have a real date, where we hold hands and talk about ourselves and don't do . . . this . . . until we're really sure about things, and then we do it in a real bed, because I think I'm going to have some nasty bruises tomorrow."

He laughed at that, but when he spoke his voice was ragged with disappointment. "OK, Birdie. I'm . . . well, I don't really care about doing things in order. I did things in order the first time and that didn't work out that well. You know?"

"I know. Same here."

"But you're right. We have some different priorities now, with kids—teenagers. I hadn't thought of that. I'd kill Greg if he had unprotected sex. Not that I think that will happen anytime soon—there aren't any girls in cartooning club. But one day. And how could I tell him, with a straight face, when I just . . . well. But, Birdie?"

"What?"

"It was different. Wasn't it? Just now, us—that was different. It wasn't just unprotected sex, was it?"

I shook my head, hid my face on his shoulder. He pulled me close, and I realized that now we both smelled of vanilla and wood smoke. And that was really neat.

"Can I drive you back to your car? Then follow you home?"

"Yes, but no. I have to—oh my God!" I started to laugh.

"What?"

"I have to stop and get some milk. I really do! I'm not just making that up!" I kept laughing while he pulled me up and led me to his car, holding on to me so tight there was no way I could run away. Even if I wanted to.

"Well, why would you?" he asked with such a sweet, befuddled look in his eyes.

I put my hand on his cheek and shook my head, unable to answer.

CHAPTER 10

So how did a struggling baker of really awful patriotic cookies become a self-made millionaire in the span of approximately two years?

And why did subliminal messages promoting these patriotic cookies wind up in a Japanese-made video game?

And most importantly, just exactly why was Tonya Nederlander so pissed off that Danny Barone dumped her, since it was well known that he'd been going out behind her back with Tiffany Marshall for at least two weeks?

These were just some of the issues weighing heavily on the mind of Super Mom.

For in order to forget about Carrie, to forget about my irresponsible passion beneath a pine tree, to protect my daughter from the evil clutches of the son of my probable archnemesis, I immersed myself in my superhero identity. It was my reason for being. What I did. Who I was.

At the store, where I worked with my face set in a pleasant, plastic smile, I noted the increasing frequency of Patriot Pop purchases, combined with a feeding frenzy over the last few plush American Justice toys. I casually questioned my customers and discovered that every one of them owned the video game.

At home I hijacked Martin's computer and searched the Internet for information. I also continued to eavesdrop on every conversation Kelly had. That's how I learned about Tonya Nederlander and Danny Barone.

And in between, I was Super Mom. I was becoming more brazen about it, calling more attention to myself than perhaps was necessary. But my press was getting really good.

WHO IS THIS SUPER MOM? asked the *Astro Daily World*.

Who is this mysterious nurturing do-gooder? What kind of person dispenses maternal justice with one hand and animal crackers with the other? Do we have our own superhero in our midst? Or just another crackpot?

"I thank God for Super Mom," Mrs. Eileen McArdle told us. "She saved my little Ian from being hit by a cement truck in a crosswalk. The normal crossing guard wasn't there, and Super Mom just pulled up in her minivan and snatched Ian up before he was hurt. And then she gave him an animal cracker and a juice box."

But others in the community aren't so sure of Super Mom's good intentions.

"She targets children," Patty Osborne, Hawthorne School District Parent/Teacher Association President declared. "Hasn't anyone noticed? She's always hanging around children. I believe she is probably some perverted sexual addict who is a danger to our town. Why doesn't anyone stop her?"

"Because," Police Commissioner Borden answered, "she's cleaned up this town—literally. I mean, have you seen the sidewalks lately? And the alleys? They're spotless. And she's turned in several merchants who were selling cigarettes and alcohol to minors. Also some small-time drug dealers we've been after. It's so adorable the way she drags them in here by their ears, lecturing them. You should see the way that woman can prescribe a time-out if they get out of hand. She's so cute—reminds me of my own mother."

So there you have it, citizens of Astro Park. Super Mom. Menace, or Mother of the Year?

"Cute." I sighed.

"Did you say something?" Carrie turned around.

"No, I don't believe I did."

"Birdie, I—"

"I'm sorry. My shift is over." I turned and switched off my light. Then I walked away, trying not to care that Carrie's eyes were red-rimmed behind her glasses, or that her bangs looked straggly and thin.

"Mom? I came up with some new ideas for the high-heel problem. I think that if we just try and—"

"That's nice, honey. Not now, though. I've got to do some research. Can I use your computer?"

"I guess." Martin's shoulders slumped. He tossed the scrap of notebook paper in the trash. But I didn't pay much attention; I was too busy figuring out how to sign up for Lexis-Nexis.

* * *

"Kelly?"

"Huh?"

"Where are you going?"

"Over to Candace's house. She's having a few people over to study."

"Is Harry going to be there?"

"No."

"Candace's parents aren't going to be home, are they?"

"Well, I was going to . . . hey. How did you know that? Were you spying on me?"

"No. Of course not. But I think you should have everyone over here, then, don't you?"

Kelly threw her backpack down. She stomped up the stairs and slammed her door. I followed and leaned against it, listening intently as she called Candace and referred to me as a "paranoid maniac who so wants to ruin my life!"

For once I didn't pay much attention to that, either.

And then one day at work, Carrie made a big show of telling me the newest issue of the *National Enquirer* had arrived. "Here you go," she said, a cautious smile on her face. "I know how much you look forward to it."

I didn't say anything.

"Birdie, I'd like to— We need to talk—" She handed me the paper while she tugged her bangs, her face full of hope, yet shy, too. She kept it slightly tilted away from me. And for a moment something caught in my chest; it was almost like a fissure in that heavy slab of stone I'd been carrying around with me ever since that PTA meeting. Maybe that's why I still couldn't fly; there was this granite slab in my chest, and who could soar carrying that around?

I looked at Carrie, her eyes pleading with me behind her glasses. "Maybe later," I said, opening up the *National Enquirer*.

"Later?"

"Maybe."

After a minute she walked away.

PRESIDENT KENNEDY ALIVE, FARMING CHICKENS IN ALABAMA, I read, tears blurring the page. REAL-LIFE INVISIBLE MAN COMPLAINS FAMILY IGNORES HIM. I concentrated on the words, staring at them until my eyeballs were dry but at least I wasn't crying anymore. Then I took a big breath and read the rest of the paper. There were the usual stories about politicians with illegitimate children, aliens bothering farmers, a new miracle diet that guaranteed to make you lose a hundred pounds in one week. And in the middle of the paper—page six, to be exact—was a photograph. A short woman, in a wide dress and an apron, a funny mask blurring her eyes, her cape a little askew. NEW SUPERHERO? the headline asked.

Could this be the first photograph of the new superhero known as Super Mom? Citizens of Astro Park, Kansas, have been buzzing about the sudden appearance of a cute little dynamo who calls herself Super Mom. This aproned avenger devotes herself to saving the children of Astro Park, as well as cleaning up the city—literally. Graffiti has all but disappeared in this bustling metropolis in the heart of the plains. But not all citizens are pleased at having a genuine superhero in their midst.

"She's a wicked one," proclaims the Right Reverend Thomas Mills of Astro Park Evangelical Baptist Christian Church. "She should be staying home with her children, not running around doing men's work. 'Wives, be subject to your own husbands!' I happen to have it on good authority that Super Mom is actually one of the whores of Babylon who cruise Twelfth Street on weekends. That apron is full of sex toys. I say to you, Super Mom, repent! The day of judgment is at hand!"

"Why, the nerve! I can't believe they'd print this!" I threw the paper down in disgust. Someone had taken my picture. Somewhere, sometime . . . I shivered a little, wondering if I was being watched, right this minute. But then I realized. I was in the *National Enquirer*! A little bloated, maybe . . . I looked at the picture again. But still. It was me! Birdie Lee! Also known as Super Mom!

"Hey, Carrie, guess what!" It burst out of me before I could think.

"Birdie?" She turned to me, her eyes wide and hopeful. "What?"

"I—oh, nothing. Nothing." That granite slab, it was too heavy. It was too big for one person—even if she was a superhero—to lift.

"Birdie." Carrie blinked and I could see tears sparkling behind her glasses. "About the other day, Birdie, I'm so sorry. I didn't mean any of it. Oh, Birdie, I need you. . . . Can't we just go back to the way things were? You seem so strange to me now; you're not the same old Birdie and I need my friend, especially now—" She stopped herself, blew her nose on her smock. Then she braved a tiny smile.

She was my best friend. Ever since her Chrissie and my Kelly were in preschool together. We'd watched the girls grow up, we'd ignored the fact that we'd both grown older. She was ferocious and kind and funny and smart; my enemies were her enemies, my friends, her friends. She loved my kids as her own.

Yet she was right. I had changed. I wasn't the same old Birdie, and I couldn't begin to tell her why, as much as I wanted to—ached to, actually.

"Carrie, I don't know. I wish I could tell—" A customer bustled up to my register and started to unload her groceries. I turned away from Carrie and concentrated on the contents of the stranger's cart: a small loaf of bread, a jar of peanut butter, tons of individual frozen dinners.

"My husband's overseas on business," she said with a guilty little smile. She was about fifty, jolly and round, with dimples.

"I understand." I smiled and finished ringing up. "I hate cooking just for one."

"Oh, don't I know it!" She shook her head and her reddish curls bobbed up and down. "Especially when you've just moved—I still can't find all my pots and pans!"

"Where did you move from, Mrs.—Cobblepot?" My hand froze as I studied the check she had just handed me: EDWARD D. AND LOLLY COBBLEPOT.

"From Japan, believe it or not. We were there for a year, acquiring some businesses. My husband is still there, closing one last deal. I had to handle the move myself."

"That's—that's a shame." I cleared my throat. "Cobblepot. Hmmm. You don't see that name every day."

"Oh, no!" She giggled and her curls bobbed again. "We're the only ones I know of!"

"Well, since this is an out-of-state check, I'll just need some information," I lied, reaching for a pen. "Your husband's employer?"

"That would be Moulton Pharmaceuticals," she said helpfully.

"Moulton? Really?" I squeaked. "And his position there?"

"Oh, he's the new CEO!"

"Right . . ." I wrote this down on the check. So the Cobblepot who spoke with Lex was CEO of Moulton Pharmaceuticals. Which just happened to be in the middle of a "Project Pied Piper." Which was . . . what, exactly? And how did it tie into the Patriot Pops and video game?

I peered into the eyes of this sweet little woman. She blinked nervously.

"They do a lot of interesting work at Moulton, don't they?"

"I'm—I'm sure they do! But to tell the truth, I never pay any attention. Edward's got his fingers in so many pies these days; he never tells me anything."

"Hmmm."

"This is our fifth move in five years," she babbled, helpless to stop as long as I was staring at her with my Merciless Gaze. "But I have to say Astro Park is the friendliest place we've moved to. That Lex Osborne—he's an associate of my husband's—was so helpful in finding us a house!"

"Really? An associate?" I looked across the street at New Cosmos; in the twilight the parking lot lights weren't yet on. But those two eyes were lit, sinister as always. "I thought your husband works at Moulton?"

"Well, CEO is just a title. It's one of many businesses he's involved in. Which is why we move so much!" She laughed nervously.

I leaned toward her and whispered, "Pied Piper."

"What?"

"Project Pied Piper?"

"What's that?" Her face scrunched up like a baby's. "I don't know what that is!"

I patted her on the arm, releasing her from my spell. This woman didn't know anything.

"Never mind. There you go!" I heaved the last bag into her cart.

"Well, thank you so much." She smiled uncertainly.

"You're welcome. And I hope you get settled in soon." I waved as she trundled out with her cart, looking back at me as if I might come running after her with knives. Then my gaze turned again to New Cosmos.

"How high up do you think that top floor is?" I wondered aloud, surveying the ornate building, counting the number of windows from the bottom up. "A hundred feet? Two? Do you think a person could somehow hang down from the top of the roof and sort of kick their way in . . ."

"What? Birdie? What are you talking about?"

"Huh?" I shook my head. Carrie was staring at me.

"What on earth are you talking about? And who was that woman, Birdie? You seem a little shaken."

"Never mind. I—I can't—"

"Say. You can't say, can you?"

I shook my head, wishing with all my heart that I could find a way out of this, find a way back to my friend, back to the way we used to be.

"Well, I said I was sorry. I really am. I guess there's not much else I can do."

"No, not right now. But, Carrie?"

She looked up, her face so pale, the tip of her nose so red.

"Thanks." I pointed to the *National Enquirer*. "Thanks for this."

She nodded. And then we both got busy, doing something . . . wiping down conveyor belts, straightening rows of candy. Doing nothing.

No matter how confident a superhero is while bashing arch-enemies into evil bits, the truth is most of them can't seem to juggle both work and family. Hell, let's be honest—most of them are too scared even to try. (What can I say? Most of them are men.)

But I didn't have that luxury. Too late: The boat had sailed on that particular subject. Not only was I a superhero, but I was the only superhero I knew of with children, a day job, a controlling ex-husband, and raging hormones (it was getting to be that time of the month). I was moving into uncharted territory. I needed help, in a big way.

And lo and behold: One morning a mysterious package showed up at my doorstep. It was a thick white envelope with no return address, no stamps. My name was written in gold ink—*Birdie Lee, Astro Park, Kansas.* No street address. A wax seal was affixed to it, the letters "JLA" written in Gothic script. Inside were a letter and a small pamphlet.

> Dear Ms. Lee (aka Super Mom),
> It has come to our attention that you are convinced you

have superpowers. Congratulations! Enclosed you will find our pamphlet called "So You Think You're a Superhero? Now What?" This will answer many questions and help you decide what to do next. Should we determine that you are a superhero, we can provide you with many resources to help you on your path to crime-fighting.

The Justice League of America is *the* premier superhero organization. You may hear from others, but rest assured, the prestige and effectiveness of the JLA is second to none. Membership is by invitation only. If you are interested in becoming a member, please notify us by returning the enclosed card. There is a set of criteria that you must meet, yearly dues that will help provide things such as life insurance (which is very difficult to get through normal companies), death benefits for loved ones, and long-term disability insurance.

But don't think that being a superhero is all hard work and no play! Membership in the JLA also gives you access to Club DC, a premier superhero vacation paradise located in the Caribbean. You may choose to rent a condo there, or perhaps buy into one of our lovely time-share units. Either way, it's a perfect spot to unwind and get away from that evil archnemesis. Rest assured, security is a top priority. We also have our annual JLA ball, to which you can invite that special mortal in your life. These are but a few of the privileges accorded members of the JLA.

Again, congratulations on your new superpowers. We look forward to considering you for membership in the Justice League of America.

"What's that?" Martin peered over my shoulder.

"I'm not sure. I think maybe a time-share presentation."

"Wow! Mom! Don't you know what this is?"

"No."

"It's the Justice League of America! Superman! Batman! The Flash! It's the big time! Wow!"

"Hold on a minute; it says it's by invitation only, and I haven't been invited yet. First I have to read this." I opened up "So You Think You're a Superhero? Now What?"

Inside was a quiz. "Go get a pencil," I told Martin as I sat down on the couch.

"OK!"

"Let's see. Question number one: 'Were you recently visited by aliens bestowing gifts?' "

"No." Martin filled in the blank.

"Number two: 'Were you the victim of an unusual accident involving chemicals, animals, radiation, lightning, or some combination of the above?' "

"Yes."

" 'Did you weaken or pass out as a result of this accident?' "

"Yes."

" 'When you awakened, did you suddenly possess new strengths or abilities that frightened you?' "

"Yes."

" 'Did these strengths and abilities linger for more than one week?' "

"Yes."

" 'Do you still possess these strengths and abilities?' "

"Yes."

" 'Has your physical appearance changed any?' " I looked at Martin. "Not really."

"Wait a minute." He poked at my spongy, grippy right palm. "This, remember?"

"Oh, right."

"That's a yes."

" 'Have you encountered any substance or situation which temporarily weakens your powers?' "

"No?" Martin looked at me.

"No," I replied.

"Good. I'd hate for you to have that Kryptonite thing, like Superman."

"Yeah, me too. One last question: 'Have you felt compelled to use these strengths and abilities for good? To protect the weak, to rid the world of evil?' "

"Yes!" Martin wrote emphatically, his eyes shining with pride. And I wished Doctor Dan could have seen him right then.

"So." I studied the instructions. " 'If you answer more than five questions in the affirmative, there is a very good probability that you're a superhero.' How many did I answer?"

"Eight. Now what do you do?"

"Well, it says I fill out this form and mail it back, and they'll be in touch with me. I may have to undergo further evaluation from their team of experts. I wonder who that would be?"

"Oh, man!" Martin flung the pencil up in the air and caught it. "Maybe you'll get to meet Superman! Or Batman! Wonder Woman! Oh, man! Can I meet Wonder Woman, Mom? Can I? If I could, like, bring her to school, so Jamie Flugal, that total asswipe, could see her—"

"We'll see."

"So, are you going to send it in?" Martin picked up the card with the same seal as the envelope and an odd postmark.

"I don't know. What do you think?"

"Well, yeah. Of course. Why wouldn't you?"

Well, I could think of a lot of reasons why not. Right now I could quit anytime. I could slip back into my old life without further risk to life and limb and family members. Taking this step—sending in that card—would make it irrevocable. I'd have more responsibilities, probably. I'd have— "Do you think I could get my own comic book?"

"Well, sure, I guess. Yeah. Maybe even a movie. Or a theme-park ride."

"Really?" I looked at the card, pressed the sharp edges into my spongy palm, ran my finger along its embossed letters— *JLA*. "My own ride?"

"Yeah. I heard Superman has one at Six Flags."

"Wow. I wonder who would play me in the movie. I could see Sandra Bullock, maybe."

"Yeah. She'd be good. Or maybe Angelina Jolie!"

"Oooh!"

We sat there a moment, imagining the possibilities. I don't know what Martin was thinking about—probably Angelina Jolie mud-wrestling Wonder Woman at his next birthday party while Jamie Flugal, that total asswipe, threw himself on the ground and wept real tears because he wasn't invited.

But I was thinking about Doctor Dan. If I were famous, if I had a theme-park ride and a movie, what would he think about me then? All those years of him complaining because I didn't finish college, because I didn't have a career; all those years of him sneering at my domesticity, my contentment with my clean little house and my clean little children. And now look at me. I could be famous, loved, revered—a franchise!

And he would forever be known as the loser former husband of me. Super Mom. Instead of the other way around.

The thought warmed me, tickling at my insides, making

me giggle so uncontrollably that it shook Martin out of his reverie of Angelina Jolie and Wonder Woman.

"What?"

"Nothing. Oh—I was just imagining what your father would say if he knew." I couldn't stop giggling; in a minute Martin was joining me.

"What's going on, you two?" Kelly appeared in the doorway, her clarinet case in her hand. She gazed at us, her gray eyes level and unblinking, until we gradually stopped our snickering.

"Nothing," I said. Martin started to giggle again.

"Honestly." Kelly turned and headed upstairs.

"Oops," I whispered, grabbing the pencil away from Martin. "Shhh."

"Forget about Dad. I wonder what Kelly will say when she finds out." Martin chewed on the end of his army jacket sleeve.

I hesitated, my pencil hovering over the card. What would Kelly say? I'd have to tell her then. Wouldn't I?

Do you wish to be considered for membership in the Justice League of America?

Yes. No. Answer unclear. I felt like one of those Magic 8 Balls. I nibbled on the end of the pencil, trying to make up my mind.

Finally Martin couldn't stand it; he grabbed the pencil and wrote in a firm hand, underlining it three times, YES!! And then he handed it to me to sign—Super Mom, aka Birdie Lee. And I couldn't help but notice that my hand was shaking so much that the letters were all scrunched up together, like tiny bugs.

We walked solemnly to the door; he opened the brass

mailbox on the side of the house and deposited the thick, embossed postcard.

Then we both stood back and looked up at the sky— hoping for a bolt of lightning, maybe, or a thunderclap. Some important, superhero-like signal that the die was cast, there was no turning back. But nothing especially dramatic happened unless you counted our neighbor, Mr. Shoemaker, yelling for his little yappy dog to "Get the hell back in here, goddammit."

"Never mind, Mom." Martin patted me on the shoulder. "When I write the comic-book version, I'll put in lots of special effects."

"Cool," I said as we shut the door. Then we went to the kitchen and microwaved some popcorn.

CHAPTER 12

"Oh, darling, we must stop meeting like this," the beautiful superhero moaned, her perfectly rounded breasts heaving in the moonlight.

"But, my sweet, whatever for? For you are the moon, the stars, the answer to all my prayers," he replied, his square jaw a monument to desire.

"But, darling, think of the gossip. The scandal. I'm a superhero—above such earthly desires. Or at least," she whispered breathlessly as he pressed himself against her, pinning her to the ground, "I should be. . . ."

"But aren't you a woman, too?" he breathed into her ear.

"You scoundrel!" She turned her face to his, meeting his hungry lips with her own. . . .

"Mom? Mom? Earth to Mom!" Martin waved a piece of paper in front of my face. "You forgot to sign the permission slip!"

"Oh—sorry, sorry." I scrambled around for a pen.

"What were you thinking about?"

"Nothing. Nothing, just nothing! Have fun on your field trip!"

"Mother, what were you thinking?" Kelly presented herself before me, her hands on her hips. "Why didn't you tell me that Harry called yesterday? You're not screening my phone calls now, are you?"

"No, I . . . he did? When? I guess I just forgot. . . ."

"Honestly. What were you thinking?" She sighed and left for school.

What was I thinking? That was my children's refrain those days as I stumbled about the house, forgetful, distracted— letting a few nefarious criminals through the cracks, too, I'm sure. What was I thinking?

Well, I'll tell you what I was thinking.

I was thinking about sex. All the time. Every minute of every day. When I was in the shower, I imagined Carl's body next to mine, imagined his long legs planted on either side of my short ones, holding me up so I wouldn't slip on the soap and fall. When I was sitting on the couch watching TV, I imagined his head on my lap, imagined stroking his brow and letting my fingers trace his nose, his lips, imagined him turning his mouth on me, taking my fingers, taking me right there on the family-room floor. When I was at work, I imagined him showing up to buy groceries, looking at me in that smoldering, befuddled way he had. Then I imagined the two of us ripping our clothes off and going at it right then and there on the conveyor belt; I could almost feel the rubber tickling my back as the belt kept rolling on and on and on and on . . .

However, the one place I couldn't imagine him was in my bed. I just couldn't picture his head on the pillow next to mine, his long body wrapped around me like a blanket—that was too cozy, too domestic. Too tame for wild, passionate creatures like us, who had made love outdoors, under a pine tree, just like in the movies. And for a person—a mother—who hadn't made love in, like, a decade, it was all a little intoxicating. Would it happen again? What would I say the next time I saw him? Would he be embarrassed? Would I? And, most importantly . . .

Had he noticed my stretch marks, my flabby underarms, the sad fact that my inner thighs were forever conjoined, like dimpled Siamese twins? I thanked God for the undercover protection of that night, the softly flattering moonlight as it had filtered down through the pine branches. I remembered Carl's hands, strong and sure, probing and stroking, and then all of a sudden, no matter where I was, I was mad for more. Weak for it, hungry for it—and from it too. I had such an appetite; all of a sudden I wanted to taste exotic foods, so I bought curry from the Indian restaurant, grape leaves stuffed with rice from the Greek place around the corner. And I imagined feeding Carl these foods while I ate them in the car with my fingers, licking the grease and oil until it ran down my chin.

And then I would panic and drive home and fix a big nutritious meal for my children that I couldn't eat. But I watched them anxiously as they chewed; I jumped up and brought them seconds, thirds, before they even asked.

And then, when I did the dishes (the old-fashioned way, because it seemed I'd forgotten, among other things, that I had the ability to clean with the power of 10,000 Swiffers), I thought about Carl. And the terrifying, exhilarating possibility of more. Sex.

"I can't believe we did this."
"Me either."

"We shouldn't have."

"I know."

This time Carl had thought to have a blanket "coinciden-tally" stashed in the back of his car. It helped, since the nights were getting colder and the ground beneath the pine tree harder.

"I was all over Kelly before I left, because I was afraid she'd try to sneak out to see Harry. She's so mad at me. And look what I did."

"*You* didn't sneak."

"I told them I had to go to the grocery store."

"Well, you did."

"Yes, and I had to run into you there."

"Sometimes I have to get milk too." He wrapped his arm around my waist, tickling the fuzz on my belly, tracing my scar from the C-section I'd had with Martin. "This is such a neat scar," he murmured, rubbing it with his long, lazy finger. The lower part of my belly tensed and quivered. "How did they get a whole baby out of such a tiny incision?"

"Doctor Dan thought it was awful. He said I'd never be able to wear a bikini again." I snuggled into Carl's sticky chest, sticky with our fluids—all of them. I'd discovered that there were certain times I couldn't control my finger after all.

"Doctor Dan is a complete dickwad, I hope you don't mind my saying. I just can't understand why he had to hurt you so much."

"Shhh. I don't want to talk about him." I closed my eyes and concentrated on where Carl had just been, between my legs, my muscles still feeling him where he'd claimed me with such urgency.

"That's fine with me." Carl tightened his arms around me;

I clutched at him, his heavy bones and ropy muscles, his sticky flesh, his surprising tufts of hair. I'd forgotten about that—hair. On a man. The roughness of it on his cheeks and legs, the softness of it everywhere else. I buried my face in his chest hair, delighted to feel his muscles dance beneath my lips.

"Now you're tickling me!"

"Good."

"Oh, Birdie," he said, and he sounded so satisfied, saying my name.

"Carl."

We lay there for a long time, entwined, complete. We lay there long enough that I had time to memorize the plains of his body, the hills, the valleys. His hip bones were sharp, yet he had a tiny little potbelly; his legs were so muscular and powerful, long and lean and hungry. His arms, too, held such power. But his chest and face were amazing in their ability to soothe and lull.

"So"—I stretched and faked an enormous yawn—"tell me about Project Pied Piper."

"What?"

"I want to know about your work—everything about you," I murmured. But he laughed.

"No, you don't. You just wanted to have your way with me, then pump me for information. You superheroes are all alike."

"Well, I did want to have my way with you. And if you don't want to tell me, I'll understand . . ."

"No, you won't." But his eyes were twinkling in the moonlight; I knew he wasn't really mad. "It's OK. I did a little snooping around, because I wanted to help you."

"You did?"

"Of course. I'm the nerdy scientist love interest, remember?"
I grinned.

"So," he continued. "What I found out is, they don't want anyone to find out. Which means security is tighter than ever before. Which means, in the pharmaceutical world, that we're either about to discover the cure for cancer or the common cold."

"But how can you work on it and not know what it is?"

"Easy. Right now I'm working on proteins. Synthetic proteins. Why? There could be a thousand different uses for a protein that's not immediately digested, which is what we're studying. Diet aids, antacids, you name it."

"But there has to be someone who knows what's going on."

"I'm telling you, security has never been tighter. Whatever Project Pied Piper is, only one person knows for sure."

"Cobblepot!" I kicked the ground in frustration.

"Well, and Lex, right? So I guess two people know for sure."

"And only one of them is currently residing in Astro Park."

"So what are you going to do? Ambush him at the next PTA meeting?"

"No!" I snorted. "*Birdie* isn't going to do anything. This is a job for Super Mom."

"Birdie. Super Mom. So who did I just make love to? Who has the cutest little"—he squeezed my butt and I squealed—"in the world?"

"Guess," I whispered into his ear, as he pulled me down on top of him. He kissed me then, so passionate, yet at the same time so familiar. I felt my body stirring once more—felt him stir too, against my thigh, my sticky thigh . . .

Thigh . . .

Thigh . . .

Chicken thighs . . .

"My groceries!" I sprang up and began to dress. "What time is it? Oh, God. I said I was getting a few groceries, and now look—what will the kids think? This is not like me at all. It really isn't. And you got ice cream! We can't do this anymore, do you understand me? This isn't right, I'm not myself, I'm not thinking right, I'm forgetting things . . ."

"OK." He grabbed at his clothes, his brow furrowed, his eyes a little dazed. "OK."

"We can't do this again," I told him.

"OK . . ."

"I mean it. We're sneaking around, taking stupid chances like horny teenagers—"

"Yesss!" He pumped his fist in the air and I had to laugh.

"But we're not teenagers. We need to do this right, Carl, have a real date, talk and . . . and . . ."

"Maybe tell—"

"The children."

"Maybe."

"Of course. Of course we should tell them." Sometime. Eventually. When they are in their eighties and too feeble to do much about it.

Carl sat up. "Birdie Lee, will you go out on a date with me?"

"Yes, Carl Sayers." I couldn't help but smile; he looked so earnest, his hand clasped over his chest. "Yes, I will."

"How about this Friday?"

"No good. Martin has a friend staying over."

"Saturday?"

"Kelly's recital."

"Sunday night?"

"A school night?"

"OK." He scratched his head. "Next Friday—no, wait. I can't. Greg has a scout thing."

We stared at each other. He was in his shirt and boxers; my sweater was halfway over my head.

"We can't keep doing this," I told him. "We can't."

"I know."

All of a sudden a flashbulb went off about twenty feet away. I heard footsteps running, a door slam, and then a black sedan—which we hadn't noticed before, being a little preoc-cupied with writhing around naked on the ground—pulled away, tires squealing.

We were frozen in place, still half-dressed; it had all hap-pened too quickly for us to move. I started to tremble, my stomach quivering; somehow I pulled my sweater down so that I was covered. But it was too late.

"Oh, God. Oh, my God. Oh, God."

"Who was it?" Carl's voice was shaking.

"I don't know. I have no idea. It could be anyone—oh, God! That picture!"

"What picture?"

All my extremities—my nose and my ears and the tips of my fingers and toes—turned to ice. "The other day I saw my picture in the *National Enquirer*. This must be the same per-son. It's my car, I guess. I mean, any fool could figure out I'm Super Mom because of my stupid car. And you!" I pointed my finger at Carl. "You! It's your fault. All I could think of was you! Oh, I'm not doing this right! The Justice League will never in-vite me now! I'm no good at this whole secret-identity thing! Oh, and if Doctor Dan sees this—oh!"

"*National Enquirer?* Justice League?"

"It's a long story. . . ." And I was far too tired to explain it to him. Just a minute ago I'd been ready to writhe around naked on the ground again. Now I was exhausted, limp, too worn out to move or think. Or talk.

"I'm sorry," I finally said. "I'm sorry to drag you into all this."

"Don't be," he said. But he hesitated for just a fraction of a second—about as long as it takes to blink. But I heard it; it was there, and I couldn't pretend otherwise.

"Carl. This is hard enough with our kids, and now this. Who knows what will happen next? Maybe we should . . . if you want to stop right now, just say so."

He didn't say so. He didn't say that I was being silly, either. He didn't say anything. He just took my hand and squeezed it. Then he led me to my car, tucked me inside like he was putting me to bed. He reached over and locked my seat belt in place, rolled up my window, and straightened the rearview mirror for me. I wanted to ask him . . . so much. But as long as we didn't talk, as long as that next sentence wasn't uttered, we were OK. I didn't have to know what happened next.

"Birdie—"

"No." I put my hand to his lips. "No. Don't say anything, OK? Just don't. Not now."

I felt his lips move beneath my fingers; I closed my eyes and willed my body, my skin, my own plains and valleys and inlets and coves to remember him, the way his lips and hands had explored and claimed, nudged and pushed, tasted, released.

Then I gently pushed him away, my fingers still on his mouth. I shut the door before either of us could say another word.

I drove away in the dented minivan that the world now knew was mine. And I pretended everything was all right. I'd be back, he'd be back; I'd feel him again draped over me, his long leg crooked over my hip bone. After all, I didn't know otherwise, did I? And then I shut everything else out of my mind but the road ahead of me, the yellow lines, the stop signs.

And when I got home, I tucked the night away in my pocket and assumed yet another secret identity. Was this the real me? Birdie? Mom? Which one was it—Super Mom? Carl's lover? It was getting too hard to keep up with them all. It was getting too hard to separate them. Sooner or later, I was bound to slip up . . .

If I hadn't already.

CHAPTER

13

It's odd when children start getting sick. It starts slowly, just one or two murmurs; then all of a sudden it's like a raging brushfire, mumbles and rumors jumping about like sparks, ready to ignite where they land. And whispers—always whispers, as if you're tempting your own child's fate to talk of another child's misfortune.

"Did you hear ..." about the Ferguson's child? Or the Davis boy? Or that sweet young man down the street?

I found out at work, naturally. I was loading Mrs. Faber's cart and noticed something was wrong. Namely, there wasn't any junk food in it. And Mrs. Faber had two preteen children.

"Wow," I said as I bagged up green leafy vegetables, low-sugar peanut butter, whole-wheat bread. "Sugar-free granola? No Patriot Pops? Who's on a diet?"

"Oh!" Mrs. Faber looked at her hands a minute, pulling at her rings. "Oh, well. It's Susie. She's—she's diabetic. We just found out. Juvenile diabetes, type two, but she needs insulin."

"Oh my God, I'm sorry. I'm so sorry—but aren't there a lot of new drugs out there?"

"Oh, yes." Mrs. Faber nodded. She kept nodding, as if she were trying to convince herself. "Yes. There are wonderful drugs nowadays. It's not like it used to be. There's even a new insulin on the market. Well . . ." She studied her hands again. "Just be thankful, Birdie. You never know. Be thankful you have two healthy . . ." She blinked her eyes, set her trembling mouth in a straight line. "Well."

I finished loading her cart. I didn't know what else to say. She pushed it away, and she looked so brave to me—this sturdy, potato-shaped woman setting her feet so doggedly in front of her, one at a time; squaring her shoulders, ready to take on the world for her daughter's sake.

Then I started noticing a change in some of my other customers' shopping habits. The Enderlins', the Wolters', the Goodmans' carts—all suddenly full of low-carb, low-sugar foods, while Mrs. Enderlin, Mrs. Wolter, and Mrs. Goodman themselves suddenly had this quiet, determined air about them, not at all inclined to linger and gossip anymore, all in a hurry to get home.

I wondered if Carrie had noticed it. I almost asked her— until I remembered that we still weren't talking. As a matter of fact, she'd seemed different lately. Distracted, subdued; I'd sometimes catch her resting her little head on her hands, too tired to read or straighten her magazines, and I wanted to run over and take her in my arms and ask if I could make it all right.

I would have, if I'd just known how to begin. It took my daughter to show me how, a few days later.

"Why didn't you tell me?" Kelly flung her backpack down on the kitchen table.

"Tell you what?"

"That Chrissie has diabetes."

"What?" I put my knife down, studied it, counting all the little serrated edges. "What did you say?"

"Chrissie has diabetes. She was really sick, they didn't know what was wrong . . . she had to have all these blood tests. Yuck. So now she has diabetes. She has to stick herself with a needle. Ugh." Kelly shuddered. "I thought you knew. You and Aunt Carrie always tell each other everything."

"Yeah, we do . . ." I remembered Carrie's face, raw and ragged. "Usually we do." And I felt so helpless, standing safe in my kitchen, my healthy daughter next to me. What kind of a friend had I been?

"Can I?"

"What?" I turned to Kelly, who was peeling an apple. "Can you what?"

"Go to Clarissa's party next week. God, Mother, didn't you hear me?"

"No." I swallowed, my throat suddenly dry, my voice hoarse. "No, you can't."

"You don't trust me at all anymore! I'm going to tell Daddy! I hate you!" She threw the apple into the sink, but before she could escape I grabbed her and held her close, buried my face in her silky hair that smelled of peaches and sunshine, stroked her warm cheek, and tried to picture the blood pumping reliably through her veins, red and strong and healthy.

"But I love you," I whispered. "No matter what."

For a heartbeat she stayed in my arms—my miracle. Then she tore herself away and stomped upstairs to her lair.

I sat down at the table and fingered the Velcro straps on her backpack—the kind that mountain climbers use, black and sturdy and heavy with books. And I remembered buying her first one when she was three, ready for preschool. Such a big girl, I thought back then. We went to the store and looked at all the tiny backpacks in primary colors with rainbows and animals on them, and she picked out a yellow-and-red one with denim pockets. She was so proud, she slept with it. And on the first day of school she met Chrissie, who had the same backpack. And I met Carrie, who cried along with me as we watched our little girls march into the building holding hands, best friends before the bell was through ringing.

I jumped up, grabbed my keys and shouted to the kids to fix their own dinner, I'd be back later.

And then I drove to Carrie's.

"Why didn't you tell me?"

"Huh?" Carrie stood in her doorway, the yellow glow of the porch light giving her skin a sallow tint. She blinked up at me like a tired, sad little mole.

"Why didn't you tell me? About Chrissie?"

She didn't reply. Which I took as an invitation to barge into her house and push her down on the living-room sofa.

"Listen. We've been friends too long. Something bad happens to you, it happens to me, OK? You should have told me."

"But we weren't talking," Carrie reminded me.

"That doesn't matter. It should never have mattered. I was so wrong." I kicked my feet against the bottom of the sofa.

"No, I was wrong, Birdie. I don't know what got into me that night. You'd been so different, going off, not telling me things, and I felt left out . . ."

"No, no, I was wrong, OK? I'm so sorry about Chrissie. I should have asked you . . ."

"I only said it because sometimes I think you're so damn smart and I'm mad that you don't do anything about it! Birdie, you could be anything you want to be, and I know you're the best mother in the world, and I know you got the short end of the stick with Doctor Dan—literally, I mean. That man has a tiny penis, doesn't he?"

"Carrie!" But I giggled. "I should never have told you that!"

"Sorry." She giggled too. "But anyway, it's your life and I had no right to say those things. I'm your friend, and . . . aren't I? Still your friend?"

"Will you stop it? Of course you are!" I patted her on the head, just like old times, and she slapped my hand away. "And I'm sorry too, for acting so strange lately. There's been a lot going on, and I didn't mean to hurt you by not saying anything—but never mind, I want to know about Chrissie. When did this happen?"

"Oh." Carrie sagged a little. "A couple of weeks ago. She'd been acting shaky and odd, sweating, having to go to the bathroom a lot. Then she passed out one day in gym and we took her in—she was just a step away from going into full insulin shock. She's got juvenile diabetes, type two, but it's insulin dependent. She has to give herself shots now, Birdie. And you know what? She can. She can do it and she doesn't even cry. She's a tough one, my little girl." Carrie's eyes, gleaming with pride behind her glasses, also brimmed over with tears.

I put my arm around her.

"Of course she's tough. That's our Chrissie! But, Carrie,

haven't you noticed? There are an awful lot of kids developing diabetes."

"Yeah." Carrie sniffed. "That's what Dr. Albright said. He said in all his years in practice he'd never seen so many kids, all at once, develop this disease and become insulin dependent so soon. He said it's an epidemic."

"Yeah. That's what I was thinking."

"But they have all these new medicines now. This new insulin—which is supposed to be longer-lasting so they don't need as many shots—Dr. Albright called it a wonder drug. And he thinks they're close to developing something even more miraculous."

"That's great, Carrie. I know they will! They'll come up with . . . who's 'they,' anyway?"

"Oh, some big drug company, Molsen, Morton—"

"Moulton Pharmaceuticals?" I sat up straight, knocking Carrie over in a heap.

"That's it."

"Moulton Pharmaceuticals?"

"Yes, Birdie. I already told you."

"Moulton Pharmaceuticals!" I jumped to my feet. "That's it! That's Project Pied Piper! Oh, Carrie!" I hugged her, dragging her around the room like she was a rag doll.

"Birdie! Put me down! What do you mean?"

"Oh, Carrie, I'm sorry, I can't—"

"Tell me?" She pushed herself away and glared at me, stomping her feet, twitching all over—just like the old Carrie. She even tugged at her bangs. "Birdie, what? What's so amazing, spectacular, earth-shattering that you can't share it with me?"

I looked at her. She was my friend. My best friend in the

world. She knew all my other secrets: that I accidentally vacuumed up Martin's hamster when he was six and replaced it with an identical one, that it was me who egged Patty Osborne's house last Halloween, that Doctor Dan was a charter member of the Hair Club for Men.

So what were a few more deep, dark secrets between friends?

"Well . . ." I grinned, put my hands on her shoulders, and spoke very slowly so she wouldn't miss a word. "For starters, Carl Sayers and I have had mad, passionate sex beneath a pine tree two times in a row."

She screamed. And gurgled. And when I picked her up off the floor, where she had fallen over in a sputtering, twitching heap, I told her about the other thing too.

CHAPTER 14

Rappelling down the side of the building, the world at her feet, Super Mom comes to rest on a narrow ledge. She pauses to catch her breath, the wind whipping her cape so that she teeters for a minute, almost plummeting to her doom. She grabs onto a brick to catch herself, says a quick prayer, and then bursts through a window, feetfirst, shards of glass falling around her like drops of rain. She lands on her feet in a feline crouch, but the office is dark, empty. Quiet as a tomb . . .

Oh, all right. It didn't happen that way, OK? I committed my first felony in the usual way, sneaking into the headquarters of New Cosmos Industries disguised as a cleaning woman, wearing a red wig. After all, I don't have all those fancy gadgets and gizmos—and butlers—like Batman has.

I looked at my watch and worried about the kids, hoping they were eating something nutritious and getting their homework done. And it occurred to me I could never have been a superhero when they were little. How could I get a babysitter at a moment's notice? I seriously doubted that there was any kind of day care facility provided by the JLA, which, after all, was a pretty testosterone-laden establishment. I sighed. Just one more example of gender inequality in the workplace.

I grabbed a cleaning cart from a closet, pulled my baseball cap over my face, straightened my wig—I wasn't in Super Mom costume, because of the need to blend in and not call attention to my criminal behavior and all, but I did have my apron tied around my overalls—and walked down the gleaming corridors of New Cosmos—A Family Place! Or so said the plaque in the lobby. Along the walls were pictures of Lex and Patty and assorted Brethren, all apparently delirious at the prospect of preparing patriotic junk food. I took the elevator up to the seventh floor. The floor with the eyes. It was dark now; the eyes were shut. I only hoped it would remain that way.

I'd been in Lex's office once before, for a PTA reception. Patty, naturally, stuck me with name tag duty. So I knew my way around. I knelt down in front of his closed office door, prepared to pick my very first lock.

I pulled a bobby pin from my hair and pushed it into the lock, moving it around a little. I poked and prodded, just like I'd seen people do on TV. But nothing happened. I frowned. Then I pulled a credit card out of my pocket, ready to slide it between the door and the frame. I'd seen James Bond do that a couple of times. But as I stood up, I bumped against the door and it fell open. It hadn't been locked at all, and I was more than a little disappointed by that. Stupid Lex.

I crept inside, pulling my cart behind me.

In the dark the office looked bigger than I remembered; even when I turned on the light the edges of the room were hidden so there was no sense of space. His desk loomed in the middle of the room.

Now, normally Super Mom would not condone breaking and entering and stealing somebody's personal files. Normally Super Mom would tremble with the fear of being caught and die of a heart attack at the thought of being locked up in jail, her children taken away to foster care or worse, Doctor Dan's. But I have to admit, I got a little thrill prowling around Lex's office, opening drawers, thumbing through file folders, hoping to discover his deepest, darkest secrets. Or, at the very least, something I could plant in the PTA newsletter. I was alarmed to learn that he had a Ziggy desk calendar; amazed to find an emergency kit of duct tape, plastic sheeting, and bottled water; amused by the discovery of a hidden stash of horse magazines in his bottom drawer. It tickled me to think of this sleek, self-made millionaire pining for his own horse, just like an adolescent girl. But then I remembered Chrissie and all of the others; I slammed the drawer in disgust and turned on Lex's computer, pulling out the diskette I had hidden in the front pocket of my overalls.

I scrolled through his files, looking for something suspicious, wrinkling my nose at all of the porn I found. "Poor Patty." I shook my head, disturbed by the flash of sympathy I felt for her.

And suddenly there it was—it had to be: the file marked Pied Piper. Unfortunately, it was password protected. I scratched my head, thought for a moment, then typed COBBLEPOT.

INVALID PASSWORD, the stupid computer beamed back at me. I frowned.

I typed again: MOULTON PHARMACEUTICALS.

INVALID, the computer barked.

"Damn," I said. How was I going to find the incriminating evidence I needed?

Maybe there was some kind of superhero hotline I could call? For a minute I thought of Carl—he'd know what to do. Or maybe Martin? He was a walking, talking superhero encyclopedia. He'd be thrilled to help out.

But then I thought of Doctor Dan. Of his smug, satisfied face, sure of my failings, so confident of my limitations. And I wondered why, when things looked their darkest and I couldn't see the next step in front of me, I always seemed to think of the men in my life.

"No," I said, and the sound of my own voice in the silent office startled me. "No, it's up to me. I have to do this on my own." And then I started typing in various words.

PTA. HARRY. PATTY. AMERICAN. JUSTICE. PATRIOT. DEMOCRACY. VIDEO GAMES. NEW COSMOS. INSULIN. SICKKIDS . . . None of them worked, and the computer continued to grin at me, blinking INVALID PASSWORD over and over. I laid my head in my arms.

"What now?" I kicked my feet in frustration, hitting something under his desk. I looked down. It was a cardboard box, and as I pulled it out I saw that it was filled with toys. Plush toys. Abe Lincolnator toys. The side of the box was marked FOR EBAY.

"That bastard!" I picked up one of the dolls, tempted to pocket it for Martin. But Super Mom doesn't condone stealing, except when the item stolen can materially benefit others in need. Which, I had to admit, was not exactly the case here.

But then I had an idea. LINCOLNATOR, I typed. And the file opened up, pretty as could be.

"Yes!" I leaped up, pumping my fist in the air, knocking over a framed picture of Patty, Lex, and Harry. It fell to the floor with a loud crash.

I froze, staring at it; then I heard footsteps in the hall outside.

"*¿Qué? ¿Hola? ¿Quién está allí? ¿Hay alguien allí?*"

"*Nada—nada,*" I sang out. "*Yo soy* cleaning! Cleaning, cleaning!" I grabbed a dustcloth from the cart and turned to swipe at some bookshelves just as the door opened.

"Who are you, yes?" A suspicious, heavily accented voice called out.

"New girl, cleaning lady. I'm just about done here," I mumbled, pulling my cap low over my face.

"OK, cleaning lady, *Ándale.* Hurry up, OK? Yes?"

"Yes! *Sí!* Yes!" I hunched over my cart, pretending to check my supplies. After a minute the door closed and I sat down on the floor, pushing my heart back down in my chest. "Jesus Christ," I whispered. Then I ran to the computer, scrolling down the file's pages. I didn't have time to read everything, but a few choice words popped out: *American Justice, Moulton, increased revenue, offshore bank account,* and a new one— *Oralsulin.* That one made me sit down in the chair.

Oralsulin, the paragraph started, *soon to be in clinical trials, should be approved (contact Senator Boothe) in less than a year. Proteins not digested and so taken orally. First trials are only for children—*

All of a sudden I heard that suspicious voice call out, "*Buenas noches, Mr. Osborne.*"

"Yeah, yeah, good evening." Lex's voice boomed, not halfway down the hall. I pulled a diskette from my pocket, shoved it into Lex's computer, closed the file, and copied it onto the disk.

"C'mon, c'mon," I begged the computer, listening to the disk drive whir and hum.

"Someone is cleaning in your office," the voice continued.

"Well, I hope whoever it is remembers to dust the blinds."

"Oh please, oh please, oh please, oh please," I whispered. Finally it stopped whirring. I popped the diskette out and powered down the computer. I slipped the diskette into my overalls just as the doorknob started to turn. Spinning around, I couldn't see a good place to hide except for one door that stood slightly ajar—his bathroom. I flung myself into it just as Lex entered his office.

"Hello? Anybody here?" he called.

"Um, cleaning, OK?" I flushed the toilet. "Cleaning bathroom?"

"Hey! What the hell—what happened to this picture?"

Damn.

"Picture?" I squeaked.

"Yes, goddammit, come out here. I want to know how this happened."

I pulled my hat down low over my face and shuffled out of the bathroom.

"You. Girl!" Lex was standing over the shattered picture, his white hair fairly bristling with anger. "Clean that up. And that frame is coming out of your paycheck. What's your name?"

"Uh, Carmen?" I knelt down to the floor and started to pick up the shards of glass; I bent my head so that my chin touched my chest.

"Carmen? Carmen's outside in the hall." Lex's shoes—polished so fine that I could see the lower half of my face in them—took two deliberate steps toward me.

"Uh, Maria?"

"What are you talking about? I asked you a simple question. What. Is. Your. Name. What are you, a half-wit? An imbecile?" I turned away, intent on the shards, but all of a sudden I felt his hot breath upon my neck. Then I was being hauled to my feet by the collar of my shirt. "Do you know who I am? Do you know who you're talking to? Do you?" His hand gripped the back of my shirt tighter, tighter; my collar felt like a noose around my neck. All of a sudden he dropped me, in one pathetic, cleaning-lady heap, onto the floor. He raised his foot. But before it could land anywhere near me, I rolled away and jumped up.

"My name? You want my name?" I lowered my voice until it sounded menacing, even to me. "I'll tell you my name." I moved toward the edges of the room, taking refuge in the shadows. "Super Mom. That's my name, Lex. Ever hear of me?"

"Super Mom?" He laughed, running his hand through his thick white hair. "Oh, please. You can't be serious."

"Oh, but I am. How is everything, Lex? All the kinks worked out at the theme park?"

"What?"

"I seem to remember—the fencing wasn't so good. A little on the cheap side. Which surprises me, given how concerned you always are for the children. Aren't you, Lex?"

"So it was you that day. I thought so. Don't worry about me, Super Mom. I'm just fine. You, on the other hand, I'm a little concerned about. Stalking children, meddling around town. And now this—breaking and entering." He took a step toward me, his pale eyes oddly gleaming, as if they were lit from within.

"Well, what are you going to do about it, Lex? Call your friend Cobblepot?"

He froze.

"Cobblepot?"

"Sound familiar?" I kept myself hidden in the shadows, as I crept, inch by inch, toward the open door. "A friend of yours? The brains of the operation?"

"The brains? I don't think so—what operation?"

"Operation Pied Piper?"

"What are you talking about?"

"Oh, just a little something I'm looking into when I'm not stalking children. It's a funny thing. Haven't you noticed? All these kids getting sick. All these kids who play American Justice and eat Patriot Pops. Odd. So odd."

"I—I don't know what you're—"

"So you want a little advice, Lex? Be careful—very careful. Because Super Mom is on a mission. And the very next house she cleans might be your own. Understand?"

"Understand? Why you—you—perverted cleaning lady!" He lunged toward me, but I was too fast; I leaped toward the door and started to run, shoving poor Carmen into her cleaning cart.

"Sorry!" I gasped, reaching into my apron. "Really I am! Here's a Band-Aid!"

"Hey!" Lex's footsteps were hot on my trail, and unfortunately getting closer and closer. "Come back here! You can't get away with this!"

"Oh yeah?" I pulled my cap down on my face again, spun around, pointed my right hand, and fired at his feet. "Says who?"

"Wha—wha— Son of a bitch!" Lex skated around, his arms flailing, his thick white hair like a cloud around his head. Then one leg buckled under and he fell to the ground, uttering a few choice archnemesis phrases.

"I'll get you for this!" he screamed as I threw myself down the first staircase I saw. "Just you wait! You'll pay for this! You'll regret the day you ever heard of me, Super Mom!"

I stuck my head back around the corner of the staircase, my cap still hiding my face.

"No, you'll regret the day you ever heard of me, Lex!"

"No, you'll regret it!"

"No, you will!"

"I said it first!"

"I said it last!"

"Shut up!" His face was purple and the veins stood out on his temple until I thought his head might explode. "Shut up shut up shut up!" He took his shoe off and threw it at me, but I ducked just in time. Then I turned and descended all five thousand, seven hundred and forty-eight steps to the New Cosmos lobby, gasping and wheezing every step of the way. I ran several blocks to my dented minivan, got inside, and roared (OK, putt-putted) away, patting the front pocket of my overalls, the diskette snug and secure. Then my hands started to shake so that I couldn't steer a straight course, and I pulled over onto a side street and stopped, shivering, my neck raw and burning from Lex's maniacal grip.

What the hell had I done?

There was no turning back now. I was a marked woman, my superhero DNA at risk of being blown to bits. The battle had been joined: Me, Super Mom, defender of children. Lex, the archnemesis, purveyor of evil. Disguised as a benevolent self-made millionaire, beloved and trusted by an entire town of brainwashed Brethren, leading them to their doom—a modern-day Pied Piper.

The Pied Piper: a character from a child's fairy tale. But now that I remembered it, was the ending really happy? Weren't the kids led off somewhere, away from their parents? Maybe to harm? When I told Kelly and Martin fairy tales, back when they were small, I had a tendency to make up my own endings if things looked grim.

And I had that opportunity, once again. Gradually I stopped shivering, stopped hurting, until all I could feel was outrage and determination. If I had anything to do with it, this tale would end happily. Children would get better. Certain self-made millionaires would end up behind bars. Maybe I'd be promoted to PTA president. Or at the very least, get my own theme-park ride.

I started the car again and headed for home—taking side streets, just in case. But I stopped at a Dairy Queen and bought myself some ice cream. After all, I'd just committed my first felony, successfully breaking into an empty office, stealing a computer file, and bringing my archnemesis to his knees.

And if that didn't warrant a little soft-serve in a sugar cone, I didn't know what would.

CHAPTER
15

"So, insulin is a protein and when taken orally is partially digested, which is why it has to be administered by a shot?" I asked.

"That's the gist of it," said Carl.

"So it would be a miracle—almost as miraculous as curing the common cold—if someone developed an oral insulin?"

"It's not a question of 'if' anymore. It's a question of 'when.' All the major pharmaceuticals are racing to be the first."

I looked up from my notes and was struck again by how handsome he was, how the rosy glow of the candle warmed his brown eyes, deepened those two long dimples on either side of his mouth, softened that adorable wrinkle in his forehead. It was so strange to be with him in a restaurant amid artificial light and noise—talking, plates clattering, chairs scraping. And among other people. I kept looking over my shoulder, afraid to see someone I knew. As if I were doing something furtive. Which I wasn't, I told myself for the hundredth time. I was having dinner with a man in a restaurant.

That's all. A man I knew from the PTA, a fellow parent, a scientist, a grown-up. Just like me. And he looked so respectable
dressed in a nice sweater and corduroys, so dignified. So tall.

"You look different with your clothes on," I blurted.

"Birdie!" He almost choked on a spoonful of soup.

"But it's true," I whispered. And it was. I was so used to
seeing him in the wild of my memory, my fantasy. Wild with
abandon, rolling on the ground, clutching, entwined—too
perfect, too beautiful, to be encased in material and buttons
and zippers. There was only the moon to show us what we
needed to see: only each other, with no one else around to
remind us that we were, after all, only two middle-aged people who talked like everyone else, sat on stiff, uncomfortable
chairs like everyone else, ate like everyone else.

"I miss the park," I said, my voice breaking.

He reached across the table and took my hand.

"So do I," he murmured. "So do I."

"But we can't go back."

"No, but we'll find a place—a place all our own, where no
one can find us. We'll feel that way again. Trust me. You do,
don't you, Birdie?"

I looked up and saw only his face. Everything else in the
restaurant faded away, and for a moment it was just the two of
us. And I did. I did trust him.

"Yes." I laid my cheek on his hand, felt his skin against
mine, and was satisfied. For the moment.

"No sign of the pictures yet?"

I shook my head.

"So what about this insulin?" He took his hand back, and
once again we were just two middle-aged people having dinner in a restaurant.

"So let's say, hypothetically, that Moulton Pharmaceuticals is the first to market an oral insulin. Coincidentally, a lot of children start getting diabetes all of a sudden—children who will be dependent upon insulin for life. And why are the children getting diabetes? Could it have something to do with Patriot Pops and a certain brainwashing video game?"

"Right. That's where you lose me." Carl continued with his soup.

"What do you mean?"

"Well, for one thing, if Lex really is involved, what's in it for him? If kids get diabetes, they'll stop eating his junk food and New Cosmos will lose money—maybe even go out of business."

"Oh. Well. I didn't think of that."

"And for another thing, it's too risky, the connection between the Patriot Pops and the diabetes. Wouldn't they think someone would catch on?"

"Who? Who would catch on? Only me—Super Mom! Remember, no one can hear those subliminal voices but me."

"But you still can't prove anything, can you? You just heard a conversation between Lex and this guy Cobblepot. So? That's not enough to bring down an evil empire."

"Well, actually"—I took a sip of wine—"I may have . . . accidentally . . . broken into Lex's office and stolen a computer file full of incriminating evidence."

"You *what?*" Carl dropped his spoon in the bowl; little droplets of soup splattered all over his tie. I made a mental note to zap it out for him later.

"I . . . uh, stole a file, got caught by Lex, but got away. I'm fine." I touched my neck, where two faint red marks remained. "Just got a couple of bruises, that's all."

"Birdie, this is getting out of hand. I'm coming with you next time."

"No!"

"Why not?"

"Because! I'm Super Mom!" The man at the table next to us lowered his menu and stared, two tiny eyes trained on me. "Because I'm Super Mom," I whispered. "Wonder Woman doesn't have her boyfriend tagging along with her, does she?"

"But, Birdie"—Carl lowered his voice too—"Lex could be dangerous."

"Could be?" I snorted. "You should see how this guy treats the hired help."

"That's just my point. And you're so little. You're so, so—"

"So what?" I glared at him, daring him to say it—just like Doctor Dan. Just like my kids. Just like Carrie. And when he did I would walk away and not be sad. I was strong enough to do that. I was steel, bedrock, granite. Nothing could move me, nothing could rock my mighty foundation—

"Dear to me," he said, fear wrinkling his brow. "You're just so dear to me."

"Oh!" I sank back in my chair, a warm tide of utter contentment flooding my chest, pushing my face into a big goofy grin. "Oh! Me too!"

"You too, what?" He smiled.

"Me too! You're so dear to me, too!"

"Well, isn't that convenient!" And then we just sat there, beaming at each other, until the man with the menu pursed his fishy lips and hid his face in disgust.

"Anyway . . ." I dug my fingernails into my wrist, trying to pull my head out of the clouds and focus on the immediate problem of fighting evil. "Oralsulin. Remember that name.

That's the name of the insulin being developed—soon to be in clinical trials—by your employer."

"Pied Piper?"

I nodded.

"But, Birdie, the fact that Lex knows about the insulin isn't exactly incriminating, is it?"

"No. That's why I think the subliminal messages are my best bet right now. Remember the good old days, when you could play a record backward and hear a message like 'Paul is dead'? Remember?"

"Yeah. These days it's all digital, these kids have CD burners and MP3 players—like a mini-recording studio, like Greg has. . . ." He put his spoon down. "Birdie, we're not thinking. We have teenage sons. We have *geeky* teenage sons. Don't you think one of them, at least, could figure this out?"

"I don't know. I guess."

"I'll talk to Greg. He'd love an excuse to play that game again anyway."

"Swell."

"You don't sound very happy about it."

"I'm sorry. It's just that here I am, relying on a man with a chemistry set in his basement and teenagers with headphones, plus I'm driving around in a 1991 Plymouth Voyager. I'm such a pathetic superhero." I threw my napkin on the table and sighed.

The man at the table next to us suddenly started to choke on a cracker. His pudgy shoulders shook, although he kept his face hidden by his napkin. A waitress came by and filled his water glass for him, and eventually he stopped coughing.

"Oh, Birdie, you're just starting out," Carl said, giving my hand a sympathetic pat. "Every superhero needs to start some-where. You just need to find a corporate sponsor or two."

"Well, when do I have the time to do all that?" I snapped. "I'm busy enough working and doing laundry and being a mom and fighting crime and cleaning up this town and breaking and entering into offices, without having to think about lining up endorsements. And who has a butler? Who? A single rich guy. It's so not fair. And I haven't heard back from the Justice League yet either. Although I did get this cheesy brochure from some other group, Avenger something."

"The Avengers?"

I nodded.

"Oh, that's the Marvel comics group—Captain America, Iron Man, those guys. Definitely low rent. Not good enough for the likes of Super Mom, in my opinion."

"Well, the JLA haven't invited me to join yet. So I may have to go with the Avengers. Typical."

"You're so cute," Carl said, his voice suddenly dropping into his throat.

"Huh?"

"You're so cute when you're talking superhero talk."

"Stop it!" I kicked him under the table. "I'm not cute, I'm a superhero!"

"Sorry. You are. Can't superheroes be cute? I love that little pout, like you're doing now—"

"I am not! This is not a pout. It's a Merciless Gaze." I folded my arms and tried to glare at him, but I couldn't keep it up; it dissolved into a grin.

"And that cute little smile . . ."

"Stop it!"

"And that cute little place, right at the bottom of your

spine, so soft and fuzzy, I love to touch it. I'm thinking about touching it right now." His voice dropped even lower, caressing the hairs on the back of my neck. "I love to feel it. Then I love to run my fingers down around your—"

"Stop it," I murmured, shifting in my seat, suddenly hot between my legs. I twitched and itched all over, hungry for his touch.

"I can't help it. I need you. I need to feel you." Carl's eyes were burning, smoldering; I had to turn away or else I'd start tearing off my clothes right there in the middle of the restaurant.

"Where can we go?" I whispered, staring at the paisley tablecloth on the table next to ours.

"Somewhere. I don't care—the back of my car—anywhere. Let's go." And Carl pulled out his wallet, flung some bills on the table, grabbed my arm, then steered me toward the exit, his hand resting on that apparently adorable spot right at the most ticklish part of my buttocks. It was all I could do to stop from pulling his hand up to my breasts, they ached so for his touch. Sometimes when I was with him, I felt like a piano that was wired all wrong: He plucked a deep bass note on my spine, and I responded with a high treble song somewhere else.

I thought I'd collapse right then, but somehow he kept me upright.

"Oh, Carl, I can't wait to get you—"

"Birdie?"

"Dan?"

Like I'd just stepped into a cold shower—the shock of coming face-to-face with Doctor Dan while having Carl's insistent hand upon my tail.

"Dan?"

"Birdie? What are you doing here?" Doctor Dan frowned down at me, his thinning blond hair flopping into his glacial eyes. I saw Dixie behind him, talking on her cell phone. "The ordinance clearly states," she said, but that's as much as I heard because I was acutely aware that Doctor Dan was glaring at Carl, who kept his hand upon my buttocks despite my efforts to remove it.

"Doctor . . . Dan, this is my friend Carl. Carl Sayers. From school? You might remember, his son Greg is in Martin's class?"

"Hmmm. Sorry, don't remember," Dan said with a sniff. "So you're a friend of Birdie's?"

"Yes. A very close"—Carl pinched my butt and I squeaked—"friend."

"Well, well. Isn't that . . . surprising? Hmm. Good to meet you, Cal."

"Carl."

"Yes. Birdie, could I speak with you a minute? Alone?"

Carl slipped his hand farther down the back of my pants, but I wiggled away. "It's OK," I hissed, although Carl was glowering and pawing at the floor just like a jealous bull. "Settle down. Don't make me put you in a Super Time Out." He smiled at that, although his fists remained clenched. I followed Doctor Dan into an alcove.

"What is it, Dan?" Dixie, I noticed, was still talking on her cell phone. She never once acknowledged me.

"Birdie. I think it's time we had a little talk."

"About what?"

"About things. About our children, Kelly in particular. She's been calling the office a lot, and it's upsetting my routine."

"She's your daughter. She doesn't need a reason to call you, Dan."

"Birdie." Dan plastered a smile on his face and waved to a couple passing by. "Lower your voice, please. Don't embarrass me. Some of my patients are here."

"Fine." I folded my arms and sighed. I could see Carl lurking around the hostess desk, pretending to sort through the bowl of dessert mints, although he was really looking over his shoulder at us. He was so adorably pathetic. "How about we talk tomorrow?"

"Birdie. Don't you know my schedule by now? You know Thursdays are my long days. Honestly."

"OK. When?"

"I can fit you in on Friday, the first appointment after lunch. One o'clock sharp."

"All right. It's my day off anyway. Oh—and, Dan?"

"What?"

"Don't tell the kids about . . . Carl. I mean, I haven't told them. Yet. I said I was going out with Carrie." I hated having to tell him this; I couldn't look at his face, knowing what I'd see there—the disdain, the superiority.

"You lied to our children?"

"Yes." My face felt hot and my skin started to itch.

"You lied to our children about going out on a date? Birdie, really."

"Don't talk to me about lying, Dan." I flung my words through clenched teeth and looked him in the eye. "You have no moral high ground in that particular area."

He fiddled with his tie and looked away.

"I'll see you on Friday."

"Friday."

Then we retreated to our respective corners: He grabbed Dixie, still chattering on her cell phone, and steered her toward the dining area. I allowed Carl to sweep me out the door and into the parking lot, where he wrapped me up in his arms and let me cry a little, although I hated myself for it. I hated this horrible, weak, helpless female feeling that came over me every time I spoke with Doctor Dan.

When I was away from him, I was strong. Let's face it—I was a superhero. But when I was with him, I was weak—an embarrassment. Just when did that happen? And why did I let it continue, after all these years?

Carl was asking me the very same thing, but all I could do was shake my head. Finally he stopped talking and just held me, never moving or fidgeting or hinting we should go. He just stood there, solid as an oak tree, and I knew he'd stay there with me forever—all I had to do was ask.

"I'm all right," I finally said. Although I remained where I was, my face inside Carl's coat, rubbing against his wool sweater, lulled by the smell of vanilla and wood smoke. I could feel his breath on the top of my head, his heart slowly, dependably pumping away beneath his skin.

"What do you want to do now?" His voice was sad around the edges.

"I need to go home." He didn't answer. But he didn't loosen his grip on me either. Not at first. And I knew by his firm, possessive embrace that he understood.

"Next time," I said, in answer to the question in his sad brown eyes. He nodded.

"Next time," he said, in answer to the question in mine. He kissed me then, a gentle, respectable kiss, entirely appropriate for a restaurant parking lot. It made me proud, to be kissed in such a normal, public fashion. But also, it made me a little sad.

"Good night," we both said together, and smiled. Then we drove off in our separate cars.

And I thought ahead to later that night. Somehow I knew that my bed would, for the first time, feel too big, the sheets too cold, the pillows too empty. I would sleep huddled up, not in my normal spread-eagle fashion, both anticipating and missing the person who should be beside me.

"Dan, Dan, Dan, Dan. Doctor—no. Dan. Dan. Dan. Dan. Dan . . ." I was sitting in my car in Doctor Dan's—no, *Dan's*—parking lot, practicing saying his name. His real name. With no "Doctor" in front of it. And I began to wonder when I started addressing him this way—Doctor Dan. And why.

He started it, really, as soon as he graduated from med school (and ran out to buy an expensive frame for his diploma, which we hung over the fireplace in our first apartment). Suddenly he was introducing himself to total strangers as "Doctor Dan Lee, Dermatology." He even signed his checks that way. So naturally I thought he'd appreciate it the first time I called him that in bed.

Well, he didn't.

"Oh, Doctor Dan," I moaned, sounding just like a heroine in a soap opera. Then I started to giggle so hard, I pushed him right out of me, and he rolled away in a huff, wrapped himself up in a bedsheet and went downstairs to sleep.

I didn't try it in bed again. But I called him that, all the time, in my head, and after the incident in second grade, when I finally gave him the divorce he'd been plotting for years, I also gave myself permission to call him that out loud. And now it's such a habit with me, I have a really hard time not saying it to his face. Which was why I was sitting in the car saying "Dan, Dan, Dan, Dan, Dan" over and over.

I checked the dashboard clock, sighed, got out of the car, and walked into his office building, firing off a final round of Dans before I opened the door.

I used to love coming here, bringing Kelly and Martin to visit Daddy. I felt that I was as much a partner in his practice as the other doctors. I'd helped him pick out the colors and the furniture, running all over town digging up swatches of bright, happy yellows and greens and oranges and buying up comfortable furniture—distressed wooden coffee tables and magazine racks for the reception area. The nurses all loved me because I brought them cookies; they let Kelly pretend to sign in patients and let Martin feed the fish in the aquarium. Dan, too, would be happy to see us, to show off his little family in the flesh, not just in their perfectly lined-up silver frames on his desk. He even seemed happy to see me, proud that the nurses loved me so much. Back then he'd even eat a cookie or two—he wasn't always watching his weight.

Then things changed—who knows just when or how. Who knows when you're in the middle of a marriage, consumed by the little details—the buying of socks, the scheduling of dentist appointments—who knows then that something big is about to happen, that someone is unhappy, that someone wants to make a change? The expression "You can't see the forest for the trees"? Well, it's true. When you're in the middle of the marriage, you don't have time to step back and see the outline of it, how it might have changed, how the balance shifted, over time.

But then one day you wake up and the person next to you is a stranger. And you don't know when it happened. You don't know if you're happy or sad that it happened. You do know that this stranger is going to disrupt your carefully constructed life in a big way. And so you do everything you can to cling to the little things, the things you can still count on. Like baking cookies. Like buying socks.

I pushed open the double doors and walked into the reception area. When Doctor Dan—Dan—married Dixie, she came in and replaced everything with chrome and purple and black leather. It's striking. But cold.

"Oh—hello, Mrs. Lee. I mean, Birdie," Stella, one of the nurses, greeted me. "Do you have an appointment?"

"One o'clock."

"Sorry, Birdie, but you have to sign in," she whispered with an apologetic shrug. I signed my name with the other patients—but bigger than theirs, taking up not one, not two, but three spaces—and smiled at Stella, grateful for her sympathy.

I sat in a purple chair and picked up a copy of *House Beautiful.* In my day, we had plenty of *National Enquirer*s lying about, which the patients really appreciated. Nothing distracts you from a microdermabrasion like reading about someone else's golf ball–size boils.

"Mrs. Lee? Birdie? The doctor will see you now."

I followed another nurse down the hall. She opened up one of the examining rooms. "The doctor will be with you in a moment."

"Wait a minute!" My feet refused to carry me a step farther.

"I am not going to see him in an examining room. I'm not here to get any moles removed! You tell Doctor—Dan that I will see him in his office. I'm his ex-wife, for heaven's sake!"

The nurse quickly shut the door to the examining room. She ran back over to the desk and consulted with Stella. I heard whispers, Stella picking up the phone and saying something in an urgent voice, then more whispers. The nurse came trotting back up to me.

"Of course, come right this way," she panted. And I followed her with as much dignity as I could muster to his inner sanctum—Doctor Dan's Dream Office.

A mahogany desk the size of an ocean freighter. Brass library lamps with hunter green shades. Diplomas framed and hung with indirect lighting. Prints of old English hunting scenes. Leather-bound books lining cherry bookshelves. A plush carpet so thick I thought I'd never see my feet again. And on the top of his desk, in a neat little row, his family—all in their little frames.

Even when we were married, I never warranted a frame of my own. The things I did—cooking, cleaning, coloring with the kids—didn't look good captured in a sterling-silver frame. But Dixie in her business suit, accepting a chamber of commerce award, she looked very nice in her frame. Same thing for Kelly in her Harvest Dance dress. Even Martin, in his soccer uniform.

Super Mom. She'd look good in one of those silver frames.

"Birdie," Dan said, leaning back in his leather chair, folding his hands into a little pyramid on his chest.

"Doctor— Dan Dan Dan," I stammered as I took my seat in front of him. I felt for the top button on my blouse, suddenly concerned that it had come undone.

"So."

"So."

"Well." He sighed and looked at his watch. Even though he had called this meeting, I almost apologized for keeping him, but something stopped me. The palm of my right hand—springy, spongy, strong—it reminded me of all I could do, all I'd discovered about myself, in the last few weeks.

So I sat back in my chair, sighed, and looked at *my* watch.

"Well," he said again, frowning at me. "How are you?"

"Fine. And you?"

"Good."

"That's nice."

We looked at each other—two strangers having a polite conversation. Yet I used to wash his underwear. We made love. I gave birth in front of him. He had seen me at my most vulnerable, most out-of-control. And now we talked to each other like two ladies having tea. Sometimes I was so sad that we had made it to this point—and sometimes I was so relieved.

"Kelly," he finally said with a paternal shake of his head. "What are we going to do about her?"

"What do you mean?"

"Kelly tells me that you're opposed to her little relationship with Harry Osborne."

"That's right."

"Well, I'd appreciate it if you'd back down a little. I can't have her so upset—she calls the office day and night."

"Dan, she's a teenager and I'm her mother and she hates me. This is normal."

"Then at the very least, she has to wait until our scheduled weekends. And I wish she'd stop crying," he grumbled. "She's always crying."

"Dan. She's fifteen and she misses her father and she hates her mother because she misses her father. She can't always wait until every other weekend to talk to you."

"Then you need to do a better job, Birdie. This is the one area I thought I could count on you to handle. You were always so good with the children before. I cannot understand," he began, leaning across the table, warming up to one of his favorite refrains, "why you always seem to make a mess of things lately. I pay you more than enough child support. I provided you with a nice home. You don't have to work if you don't want to, and why you persist in remaining at that place is a mystery to me. It's embarrassing when my patients come in and mention they saw my ex-wife bagging groceries—"

"Dan."

"Anyway, no one has it easier than you, Birdie. Yet our daughter is miserable and our son is hostile to me and living in a fantasy world."

"They're teenagers now. It *is* a mess—it's going to be a mess. But then, you were never all that good with messes, were you?" I struggled to keep my voice tea-party pleasant. "Dan, Kelly needs you now. Maybe it's a daughter-father thing. I don't know. But lately all she does is pick fights with me, and while I understand why, I'm getting a little sick of taking the blame for what you—"

"What I what?"

"What you did. You know very well what I mean." I looked at him without flinching. He smiled.

"You forced me into a very unpleasant situation, Birdie."

"I did not—and even if I did, you went too far. And then to get the tapes mixed up—in front of the entire second grade and their parents!"

"That was unintentional. But subconsciously, I suppose I

felt I had to do something desperate in order to make you understand how much I wanted out of our marriage."

"No. There's no excuse for what you did and how you did it. None of those kids will ever be able to go to a career day again!"

"Everyone grossly overreacted to the situation. The tape was of poor quality, anyway. No one saw anything—unpleasant."

"Martin did."

"Oh, posh. He was only eight. He doesn't know what he saw."

"Fine," I said, although I wanted to jump up on his desk and punch him in the face. The memory of that afternoon, the shame, made me shake so that my right hand started to itch and twitch and I was afraid I would spurt all over him. I pinched myself until I calmed down. "Fine," I repeated.

"So ease up on Kelly and Harry." Doctor Dan looked at his watch. "Lex and Patty Osborne are powerful people in this town. They employ hundreds. They're self-made—"

"Millionaires." I pursed my lips.

"Precisely. So my daughter—"

"*Our* daughter."

"Our daughter dating their son is a good thing. It can only be advantageous to me. I mean, to Kelly."

"Right. To Kelly."

"Of course. I'm only thinking about her future. Harry Osborne is a fine, upstanding citizen."

"Yeah, well, that's not what Super Mom says."

"Who?"

"Super Mom."

"Super Mom?" He laughed. He threw his huge stupid

head back and laughed, his thinning hair flopping back over his scalp. "Super Mom? That nutcase?"

"She is not!"

"Birdie, she's a loon. She's crazy. She's a sick person dressed up in a Halloween costume."

"She's a superhero who is making Astro Park safe for children," I said, enunciating every syllable.

"Right. Well, I just wouldn't take anything she says seriously. The day she actually does something worthwhile is the day I eat my hat."

"Really?" I leaned forward with a smile. "Would you care to make a little wager on it?"

"What do you mean?" He looked at his watch again and started gathering up some charts.

"I mean I'll bet you that Super Mom does something really heroic, like uncovering a major scandal that involves the health and welfare of the children of Astro Park—or something like that—and if she doesn't, I'll do something for you. But if she does, you have to do something for me."

"Like what?"

"If she turns out to be a nutcase, like you say—I'll quit my job at the grocery store."

"Really?" He stopped fiddling with his charts and looked at me.

"Yes. Really."

"Go on, go on. What do I have to do?"

"Well," I said, unable to contain a smirk. "You have to apologize publicly for the incident in second grade. And you have to tell Kelly exactly what happened when you left. She has to hear it from you. I think you owe me that, Dan."

"What? I don't think so. You're out of your mind."

"Fine." I got up to leave. "I didn't want to quit my job anyway. I love bagging up all your patients' Froot Loops and Tater Tots. And you know what, Dan? I'm really good at it too. The best there is."

"Wait a minute"—he stood up—"you'll really quit if this Super Mom turns out to be a fraud?"

"Yep."

"All right." He shook his head. "All right. Easiest bet I ever made. You go tell your friend Super Mom I can't wait to see her carted away to the loony bin."

"Oh, I will, I will. I'll tell her. And you promise, right?"

"Yes, yes." Doctor Dan waved his hand at me, dismissing me. "Oh—and Birdie?"

"What?"

"About your . . . friend? Cal?"

"Carl."

"Yes. Well. Try to control yourself. I don't want him sleeping over in my house."

"Your house?"

"Yes. My house. That I paid for, that my children are living in. If he must . . . be with you . . ." His nose wrinkled up as if the thought of being with me was the most unpleasant prospect in the world. And I wanted to rip off my clothes and do a mad striptease on his desk, just to show him what he'd been missing all these years. But for the sake of the children, I didn't. "Be careful, Birdie. Don't do anything that would—"

"Embarrass you. Right. I believe I've heard that before." I started to leave; I couldn't wait to get out of there. But when I got to the door, I looked back at Doctor Dan. He was frowning at a chart, reaching for the phone. Already forgetting I'd ever been there.

And it made me mad. For once I shook off the weight of his disdain. For once I allowed that small flicker of indignation to flame up; I even fed it, coaxed it to burn brighter. Bright enough, hot enough, to propel me back across the room, where I grabbed the chart out of his hand and disconnected his phone.

"Me? Embarrass you? Think back, Doctor Dan. Think back to what you've done to me, to your family. Then we'll talk about embarrassment. Until then, I will be with Carl. Carl. C-A-R-L. Whenever and wherever I want. And I will not feel guilty about it. I will not let you do that to me. I am not that person, Doctor Dan. I am not that Birdie. Not anymore."

Doctor Dan stood with the phone still in his hand, his eyes blinking. Then he curled his mouth into a sneer.

"Well—who are you, then?"

I straightened my shoulders, lined up my loafers in a parallel line, pointing right at him.

"You'll find out. Soon enough, Doctor Dan. You'll find out." Then I swept out of his office, not looking back.

And I didn't even sign out at the front desk as I left.

CHAPTER
17

"This is all so fascinating. Tell me more."

"Oh, Carrie," I groaned, stiff from lying on my loveseat, which was too short even for me to recline on all the way. But Carrie insisted that I lie on a couch for our sessions.

She was analyzing me. She was convinced that my becoming a superhero had something to do with my failure to dream. And something to do with my thwarted ambition, or lack of ambition, or stifled ambition—I wasn't exactly clear. Also something to do with my own mother. And a lot to do with Doctor Dan.

I didn't care. I didn't really want to examine any of it too closely. I just wanted to be. But Carrie had a sick child and she was my best friend and I was sorry for keeping secrets from her. So I played along, sometimes making things up that I knew she'd like.

"But don't you see? All your adult life you've been identified as a mother. You were never something else—and now all this frustration manifests itself as Super Mom! It's priceless!"

"Carrie, I wasn't frustrated about being a mom. I liked being a mom. I still do. And my powers are real, not some figment of my warped, frustrated imagination." I zapped a cobweb above her head just to prove my point.

"I know, I know—I'm not saying your powers aren't real. But I have a theory—bear with me—that most superheroes do tend to build on their weaknesses. Like Aquaman. I wonder . . . do you think he couldn't swim as a child? Maybe he almost drowned! And that's why he became Aquaman! Oh!" She scribbled furiously in her notebook, her nose all wrinkled up. "I may have found my thesis!"

"Good for you." I rolled over, trying to get comfortable. "But I never thought being a mother was a weakness. Now, Doctor Dan did, that's for sure—"

"Of course! He hated it that you were just a housewife—"

"Stay-at-home mom," I corrected her.

"Stay-at-home mom," she repeated. "So despite your contentment, you must have felt some sense of futility. Some low self-esteem. You still do most of the time. Especially around men—and Doctor Dan in particular."

"Well . . ." I smiled, thinking of the past few days. "Let's see how Lex is walking at the next PTA meeting. Then we'll talk about low self-esteem—"

"And if my theory is correct, that may mean you have stronger powers when you're around Doctor Dan! Maybe he's your reverse Kryptonite! Ooh!" Carrie started writing again.

"My what?"

"Kryptonite makes Superman weak. So a reverse-Kryptonite concept would mean there's something that makes you stronger."

"So you're saying being around Doctor Dan makes me stronger? A better person?" I had to sit up—this was too much to take lying down.

"Well, not a better person, but you know the old saying? 'What doesn't kill you makes you stronger'? I wonder if literally it could be true. Did you happen to fight any criminals when you were around him?"

"Oh, sure, sure, I did. I took out a posse of acne-scarred bank robbers." I flopped back down on the loveseat. "Since when did you know about all this superhero stuff, anyway?"

"Since the other night. I've been reading up. I tell you, my thesis is going to be brilliant! Probably even published! And it's all thanks to you!" She beamed at me.

"Well, I do what I can."

Suddenly there was a thump outside my door. We looked at each other; then I went to the door and cautiously opened it. At my feet was a large white envelope. But there was no one around, except . . .

Out of the corner of my eye—did I just see a red blur streak down the driveway?

"Nah, it couldn't be." Then I picked up the envelope: *JLA*, embossed on the cover.

"Oh, cool!"

"What's that?"

"Let's see." I opened it up. " 'Greetings, Birdie Lee, aka Super Mom,' " I read aloud. " 'Thank you for submitting your name for consideration for membership in the Justice League of America. As we outlined in our previous correspondence, membership is by invitation only. We have determined that you do meet the first qualifying set of criteria. It is obvious that you do, indeed, possess superpowers—' Yippee! Carrie! I'm a superhero!" I hugged her.

"Well, yeah," she said, pushing her glasses back up on her nose.

" 'Now for the second step,' " I continued. " 'As you indicate, you have chosen to use your powers for good. This must be validated. At some point in the near future, you must either: Destroy an evil empire or reduce the crime rate in your hometown by seventy-five percent in cooperation with your local law enforcement. We must be able to contact your local law enforcement to confirm your partnership, or we must have proof—either a dead body or incarceration in a federal prison, whichever is more convenient—that the evil empire has been destroyed.

" 'We will monitor your activity and contact you when we feel you have accomplished your mission. At that time, if we deem you to be worthy of JLA membership, you will be assigned a superhero mentor who will guide you through the initiation and first year of membership.

" 'Sincerely,

" 'The Justice League of America.

" 'P.S. It has come to our attention that the Avengers have also tried to contact you. Although their offer may be attractive, please know that they can offer but a fraction of the benefits that membership in the JLA can provide. Once you have become a member, we will invite you and your family to a special presentation at Club DC, where you will have the opportunity to take advantage of a special onetime low-interest offer on a vacation home in our lush Caribbean island paradise!'

"Man, I still can't figure out if this is just a time-share scam or what." I handed Carrie the letter. "But Carl and Martin both say the Justice League is the really cool club, so I guess they're legit. And that part about being assigned a mentor! That sounds really neat!"

"Yeah." Carrie scanned the letter. "I wonder who you'd get."

"Ooh, Superman is so dreamy!"

"Yeah, but Green Lantern is pretty hunky too."

"True."

"Carl might get jealous," Carrie sang as she wagged her hips back and forth.

"Stop!" I pinched her. "Do you think so?"

"Definitely. Superman? What man wouldn't be jealous of his girlfriend hanging out with Superman?"

"Well, I'm not really his girlfriend, anyway."

"Of course you are. I mean all that sex?"

"Twice. We've made love," I whispered, even though I knew the kids weren't home. "Twice. And we went out on a semi-date. So I don't think we qualify as boyfriend and girlfriend. And besides, Carrie, it sounds so stupid that way. Anyway"—I got myself in position on the couch, because I knew she'd have a field day with this—"I haven't told my kids yet, and I just don't think I can."

"Birdie!" She ran to her chair and picked up her notebook. "Tell me more!"

Well, I didn't have to tell her more, because she was a witness to "more" at the next PTA meeting.

Lex limped into the cafeteria on crutches, his leg in a brace.

"Oh dear," I clucked, shaking my head. "What happened, Lex?"

"Freshly waxed floors at work," he grumbled.

"That's a shame. But at least the cleaning person was doing her job." I turned away, hiding a wicked little grin. Behind me, Lex started to sputter but was soon soothed by assorted Brethren who swarmed all over him, putting cushions beneath his elevated leg and behind his back—practically mopping his brow. I took my seat next to Carrie, who looked at Lex, then at me, and raised an eyebrow. I nodded. She grinned. Then I felt a hand on my shoulder, and I turned to see Carl pulling out the chair next to me.

"Hi," he said, swooping in to kiss my cheek.

"Carl!" I ducked away, looking around to see if anyone had noticed.

He made a face and sat down. Next to me. In the PTA meeting. Right there in front of Patty and Mary and Marge and everybody.

"Got your radio ready, Carl?" Carrie whispered. He grinned.

Patty was rapping her gavel at the podium. "So once again, it is up to the PTA to address the problem of this so-called Super Mom."

Carrie and Carl both looked at me, then at each other; then they giggled.

"Oh please," I hissed. "Grow up, you two."

Carl leaned back, stretched his arm, then placed it around my shoulders. Right there in front of Patty and Mary and Marge and everybody.

I bent down like I had to tie my shoe, and his arm slipped off my shoulders.

"Not content to endanger our children, she has now seen fit to threaten the very backbone of our community—New Cosmos Industries!" The crowd gasped. "Yes, my friends— my Brethren, if I may—Super Mom was seen breaking and entering into our own beloved CEO's office. Not only that, but she made malicious, fraudulent accusations of the most insane nature. It is only too clear what her plan is. . . ."

Carl wrapped his arm around my waist and hooked his thumb in my belt loop.

"She wants to destroy our cherished town. She wants to harm our children, put everyone out of work, force us all to eat imported snack food," Patty continued. "Unfortunately, our police chief isn't as alarmed as one would expect. So it's up to us, the PTA—the first line of defense in homeland security. One must take one's duties as PTA president seriously, and as such, I have designed an elaborate plan of preparedness." Someone dimmed the lights and Patty switched on an overhead projector with a dramatic flourish. "A color-coded phone tree. Green is all-clear. Yellow means she has been seen but her current location cannot be verified; go about your usual activities but be alert. Orange means there's an upcoming event at which children are at risk; extra police presence will be on hand. Red alert means a Super Mom sighting is currently in progress; grab your children and take shelter immediately. Birdie!"

"What?!" I leaped up, shaking off Carl's probing hand. "What? What do you want me for?"

"Birdie. Please. I just want you to pass these phone-tree sheets out."

"Oh! OK. Hey, why do I always have to do it?"

"Well, because . . . just because." Patty dropped her gavel and stared at me. So did everyone else.

"Well, maybe you need to look at my job description. I don't think it says 'lackey,' " I snapped, sick and tired of Patty and Lex and Carl and everyone else in the stupid Hawthorne School District Parent/Teacher Association.

"Why, Birdie, what's gotten into you?" Patty asked.

"Oh, forget it." I stalked over to her, grabbed the sheets, and passed them out. When I returned to my seat, I whispered to Carl, "Please, don't do . . . what you've been doing. Not here."

"What do you mean, 'not here'?" He turned to me and his eyes, which were always so soft and kind, suddenly glistened like hard little pebbles.

"Here. In the PTA meeting. It's not exactly the best place, if you know what I mean. We're around all our friends, Carl, we can't be seen—"

"Seen doing what?"

"Let's talk about this later," I hissed, turning to face Patty.

"Yes, let's," he said in a voice so icy I thought my fluid would freeze.

I sat there and listened to Patty proclaim the evils of Super Mom and her "un-American desire to bring down a capitalistic society based on free enterprise and entrepreneurship" and I just sighed. If I'd wanted to, I could have brought her down with one carefully aimed flick of my right index finger. (Not that Super Mom condones the use of violence except when absolutely necessary in life-threatening situations.) But how to take care of the smoldering scientist sitting beside me, wanting—needing—so much?

And all the while Carrie, when she wasn't jumping up now and then to vehemently defend un-American superheroes, scribbled notes down on the back of the phone tree, my body language providing her with even more rich material for her thesis.

"And so it is our duty as parents and patriots to bring this villain to justice!" Patty thumped the gavel down with glee.

"I don't want to lose my job," someone called out.

"Me either! And she gives me the creeps, the way she stalks our kids!"

"People, people!" Lex struggled mightily to Patty's side, and everyone burst into applause when he finally made it.

"Oh, please," Carrie whispered. "It's not like he's in the Special Olympics or anything!"

"People, please!" Lex gestured for the applause to stop. "Please don't harm Super Mom. Violence is never the answer. She must be brought to justice. After all, our Constitution provides for a fair and speedy trial. Even for misguided so-called superheroes. No, I'd much prefer it if Super Mom was unharmed so I—we—can ensure that she gets a fair and proper punishment."

I swallowed hard.

More applause, admiring glances, and even a few tears. Then Patty gaveled the meeting over before Carrie, who was twitching and jumping beside me, could get in a final word.

"Just another day at the office." I sighed, turning to Carl. But he was already gone, walking down the hallway so fast I had to sprint to catch him.

"Carl! Carl, wait!"

"What?" he asked, not slowing down a bit. "So now you're not ashamed to be seen with me?"

"Ashamed? I was never ashamed," I panted, tugging at his sleeve.

"Oh, really?" He finally slowed down. "Well, you certainly had me fooled."

"No, Carl—wait." I stepped back and flattened myself against a locker as Marge and Mary walked by. They looked at us and giggled.

"Hey, you two! Watch out for Super Mom!" Marge winked.

"Yeah! She might put you in a Super Time Out for necking at your locker!" Mary simpered.

"See?" I hissed as they skipped away. "That's what I was afraid of."

"Afraid of what?"

"Afraid of people knowing. About us."

"So? So what if people know?"

"Well, they might . . . we might . . . I don't know, but it just doesn't seem right!"

"Birdie, why are you afraid? What's so wrong about you and me? What's so horrible about it that you only want to be seen with me in dark, out-of-the way restaurants? Or secluded parks? Why won't you let us just be—in the open? In front of everyone?"

"Because." I looked down at my shoes; my laces were frayed and dirty. "I'm not ready for that. Look, I'm just learning all sorts of things about myself that I never understood before, and I need to get used to it. Plus there happens to be a bounty on my head, in case you didn't notice. And yes, I'm afraid. I'm afraid of what my kids will say, of turning their lives upside down. I'm afraid of needing—" Then I looked up, right into his hard brown eyes, judging me, testing me. And I couldn't remember what he looked like, how he felt—before. Already I missed him.

"I'm afraid to lose you," I stammered. "To lose us, how we felt. How we feel, when we're so together. But if we start to mess with it, if we bring the real world into it, I'm afraid we'll ruin it. And it's been so perfect, hasn't it? Just the way it's been, just the two of us?" There was a tightness in my chest. I was afraid to breathe—afraid if I did, I would rupture something tender and innocent inside me. I couldn't bear to look at Carl just then. I couldn't bear to see what was waiting in his eyes.

"Birdie," he began. Then he stopped. I could hear him breathing, could feel him so close to me. I knew how his skin felt on mine and so I could imagine he was holding me, caressing me. But that's all I could do—imagine it. For he didn't move toward me. He didn't move at all. He just stood, like a man struck by some horrible realization.

He cleared his throat, and when he finally spoke, his voice was thick and strange.

"Birdie, I don't know. I don't know about your kids. I don't know what you're afraid they'll do if they find out about me, and I don't know why you seem to feel like you owe them for something that wasn't even your fault. All I know is that I want you in my life all the time, not just under a pine tree whenever we both can clear it on our calendars. All I know is I can't wait to tell Greg about you; I can't wait to tell everyone I know about you. Or, at least, I couldn't wait. Now, I'm not so sure."

"You're not?" I still refused to look at him; my eyes felt small and raw as I fought the tears.

"No."

"Oh."

"I'm not a stupid man, Birdie. I waited a long time to find someone like you, but I'm not a love-struck teenager. If you can't do this, I won't die. I'll just go on, and we'll see each other like we used to, at PTA meetings and bake sales. I can do that. Although . . ." His voice shook a little, and he took a step away from me. "Right now, just thinking about it makes me . . . I don't know how I'll see you and . . . well." He cleared his throat again.

I didn't know what to do. I didn't know what to say. Not for the first time lately, I was lost, stuck in a timeless place where all I could do was watch my life happen without me, watch as my life suddenly turned a corner and headed in a direction I wasn't prepared for it to go. But I had no idea how to stop it—or even if I wanted to. Did I really want to turn it around again and make it come back to me, to Carl—to us?

"Well, OK, then." Carl punched his hands in his pockets and kicked at a locker. "I guess I'll be seeing you, Birdie."

"I—but—"

He started to go. He didn't look back.

I stood where I was and couldn't stop myself from looking as he walked farther and farther away from me.

"Carl?" I said in a voice as small as I felt. "Carl?"

But it was too late. He couldn't hear me; he was already out the door. And what I felt when I saw the door swing shut surprised and terrified me: I felt relieved, free—lighter, somehow. Life, so complicated lately, would be simpler in one aspect at least.

"Birdie?" Carrie suddenly materialized. "Birdie? What's wrong? Where's Carl?"

I spun around and grabbed her by the shoulders.

"He's gone, OK? It just didn't work out. I made a mistake. This wasn't the right time for this. He couldn't really handle . . ." But that wasn't true. It wasn't Carl who couldn't handle this. "But anyway"—I raised my chin and tried to smile confidently—"it's all for the best. I have a lot of work to do, you know. I'll see you later."

"But, Birdie, I just don't understand. . . ."

But I thrust my arm out at her and shook my head. I couldn't, wouldn't, speak, because all of a sudden I didn't feel so relieved. I worked my mouth, trying to keep every-thing inside that suddenly wanted to cry out—for Carl, for me, for that perfect pine tree with the branches so low I knew how the needles felt when they rubbed against my skin.

I shook my head again. Then I walked down the hallway, alone; to go home, alone; to go to bed, alone. Just like I was used to, just like I deserved. For right now I wasn't a super woman after all; I was just another mother and an ex-wife who had made mistakes—who was still making mistakes. And an empty bed and an empty heart were safe places, where I could be trusted not to hurt anyone else.

CHAPTER 18

Dear Super Mom,

Please meet me on Tuesday at 7:00 P.M. at that place. You know what I mean. I have something that will be of interest to you.

J. Nelson.

And that's all it said—a small note, folded carefully in half, tucked under the windshield wiper of my dented minivan. I found it one evening as I was leaving work.

So on Tuesday I put on my costume, got in the van (for which I'd just gotten an estimate to see how much it would cost to repaint), and drove to that place. Which was our place. And that's when I understood the price you pay for being an Amazon. Because as soon as I pulled into the parking lot and realized that Carl wasn't sitting on the picnic table waiting for me, I felt a physical ache—like something had been carved out of my flesh. And to look at this place without him, without the magic we would weave around ourselves beneath the pine tree, made me see how shabby it was. The broken tetherball pole, the rusty trash can, the weathered and splintered picnic table. It was really a sad, sorry little place. As seen through sad, sorry little eyes.

Then a black sedan pulled up beside me. I adjusted my mask, smoothed my apron. And I calmly got out of my car, because I was Super Mom now. A strong, resilient defender of good; a warrior who had no time for a broken heart.

"Super Mom, I presume?" A short bald man with round eyes got out of the sedan, looking vaguely familiar. He had a camera around his neck, a mini–tape recorder, and a large envelope. He mopped his forehead, even though it was forty degrees out with a stiff wind blowing.

"Yes." I stood, impenetrable as a fortress.

"Wow. You're a lot smaller than you look in your picture."

"That's what everybody says."

"Well, let's get this show on the road. Shall we sit over there?" He pointed at the picnic table.

"No!" I shouted, pointing my finger and forcing a solid stream of fluid, like a wall, between him and the table. He jumped backward about five feet.

"Don't shoot!" His bulgy fish lips puckered up like he might cry. "I'm unarmed!"

"Sorry." I dropped my hand, ashamed. "Sorry—that table has sentimental value to me. Hey, don't I know you from some-where?" I peered into his face, trying to place him.

"No. No, you don't. Never saw you before in my life. I have no idea what you're talking about. So, Super Mom, I happen to possess a picture that I believe you might be interested in."

"I'm sure you do." I held my hand out.

"Not so fast. Don't you even want to know who I am?"

"Not particularly."

"I'm Jimmy Nelson, from the *National Enquirer.* We—"

"You're from the *National Enquirer?*"

"Uh, yeah . . ."

"Oh my God! That is so cool!"

"Gee. Most people get really upset when I tell them."

"Oh, no! I love the *National Enquirer!* 'World's Fattest Pig Gives Birth to World's Fattest Piglets!' I loved that story!"

"Really? That was one of mine!"

"Get out!" We beamed at each other.

"Well," he said, wiping the smile from his face with his hand. "Now about this picture . . ."

"I know, I know." I sighed. "You have a seminude photo of me and an unidentified male underneath a pine tree."

"Yeah." He sounded apologetic.

"We broke up."

"Huh?"

"Me and the unidentified male. We just broke up." I sat on a big rock. Jimmy wheezed as he sat down next to me.

"Aw, that's a shame. Really it is. Why?"

"Well, for one thing, he wanted me to tell my kids, and I wasn't ready. I was so stupid. I don't know why I can't tell them."

"It's tough, when you have kids. How old are yours?"

"Thirteen and fifteen."

"Mine are ten and twelve." He reached into his wallet. "Do you want to see pictures?"

I nodded, and he showed me two school pictures: a little boy who looked like he was already balding, and a little girl with fish lips.

"They're adorable!"

"Yeah. There's nothing's like it, is there? Parenthood?"

"Nope."

"Sorry about your boyfriend. From the looks of the . . . well, from what I've seen . . . I mean, he seemed really nice. Have you tried talking to him? Maybe send him a card? It might not be too late for you to—hey! Wait a minute. Jeez. You threw me off track. Now"—he cleared his throat—"what I have here is an interesting photo. One you would most likely be eager to, shall we say, have destroyed?"

I nodded.

"So let me make you a little deal, Ms. Super Mom. Or is it Mrs. Super Mom?"

"Just Super Mom is fine, thanks."

"OK, Super Mom. You give us an exclusive interview—the world's first glimpse of this maternal dynamo known as Super Mom—"

" 'Maternal dynamo'?"

"Aw, I'll come up with something better. You'll see. Anyway, you give us an exclusive interview, and we'll give you the picture."

"Sure." I shrugged. "Why not?"

"Really?" He dropped the envelope. "That easy?"

"Yep. What do you want to know?"

"Hold on, hold on—I wasn't prepared for this. Nobody ever says yes." He fiddled with his tape recorder. "This thing—I don't even have a tape for it. Nobody ever gives us a real interview! We just make things up!"

"Not all of it, do you? Some of it's true, isn't it?"

"Whaddya mean?" He was searching through his pockets now. "I coulda sworn I had a tape somewhere. . . ."

"But the three-headed cow with the six-uddered calf! That was true, wasn't it?"

"Are you for real?" He stopped searching through his pockets. "Are you . . . Yeah," he said, looking away, "sure. Some of it's true."

"I knew it! And Birdman, and that one about Superman . . . I knew it!"

"Well, yeah, those guys—they're nuts. Most of them won't even give you the time of day—I've been wanting to get something on Batman for years. It'd be nice to get a big one. I could use it. Things are a little tough right now. They're talking about layoffs and—"

"Really? Oh, that would be a shame. Why, you're the fattest-pig guy! They need you there!"

"Yeah, well, times are tough with reality TV and all. People just aren't reading like they used to."

"I know, I know. I can't get my kids to read anything anymore."

"Yeah. Does your boyfriend have kids?"

"One—a boy."

"You know, I bet you could work things out. The two of you looked really nice together the other— I mean, in the photo . . ."

"That's it!" I straightened up and glared at him. "At the restaurant! You were the guy choking on the cracker!"

Jimmy nodded and turned his head, trying to avoid my Merciless Gaze.

"What did you hear?"

"Nothing! I swear! Nothing. I didn't hear anything about anything; I was just eating my dinner and minding my own business. . . ."

"Sure you were." We were silent for a minute, although I could hear Jimmy breathing heavily, wheezing a little as he kept fiddling with his tape recorder. I tapped my finger to my nose, thinking. "You know, as long as you were eavesdropping . . . I might be able to help you out. And you'd be doing me a favor too. How would you like to tag along with Super Mom as she brings down a self-made millionaire's evil empire? And maybe, if all goes well, I can get you an interview with the Justice League."

"The JLA? You're kiddin'. She's kiddin', right?" He turned around to address the rock next to him. "The JLA? Me? Well, yeah. I could use that!"

"And maybe it will help readership? Improve revenue? We can't let the *National Enquirer* go out of business."

"How would I feed my kids?" He shook his head.

"OK, then. Do we have a deal?"

He nodded.

"Give me the picture."

He handed it to me. I didn't look inside the envelope; I trusted him. Plus I didn't want to see myself with Carl. I didn't want to see us caught like that, all awkward and frozen and ashamed. I wanted to remember it as perfect, natural—that the bulb never flashed at all.

"The negatives?"

He mopped his forehead.

"Yeah, the negatives . . . Funny thing, I meant to bring those, and . . ."

"No negatives, no deal. You bring them to me next week, same time, and I'll have something for you. A little scoop about a pharmaceutical scandal. Interested?"

"Interested? You bet!" He jumped up and helped me to my feet. We shook hands.

"Gee, Super Mom, thanks."

"Don't mention it. Now, drive home carefully; it's dark out and you don't know the neighborhood."

"I will."

"Oh," I said, reaching into my apron, "and have some animal crackers. You probably missed dinner."

"Super Mom, you're one hell of a— I mean, you're the greatest!"

"Well, aren't you sweet!" I stood as he rushed to open my car door for me. "And don't talk with your mouth full!"

Jimmy nodded, his cheeks bulging like a chipmunk's. He climbed into his car and started to drive off, but when he caught my eye, he stopped.

And then he buckled his seat belt.

CHAPTER
19

It's a little-known fact, but true: Most of the major super-heroes started out in life as geeks. Take Peter Parker, for instance, always getting beaten up at school until he was bitten by that radioactive spider. The Flash—geeky scientist before that freaky thunderstorm in his lab. Hawkman—geeky archaeologist before he happened to discover he was really the reincarnation of an ancient Egyptian prince.

So really, I shouldn't have been worried when Martin started coming home late from school, panting and wheezing, usually missing something—a button on his shirt, a hat, homework. After all, he had superhero in his genes.

But I did worry—I'm a mom. A Super Mom. When I asked him what was happening, he said it was nothing. When I sat him down in the kitchen with milk and cookies, he still said it was nothing.

When I looked him in the eye, he produced sunglasses that shielded him from my Merciless Gaze. Pretty smart, even for a trusty sidekick.

So I did what any self-respecting Super Mom would do. I

took advantage of one of those rare disturbances in the space-time continuum when Kelly was actually speaking to me, and bribed her to rat out her brother.

"Jamie Flugal," Kelly said as she calmly palmed five bucks.

"The Total Asswipe?"

"The one and only. He has it in for Martin, and no one knows why. He said he just doesn't like the way he looks."

"Well!" I started to twitch all over, my Super Mom Sense kicking in. My eyes burned like lasers, my skin flushed hot with indignation, and my hands itched to grab that total ass-wipe by the ears.

"He won't let Martin ride the bus anymore. That's why he's been late. He stands outside until the bus is ready to go, and he won't let Martin on—usually he shakes him down some, too."

"Well, why won't the bus driver do anything?" I stalked toward the phone in the kitchen. "I'm going to call that school right this minute!"

"Mother." Kelly shook her head at my ignorance. "That would only make things worse. They'll throw the Total Ass-wipe in detention for a week; then when he's out he'll go af-ter Martin worse than ever."

"Hmmm." I looked at my wise daughter. "You're right. So, any suggestions?"

"Just let Martin figure it out. You baby him too much. He needs to learn to deal with stuff like this."

"Yeah, maybe." I nodded, like I was agreeing with her.

But I wasn't. I had a secret identity or two up my sleeve.

Super Mom tried not to go near school when it was in ses-sion. Patty, after all, had the phone tree on yellow alert. And even though the principals were secretly on my side, the truth was that these days even a superhero hanging around a schoolyard was going to cause some concern.

Plus, I set off all the metal detectors with my scissors.

But lo and behold, I happened to be driving by one afternoon when school was letting out. And lo and behold, among all the scuffling and pushing and shouting, I came upon one large lump of a boy with spiked black hair and boils on the back of his neck holding, with one grubby, sausagelike hand, a smaller boy with floppy blond hair and an army jacket.

"Hello, boys!"

The Total Asswipe kept a grip on Martin, who kept flailing his puny little arms.

"Super Mom?" the Total Asswipe said, his jaw dropping open to reveal a gold tooth.

"Yes, Super Mom. So what have we here? What's the problem?"

"Nothing." He still kept his grip on Martin, who was only occasionally flailing by now.

"Well, Mr. Flugal, I strongly urge you to drop this boy right now."

"Why?" He looked at me, his face a blank, not comprehending.

"Because it's not nice to beat up boys who are smaller than you," I said sweetly, although I was pinching my right hand hard so that I wouldn't fling cleaning fluid right into his red little pig eyes.

"Tough shit," the Total Asswipe said.

"OK, that's it. I asked nicely. Now it's time for you to let Mar— that boy go. I said now!" I raised myself up, peered into his pig eyes with my Merciless Gaze, and watched as his face slowly melted—his eyes turning watery, his nose getting runny, and his chin starting to tremble.

But still his hand gripped Martin.

"I said, now. You should be ashamed of yourself! Does your mother know you beat up little boys?"

"Mo— Super Mom!" Martin yelped.

"No," the Total Asswipe muttered.

"Why, hello, Super Mom! This certainly is a pleasant surprise!" Principal Davis came running up.

"Hello. I was just driving by when I sensed a problem here. Just doing my job, you know."

"And a fine job it is. We really appreciate it! Now, Jamie, why don't you release little Martin Lee? C'mon, let him go."

Jamie—aka the Total Asswipe—blinked at us both. But still his hand gripped Martin, who had given up any pretense of fighting back. He just hung there like a doomed fish on a line.

"I—I can't do it," Jamie stammered. "It won't let go!"

I sighed and grabbed his arm. Mr. Davis started to sputter.

"Oh no—no, Super Mom, we have a strict policy about not physically reprimanding our students!"

"I'm not physically reprimanding him." I shook Jamie's arm until his grip relaxed and Martin fell to the ground. "See? No harm."

"Super Mom hurt me." Jamie started to sniffle.

"I did not!"

"Yes, she did—see? I have a bruise!" Jamie presented his flabby arm to Mr. Davis, who shook his head and clicked his tongue.

"Super Mom, I'm sorry, but we have to document all incidents of suspected child abuse—"

"Child abuse!"

"Technically, I'm afraid this qualifies. I'm so sorry, but I'm going to have to report this to the police."

Martin, meanwhile, picked himself up and started to inch away.

"Oh, please. I didn't hurt anybody. And besides, if you'd done a better job of making sure this school was safe for little defenseless kids like that one"—I pointed to Martin—"none of this would have happened."

"Well, I'm sure we'll review our policies, but meanwhile I think you'd better go now, Super Mom."

I looked around. A crowd of kids had gathered, and one by one they looked at me and started to whisper.

"Did you see that? Super Mom beat up Jamie Flugal."

"The Total Asswipe?"

"Yeah! She totally flattened him!"

"She picked him up and threw him down on the ground!"

"She stomped on him! I saw it! I saw it all happen!"

"Well, really!" I huffed. "You should all be ashamed of yourselves, lying like that! What would your mothers say?"

"All right now, Super Mom." Mr. Davis ushered me down the sidewalk. "There's no need for name-calling."

"Oh, puh-leeze!" I shook him off and stalked to my minivan, passing a hunched-over Martin on the way. "C'mon. I'll take you home."

"No."

"C'mon, Martin. Let's go. Now."

"No," he said in a quiet voice. Quiet, yet firm with resolve.

I stopped and looked at him. His face was pale and his clothes were all rumpled, but there was steel in his eyes that chilled me.

"I'm walking home. I don't want to go home with you. I don't want to go home with Super Mom. You ruined every- thing. Why did you do that? Why?"

"But, Martin! I just— Why, you were in trouble and I just thought you could use some help—"

"I don't need you to rescue me!" He started to walk away, taking long, quick strides like a man. "I don't! I'm thirteen now, get it? I don't need you! And I don't need Super Mom!"

"But, you did! You did need me. That kid was bigger than you. He's been beating you up and you're so little; you're my baby and—"

"I'm not!" He whirled around, his face red and pinched, and I knew he was trying so hard not to cry. "I'm not a baby! Is that how you think of me? I thought—"

"No. No, Martin, I didn't mean it. I didn't! Of course you're not a baby; you're a young man now and I didn't mean it—"

"But you did. You *did* mean it! Now all the kids will think— oh, forget it. Just go away! Just leave me alone!" He started to run.

"Martin! But . . . Martin!"

I stood there, watching as my son ran farther and farther away from me. Down a sidewalk filled with cracks he kept running, running, his shoelaces untied and flapping so that I was afraid he would trip. I took a few steps too, as if I could chase him. The wind caught my cape and lifted it off my shoulders. But still my son kept running. And it was just like in my hallucination: my son running away from me, the wind catching a cape—only the cape was mine.

But this time I couldn't run after him; at least I knew that much. So I stopped and did the only thing I could think of, the only thing that made sense: I went home and waited for him. And while I waited, I made his favorite meal for dinner.

And when he finally came home—pale and ragged yet quietly dignified—and refused to eat it, I wrapped it up and put it in the refrigerator.

Just in case he got hungry, later.

CHAPTER 20

SUPER MOM BEATS UP STUDENT! the headline screamed.

Witnesses at Jerome Siegel Junior High and High School insist that Super Mom went berserk during an altercation involving two students.

"She just flipped. She totally slammed this dude. She broke his arm, I heard," said Tristan Wright, a seventh-grader.

"I heard she stomped on his face. I mean, the guy's a total [expletive deleted], but he didn't deserve that," said Kerry Fellows, eighth-grader.

Patty Osborne, Hawthorne School District Parent/Teacher Association President, declared herself unsurprised by the turn of events.

"Lurking about at school dances, breaking and entering, and now this—physically attacking a defenseless student! Where will it end? Our police commissioner and city council have been reluctant to take any action against Super Mom. One hopes that this will serve as their wake-up call.

And please remember, PTA members, we're still at yellow alert."

Police Commissioner Borden expressed concern and sadness over the incident.

"I really hope Super Mom has a good explanation for her actions. She's been a passionate protector of children in this town, not to mention one heck of a cleaning lady. I find it hard to believe she would deliberately harm a child. But it's my duty to investigate the incident."

The child in question, who is a minor, has been treated and released from a local hospital. His parents are deciding what charges, if any, will be filed.

"Jesus Christ, Birdie!"

"Oh my God." I sank down on Carrie's sofa. "What do I do?"

"I don't know." Carrie sat down beside me. "This is terrible. You didn't . . . I mean, you really didn't?—"

"Of course not. I just shook his arm a little so he would let go of Martin. He didn't even bruise! This is so ridiculous. But I'm scared, Carrie. What if—what if they arrest me? Then they'll find out my secret identity."

"And Doctor Dan will spontaneously combust," Carrie clucked.

"Worse than that. What if they take the kids away from me?" My stomach flopped over; I pressed my face into a sofa cushion to keep the nausea from rising up into my throat.

"That won't happen. It just won't. It can't."

I didn't move, waiting for my stomach to settle down.

"Why are they doing this to me? Why? All I want to do is help these kids."

"Who knows? It's a mob mentality, for one thing. And it has the backing of Lex and Patty. The thing is, what are you going to do about it?"

"I don't know," I mumbled, my mouth full of upholstery. "Who says I have to do anything? What if I can't do this, Carrie? What if Super Mom just disappears—"

"Mom?"

I looked up. Chrissie was standing in front of us. Her face was white, a mask with two big eyes dark with fear; she was shaking and sweating.

"Mom? I kind of forgot to eat lunch today. . . ." She plopped down on a chair as her legs gave way.

Carrie jumped up like she'd been shot from a cannon. She raced to the kitchen and came back with some apple juice, a cookie, and a cold washcloth, and pressed the cloth on Chrissie's neck while she murmured soothingly.

"It's OK, sweetie, just take this. Drink up now, there's a good girl. Now, eat the cookie—slowly, now. It's all right. You'll be all right."

I watched the two of them—this trembling girl and her frightened mother—huddled together in their own little world, trying to fight a disease that was bigger than they were. And it wasn't right. Chrissie should have been yelling at Carrie; Carrie should have been rolling her eyes and taking it. That was what teenagers and their parents did.

But not the teenagers of Astro Park. Not anymore. And I alone knew who was responsible.

I stood up. Carl, Doctor Dan, my children—I'd been too distracted lately, worrying about their needs, worrying about my own. I'd forgotten what was really important—what was happening here in this living room, in this town—children getting sick. Parents too frightened to do anything but hunker down and concentrate on just one thing—getting their children through this, day by day.

I could change this. I couldn't make it better—I couldn't cure them. But I could make it easier for them; I could stop it before it happened to more children. I—Super Mom—Birdie—all one and the same. A woman with responsibilities, sure—what woman wasn't? But for too long I'd hidden behind those responsibilities; I'd hidden behind the fact that I was a mother, a good mother, even. I'd used it as an excuse—to let Doctor Dan roll right over me, to let Kelly blame me for everything, to let Carl slip away.

But not anymore.

I raised my hand to the light, flexed my fingers, and remembered that first night under the stars, alone, with only the wind a witness to my wonder. When I raised my hand to the moon, mesmerized by its outline, like a map of some new world. Uncharted, full of mystery, hidden treasures. Untapped power.

I held so much power—because I was a mother. I was strong enough to bring down an evil empire, all by myself; I didn't need anybody's help. Or anybody's approval.

All I needed was this hand, these eyes, this indignation quivering in my chest—my strong, unyielding chest with an orange "S" emblazoned on it, for all the world to see.

"I know what to do," I told Carrie after Chrissie had stopped shaking and a hint of normal color had returned to her cheeks.

"What?"

"I know what I have to do. And it might make the people of Astro Park forget all about this silly thing with the Total

Asswipe. It might even get me into the Justice League of America. But that's not why I'm doing it. You know that, right?"

Carrie didn't say anything. She just kept coaxing Chrissie to sip her apple juice. But her eyes, red and tired behind her glasses, turned to me, gleaming with approval.

"Thank you, Birdie. Thank you."

"No." I whispered, smiling, flexing my powerful, amazing hands. "Thank Super Mom."

"No," Carrie said slowly, as if she were talking to a child. "Thank *you*, Birdie."

I looked at her. It was just like that time in college with Dan: It was just like hearing my name, spoken for the very first time. Only this time it sounded harder, the consonants cruel and clipped. Not quite so soft, not quite so pretty. But stronger. Infinitely stronger.

"I'm sorry to bother you. But it's important." I kept my trembling hands shoved tightly in the pockets of my coat.

"All right." He held the door open and showed me in, as gracious—and impersonal—as a doorman at a fine hotel.

"Thanks for letting me come over."

"You're welcome."

Carl led me downstairs to his basement. He turned on the light and stood with his back to me, fiddling with his chemistry set.

"I need a little help. Just a little, and I wouldn't have come if it wasn't really important . . ."

"I know. I read the paper."

"Oh—that!" I'd almost forgotten all about the price on my head, courtesy of the Total Asswipe. "No, that's not what I meant. But, well, what did you think?"

"About what?"

"About the article. Did you . . . that is, did you think—"

"I didn't believe it, Birdie, if that's what you're asking."

Tears sprang to my eyes, but I turned my head away from

him. I couldn't let him see how happy that made me—and how sad, too.

"Thank you. That means a lot to me." I looked at his back, his flannel shirt, the way his broad shoulders filled it out, the way his slender waist tapered in. Just to be with him, but not to be able to touch him or reach out to him in any way—it was like being denied Christmas. And Easter. And Halloween. And every insignificant, beautiful day in between.

"So what did you need, Birdie?" He didn't turn around.

"I need help with the video game, the voices. It's time. I need to get Lex, once and for all. I've seen what he's done, I saw Chrissie—Carrie's girl—almost crash the other day." Carl turned around, his face a blur of concern. "Anyway, I can't let this go on any longer. I have to stop it now. But I need your help."

"Oh."

"So . . . can you? Help, I mean?"

"Yes, I can help . . . Super Mom. That's who I'm helping, OK? Do you understand?"

"Yes." I took a big breath. "I understand."

"OK." Carl's eyes were even and hard, his mouth just a grim line, his face full of sharp edges. Not at all the kind, comforting face I remembered. "OK," he said again. "Come with me."

I followed him up the stairs, past the family room with the little blue footstool that made my heart catch in my throat, up more stairs, to a closed door papered with threatening signs: CAUTION! ENTER AT YOUR OWN RISK! BEWARE OF ATTACK DOG! TOXIC WASTE SITE—DO NOT ENTER!

"Greg!" Carl hammered on the door.

No answer.

"Greg!" Carl pounded again.

No answer.

"Gregory!" Carl pounded once more, then put his shoulder against the door and pushed. The door flew open, revealing—

A recording studio. With a twin bed wedged into a corner, surrounded by speakers and computers and receivers and tweeters and woofers and all sorts of gadgets with dials and buttons. And sitting at the main computer, headset on, eyes closed, head nodding to earsplitting (at least to me; Carl couldn't hear it) music, was Greg.

"Greg!" Carl went over and shook his shoulder. Greg looked up, surprised.

"Greg." Carl removed his earphones. Greg sighed and punched a button on his computer. I dropped my hands from my ears as the music faded.

"Mrs. Lee is here. Remember the video game? The subliminal messages?"

"Oh, yeah." He glared at me; I grimaced back. "Thanks for ruining a perfectly good game."

"Greg!"

"Sorry. Anyway, yeah. Those messages. Got 'em."

"You do?" I wanted to hug him right then and there, but something—probably the stark look of hatred in his eyes—stopped me.

"Yeah. It's weird. Most subliminal messages are imbedded backward—it's called back-masking—and it's all done with computers now. So I can just press a button and un–back mask it. But this stuff was different. It was like really low rumblings—like on a string instrument or something—that mimicked speech. Anyway, I had to use a base two-fifty-six system to convert it. Pretty simple once I figured it out. Here you go." And he flipped me a CD.

I stared at this small sullen boy. Last time I'd seen him, he'd been whining for Patriot Pops. "Is he always like this?" I asked his proud father.

Carl grinned, his brown eyes shining. "That's my boy!"

"Well, thank you, Greg. Thank you very much. You don't know what you've done, but it's very important."

"Yeah. Whatever." And Greg put his earphones back on and punched up the music.

Carl and I went downstairs. I put the CD in my purse and grabbed my coat.

"Well," I said, not looking at him.

"Well."

"Tell Greg again that I thank him. He's pretty special."

"Yeah, he is."

"And thank you, too. For helping me. I mean, for helping Super Mom." I pinched my right hand, hard—not to stop my fluid from spurting, but to stop my tears.

"Well, she's a good person," Carl said softly. "Super Mom. She means well."

"Yeah. She does." I looked up at him, and it was hard to see his face through my tears. "She really does mean well."

He didn't say anything. We just stood there looking at each other, each balancing on our own end of this tightrope between us, each afraid to take a step toward the other. Because if we did, we might lose our balance and fall.

He opened the door for me. I put my coat on. Then I left, with one backward glance to see if he was still looking. And he was.

But wouldn't you know it, on the way home, my Super Mom Sense kicked in.

I told myself to ignore it. I told myself I couldn't risk going near children until this whole Super Mom/Total Asswipe scandal blew over. I told myself I wouldn't look good in an orange prison jumpsuit.

But somewhere a child was in danger.

So when the back of my neck and the top of my head were vibrating like violins—high-pitched, staccato—I pulled my minivan over to the side of the road, reached into my paper bag, and pulled out my Super Mom costume—a little wrinkled now because that treated dustcloth material was murder to iron. And when I had changed clothes, I stood on the sidewalk, unafraid, defiant, because all of a sudden I felt invisible in my costume. Somehow I felt like the fabric enveloped me like a mummy; the mask hid not just my eyes, but my soul. No one could harm me, no one could touch me, when safely hidden inside Super Mom.

The night was crisp and clear, stars hanging low like they do when winter is approaching. I held myself still, listening only to the wind and the quivering strings in my head. Then my whole body began to tingle and quiver, my right hand pointed due west, and I followed it without hesitation across two empty lots and past a dark alley, straight to a house with lights blazing and music blaring. And an orange station wagon parked in front.

My chest felt like it would split in two. I had to concentrate on gravity—I had to remember it, imagine it, in order to stay firmly on the ground so I could do what I had to do.

I stalked toward the house to the beat of bass guitars. I was just about to ring the doorbell when I heard voices around back and smelled smoke, like burning leaves. I crept around the house, flattening myself against the side.

Gathered around a fire pit was a group of kids. Nice-looking kids, really. They were roasting marshmallows and talking all at once; innocent conversations bounced off one another so that I couldn't figure who was talking to whom. But the kids could; they looked happy and contented, firelight dancing in their eyes, their faces rosy from the heat.

Danger wasn't here. Danger couldn't be here. Yet it was; I felt it.

Then one of the faces looked up from the fire. Long ash-blond hair, freckles playing across her nose, a cautious smile on her face.

"Kelly!" I gasped, before I could stop myself.

Conversation ceased. Kelly looked around for whoever had called her name.

"Look! It's Super Mom," someone called out. And in an instant, I was surrounded.

"Hey! Is it true you beat up that kid?"

"No," I said. Then Kelly snapped her head up and looked at me—right through the holes in my mask. "No," I repeated, lowering my voice an octave.

"I heard you stomped on his arm and broke it."

"You heard wrong."

"You know, the police are after you."

I shrugged.

"I heard the PTA has a reward out for you."

"Figures," I said, disgusted. "Well, kids, this is all very nice, but I would like to talk to the parent in charge if you don't mind. There is a parent in charge, isn't there?"

Guilty glances, hands in pockets. A few kids started backing away.

"Right." I sighed. "When will you guys learn? All right, party's over. But before you all go home—it's almost past your curfew, by the way—would somebody point me in the direction of the owners of the orange station wagon I saw parked in front?"

Nobody answered.

"OK. Fine. I'll find them myself." I whirled around and walked to the patio door.

All of a sudden a young man blocked my path. A tall, suave young man with light blond hair—almost white. And eyes that met mine with chilling arrogance.

"Where do you think you're going?" Harry Osborne asked.

"To find whoever's in charge."

"That would be me."

"Would it?"

"Yes. So what's the problem? We're just having a little party." He winked at the gathering crowd; there were a few nervous giggles, but mainly the kids were quiet, watching. And I got the impression that no one really liked Harry. No one was moving to stand beside him; no one was repeating what he said.

"And the drug dealers who own the orange station wagon? Were they invited too?" My stomach felt like cold hands were twisting it in two.

"You could say so. You could say they were the guests of honor."

"All right, I hate to do this, young man, but I'll have to ask you to step aside."

"Make me."

"What?" I looked at him. Sure, he was two feet taller than me, but still. I was a superhero! Or hadn't he heard?

"I said, make me. You like to beat up little kids. Why don't you try one more your own size?"

"Harry"—Kelly grabbed his arm—"what are you doing? Are you nuts? And what stoners? You told me—"

"And you believed me, didn't you? So shut up." He gave her a shove and she stumbled backward a little; I ached to catch her, but I knew I couldn't. She'd know it was me; I couldn't put her in that kind of danger.

"Like father, like son," I growled. "Fine. I really hate to do this, but you give me no choice." And I flung my fluid at a flowerpot hanging over his head; it fell, just missing him, and shattered on the ground.

Harry laughed at me. "Need some glasses, Granny? Your aim's not so good." Then he slowly, deliberately, pulled a cell phone out of his pocket and hit a button. "Mom? Yeah. She's here."

And that's when I knew I'd been had.

Sirens started blaring; red and blue lights were flashing from the other side of the house. In an instant there was chaos.

"The police!"

"Oh, shit!"

"Who called them?"

"Relax, they only want her."

"Yeah, but they'll find all the other stuff, and my parents will kill me!"

"Run!"

Someone knocked over a bag of marshmallows; kids came pouring out of the house while at the same time other kids were trying to run into the house. And meanwhile I was frozen, staring at Harry in horror.

He laughed again. Then he grabbed Kelly, who was turning to flee.

"Hey, babe, what's the hurry? This party's for you, remember? Well, this is the entertainment portion of our evening.

Don't you want to stay and watch the fireworks? Don't you want to see the police catch this super freak?"

"No!" Kelly struggled, but his grip tightened; I could see his hands digging into her wrists, branding her flesh. I slowly unfroze, thawed by blistering rage. I narrowed my eyes, pointed my hand, and—

"Super Mom, come out of the building," Police Commissioner Borden called through a bullhorn. "Come out with your hands up. No, wait a minute—come out with your hands in your pockets. We have a warrant for your arrest."

"Red alert! I repeat, red alert! Super Mom has been sighted!" Patty Osborne's voice screeched over the din. The music was still blaring, the sirens were wailing, and kids were running all over the place.

I dropped my hand just as Kelly kneed Harry in the groin. He doubled over in pain as she ran around the house—in the opposite direction of the bullhorn. So I knew she would be safe.

Meanwhile, I found myself strangely unable to move. I was no longer invisible inside my costume; I was acutely aware that I had a giant orange "S" and a giant orange "M" across my chest that clearly stood for "Shoot Me." My heart was beating so fast, I thought it would blast off into space. My feet were faced with so many decisions—run, hide, go help Harry, go kick Harry—that they shorted out and couldn't be moved.

Finally a kid—I don't know who he was, but I'll never forget him—appeared in front of me, calmly stepping over the weeping Harry. He had big eyes, a buzz cut and a mouthful of potato chips.

"Run, Super Mom! You've got to run! Get out of here!"

"Right!" I shook myself, gave him a hug (but no animal cracker; I was in a hurry), and started to run. I tripped over some firewood but kept running; I heard voices behind me urging me to stop, cease, desist, halt in the name of the PTA.

"Just shoot already!" It was Lex.

"Are you crazy?" Police Commissioner Borden sounded appalled. "With all these kids?"

"I don't care!" Lex screamed.

"We could try the dogs," someone said. And then I heard whistles, barks, and pounding feet.

"Oh, shit!" I ran faster, turning around and firing cleaning fluid at my footprints to throw the dogs off the scent. I zigged and zagged, in and out of houses, jumping over sandboxes, tripping over sprinklers—pausing just once to zap out a stain from a shirt that was hanging on a clothesline. (Red wine on silk? No way was that going to come out in the wash.) Behind me the feet kept pounding, but suddenly the barking sounded confused. Lex and Borden were shouting to go this way, no, that way—"What's the matter, you stupid mutts?"—and finally I heard a loud thump and a pathetic yelp, like a dog had run into a tree.

And still I kept running until I found my minivan around the corner. I threw myself into it, ripped off my costume and stuffed it into the paper bag, pulled on my regular clothes, and was just about to climb in the driver's seat when I saw a familiar figure running down the street.

"Kelly!" I held my side, trying to catch my breath and act as if I hadn't just outrun a pack of wild dogs.

"Mom?" She stopped under a streetlight, leaned forward, and peered in my direction. "Mom? What are you doing here?"

"I"—gasp, wheeze—"was just out in the neighborhood"—cough, pant—"checking—"

"Checking up on me? Spying on me?"

"No. Well, yes. But no. But excuse me, young lady, I hardly think you're in any position to question me. What the hell are you doing out this late? Why aren't you home?"

"I—I— There was this party . . ."

"A party? You're not allowed to go to any parties!"

"Oh, right. I forgot. You've forbidden me to have any social life." I could have heard her teeth grind half a block away.

"Get in the car. Now. We'll talk about this later." Sirens were still blaring somewhere, although the barking had ceased.

"No. Let's talk about it now. I have had it with people tonight!"

"What do you mean?"

"I'm sick and tired of people lying to me!"

"Honey, do you mean—"

"Harry! Yes, OK? So there—are you happy? Are you? Because you were right about Harry?" She was sobbing now.

"No! Of course I'm not happy! Especially since this party was for you—"

"What?" She wiped her eyes with her sleeve. "How do you know about that?"

"I . . . well, I just guessed. . . ."

"No, you didn't! You've been listening in on me on the other phone, haven't you?"

"Well, not exactly—"

"And checking my e-mails when I'm at school?"

"I don't do that, really—"

"Yes, you do! Why won't you just admit it!" She ran toward me, punching the air. "Why won't you just admit you've been spying on me? Why won't you trust me anymore?"

"Because I saw you!" I couldn't help myself. "I saw you! At

the dance! I saw you with Harry and those guys in the orange station wagon! You were about to buy pot, Kelly. I saw you!"

She didn't move. I saw her shoulders heave like she was going to be sick. Then I heard her voice, tight, angry—accusing.

"I wasn't. I wasn't going to do it. I just went along with Harry and I was about to leave, but that weird person popped out and all those parents came running—and so I ran too. But he knows I don't smoke pot. And then he told me he was going to stop too. For me. But I didn't do anything wrong. I wouldn't do that. I thought you knew that about me." Her voice broke.

"I thought I did too."

"I haven't changed any," she whispered, and I could see tears in her eyes, catching fragments of moonlight so that it looked like there were stars rolling down her cheeks. "But you have. You used to trust me."

"Kelly, I'm sorry— I . . . things have been strange lately, I guess. I've seen a lot of things and I'm sorry—"

"I want to go to Dad's."

"What?"

"I want to go to Dad's. He trusts me. He loves me. Take me there, please. I want to stay with him."

"What do you mean?" I felt like I'd swallowed a chunk of ice. "Stay with him?"

"I want to stay with him. From now on. I don't want to live with you anymore, Mother. Get it?"

Her words were poison darts aimed right at my heart, and they hit their target with beautiful, deadly precision.

"Yeah," I whispered. "I get it."

She got into the car and waited for me to get in the driver's seat. We drove home and I stayed in the car while she went upstairs to pack a bag. Then I drove her to the big house on the other side of town. It was a long drive. Neither of us had anything to say.

I pulled into Dan's driveway. I turned to my daughter.

"Kelly, wait a minute. Before you go in— Your father— You need to know he—"

She looked at me, her face so young and yet so hard— she thought she knew. She thought she knew about me; she thought she knew about her father. She had lived with her own story for years. And I realized it was time she knew the truth. Even if it would break her heart. Even if, by letting her out of my car, letting her walk up that long sidewalk with its beautiful pavers and inlaid lights, letting her knock on that big wooden door—her father's door—unannounced, I was letting her in for the biggest disappointment of her life. But I couldn't—shouldn't—protect her anymore.

"Never mind," I said, and I smiled at her—my beautiful daughter. Nothing she said could ever make me not love her, no matter how hard she tried. "Go. I love you, you know."

She blinked, then chewed her fingernail.

"OK." She got out of the car, reached into the backseat, and grabbed her bags.

Then she walked up the sidewalk, and I drove off before she could even ring the doorbell, because I couldn't bear to see the look on Doctor Dan's face when he saw her standing there.

On the way home I listened to the radio. An APB was out for Super Mom, who had resisted arrest and was last seen fleeing the scene of a teenage party. And the Hawthorne School District Parent/Teacher Association was offering a reward for any information leading to the arrest of this aproned pervert—a thousand dollars and the opportunity to be principal for a day at the elementary school.

I drove to Carrie's.

"Can I switch cars with you? Just in case?"

She nodded, moved her car out of the garage, and I pulled my dented minivan in.

"Thanks." I sighed. "It was a trap."

"What was?"

"That party. It was a trap. Lex and Patty—they must have planned it. The police were right there. That little shit of an Osborne was way too cool about it all. And they used kids as bait—Kelly, too. Can you believe that?"

"Oh my God!"

"And *I'm* the one they think is dangerous to children?"

"Be careful, Birdie, OK? Promise me?"

"Yeah, I will. But this thing isn't over yet. Thanks for the car— Oh, wait a minute." I went back to my minivan to retrieve my costume.

Only it wasn't there.

I stuck my head under all the seats, I searched the glove compartment, the back of the van, everywhere. My crumpled-up bag wasn't there. And then I remembered—Kelly grabbed her luggage when I dropped her off, from the backseat—where my bag had been.

"This night just can't get any worse." I slammed the door and sat down on Carrie's garage floor. I was so tired, so sick. I realized I hadn't eaten in about two days, and I just wanted to go to sleep right there on the floor and have Carrie take care of me, cover me with a blanket and feed me soup and read me a bedtime story.

"What?" Carrie came running over, tugging on her bangs.

"Kelly has my costume. At Doctor Dan's."

"What?"

"Yep."

"Oh, Birdie!"

"Yep." I closed my eyes and leaned against the car. The gas fumes pricked at my nostrils.

"Now what?"

"I don't know. I'm tired of trying to figure out 'now what.' I want someone else to do it for me."

"Go home. You need to go to sleep. Worry about all this tomorrow."

"I can't. I have to go back to Doctor Dan's and get my bag. Hopefully before he looks inside it."

Chrissie popped her head into the garage.

"Mom? Aunt Birdie? Somebody's on the phone for you."

"Me?" She nodded.

I pushed myself up and walked to the phone on legs that felt like bags of sand.

"Hello?"

"Birdie?"

"Dan?" Suddenly I was wide awake and tingling all over.

"I called you at home; Martin said you weren't there. I believe I have something that belongs to you?"

"Yeah," I said, licking my dry lips. My voice sounded like it was coming from inside a deep tunnel. "You do."

"Would you please come over right away?"

"Yes."

I hung up the phone.

"He found it," I said to Carrie, who was still tugging on her bangs.

"What are you going to do?"

"Go get it."

"Then what?"

"I have no freakin' idea." I took her keys and drove off, safe at least from the posse of PTA parents out to get me. But not safe from the wrath of Doctor Dan. Which I faced when I dragged my sandbagged legs up his *House Beautiful* walk and rang his gold-plated doorbell.

"Well," he said, displeasure etched in every line across his face. "Well."

"Well?" I stood on the porch; he didn't invite me in.

"We need to discuss this."

"OK."

"So you just dropped this off on my doorstep?"

"Well, no, Dan, I didn't just— Kelly? Honey?"

Kelly was suddenly pushing her father out of the way, her eyes streaming, her nose red.

"Just take me home, OK, Mom? Just take me home."

"Dan?" I looked at him. "You meant Kelly? You meant Kelly was the thing—the *thing*—that belonged to me? That I just dropped off on your doorstep?"

"Well, Birdie, it's not my weekend to have her. You know my schedule. I'm surprised at you both—"

"That's what you meant? That's what you wanted me to come pick up? Oh Jesus, Dan, you are pathetic. Just pathetic. She's your daughter! She is not a thing! You don't deserve to have her, you know that? You don't deserve to have either one of them!" I couldn't bear to look at him any longer, that smug, superior face that once had held enchantment for me. How could that be? How could I ever have loved this man, wanted this man, felt betrayed by this man? He wasn't a man. He was just a sperm donor. That's all. And he didn't even do that particularly well—

"You—you . . . needledick!" I screamed at him. I could have sworn I heard Dixie cackle from the living room. Then I turned and ran after my daughter, who was sitting in the front seat of the car crying, great gulping sobs that threatened to split her in two.

"Sweetheart, don't," I said as I started the engine. "Don't. He isn't worth it."

"Oh, Mommy," my daughter sobbed, and I raced to get home so I could hold her, rock her, make her feel loved again.

"You knew he didn't want me, didn't you? Why didn't you tell me?"

I stroked her silky hair. She was lying in my arms, both of us stretched out on my bed.

"Honey, sometimes you have to let people make their own mistakes. That's what I had to do tonight. If I'd said you couldn't go, what would you have done?"

"I would have screamed and said I hated you."

"Exactly. And Kelly, I've let you do that for a long time now. Tonight, I had to let you get hurt so you could find out for yourself. And it's not that he doesn't want you, Kelly. You have to remember that. But he . . . well, he doesn't want to do this every day, being a parent. He has his life now, his schedule. But he does love you."

"I doubt it," she said, her voice dry and skeptical. "Mommy?"

I smiled and kissed the top of Kelly's head. I hadn't heard that in such a long time.

"What?"

"Why'd you marry him?"

"Because he asked."

"No, really."

"That's not that far from the truth." I sighed. "Oh, I loved him, I really did. And he loved me, in his own way. And I wanted to get married, have babies—as uncool as that sounds—it's what I wanted."

"But . . ." She wiggled around, trying to get comfortable in my arms; the last time we'd cuddled, she hadn't been taller than me. "Then why did you get divorced? If you loved each other once?"

"Oh, honey, we've talked about this. Sometimes two people fall out of love. But it doesn't mean they don't love their children. It just means that sometimes they change—"

"Mom. Cut the crap."

"Kelly!"

"Mother, seriously. I know all that, but it doesn't tell me anything. Why? What did you do? What did he do?"

"Kelly." I wanted to tell her—oh, so much! If ever there was a time to tell her, this was it. But we'd made a deal, Doctor Dan and I. And I intended to make him stick to it. "We were both idiots, OK? I pretended everything was all right when it wasn't, and he . . . well, he'll tell you. One day soon. But it just happened, and it happened long ago, and it's time we moved on. You and me. Especially me."

"Men are such shits." She sighed.

"Kelly!"

"Sorry," she murmured drowsily, yawning. But then she sat up, sliding out of my arms. "Oh! Mom! I found something tonight. I think it belongs to you." And she reached over the side of the bed and produced a bag. A crumpled-up brown paper bag. "It's you, isn't it? You're Super Mom." And she didn't sound surprised.

"Well." I blushed. "Well, yes. Yes, I am."

"Wow. You know, I thought—little things—like tonight at the party: When Super Mom said something, it sounded like your voice. But then things got so crazy, and Harry—"

"Harry put you—all of you—in a very dangerous position," I said, even though I really didn't want to hurt her anymore. But I had to make sure she understood how evil he was. "Just to get to me. That's the kind of a person he is."

"I know." She turned away, blinking her eyes. "But . . . you. How long have you been Super Mom?"

"Ever since that day when you guys found me in the bathroom. The day of the Horrible Swiffer Accident."

"Wow. So you've been sneaking out? Fighting crime? Did you really deck the Total Asswipe?"

"I did not, and I can't believe people are so upset about it—"

"Why didn't you tell me?"

"I don't know." And right then, sitting there talking *to* my daughter instead of *at* her, I really didn't know. "It seemed easier, I guess, for you not to know—"

"Does Martin know?"

I took a big breath. Then I nodded.

She looked away.

"Didn't you trust me?"

"Oh, Kelly! Of course I— Well, no. I didn't trust you not to tell your father. And if he found out . . ."

"Oh." Her voice was small and she moved away from me when I reached out to her. "And Martin wouldn't have told. I understand."

"But I wanted to, really I did. There's so much I've wanted to tell you lately—"

"Mom? Kel?"

We both turned. Martin was standing in the doorway.

"Is everything all right?" He hung his head, his hair flopping over his eyes.

"Yes, honey, everything's all right. Kelly just had kind of a rough night. So did I."

"OK. I'll be in my room, if you need me. Mom, I changed the lightbulb on the porch. It was out."

"Was it?" I turned my head so he wouldn't see my smile. "Thanks, sweetie."

"OK," he said again. He met my gaze for the first time since the day of the Total Asswipe.

"Martin?"

"Huh?"

"I need to apologize to you for the other day. It seems I haven't trusted my children lately, and I'm really sorry about that. Can you forgive me?"

Martin shrugged, hunched his shoulders, made his hands disappear into his raggedy sleeves. But I saw a glimmer of something soft in his eyes—like snow beginning to thaw. I smiled and patted the bed next to me, and all of a sudden he grinned and went flying through the air, jumping onto the bed and bouncing us like we were on a trampoline—the Amazing Lees, Circus Performers Extraordinaire. I grabbed my children's hands and we bounced and bounced. Just the three of us, just as it always had been, just as it always would be—unless . . .

Well. Unless.

I fell back down to earth with a gentle thud.

"I have something else to tell you guys. There've been too

many secrets in this house lately. So I think you should know that I've been seeing someone."

"You have?" Kelly turned around, her gray eyes enormous in her face. "You've been dating? A guy? You?"

Martin was quiet. He picked at the hem of his jeans.

"Yeah." Suddenly I grinned and covered my head with a pillow.

"Mom!" Kelly squealed and snatched the pillow away from me. "Who? Who is it? Is he cute?"

Martin groaned.

I reached over and pulled him to me. "Yes, he's cute, I guess. All right." I took a big breath. "You know Greg Sayers, in Martin's class? His dad? The guy who does the cartooning club?"

"Mr. Sayers?" Martin squeaked.

I nodded. Kelly's eyes got even bigger.

"Oh my God, Mom. He's, like, a total hottie! He likes you?"

"Don't sound so surprised. Yes, he likes me. Or, at least, he did. He's . . . well, he's mad at me now, and one of the reasons is because I was afraid to tell you guys."

"Afraid of what?" She reached over and pulled something out of my hair—a tiny leaf.

"Afraid of upsetting you. Afraid of disappointing you."

"How? I mean, please, Mother. It's about time. You're—what, forty?"

"Forty-one."

"Wow. Seriously, you are not getting any younger. If you're going to date somebody, you'd better get on with it."

"Thanks, Kelly. Martin?" I turned to my son.

"Hmm?"

"How do you feel about this?"

"Weird," he said. Kelly opened her mouth, ready to lecture, but I stopped her.

"It's OK to feel weird, you know. It *is* weird—even for me. That's why I wanted to keep it a secret, but it was wrong. It was wrong not to tell you, it was wrong for Mr. Sayers— Carl. I hurt him."

"Is he really mad at you?" Martin asked.

I nodded.

"He's a nice guy, Mom. I mean, in cartooning club? When people just sit there and goof off? He never says anything. I bet he won't stay mad at you forever."

I smiled and kissed his forehead, wishing children could run the world.

"I think you should apologize to him," Kelly said with an emphatic nod.

"And it wouldn't upset you? If I—we—were dating?"

"Well, no. Not really. I mean, I never thought you and Daddy would ever get back together. As much as I wanted that, I never thought it would happen. And, I don't know . . . it's kind of weird that you just seem to be all wrapped up in Martin and me. Seriously, Mother, I'm not sure that's healthy."

"Yeah, it's way not healthy. You need a life, Mom." Martin patted my hand.

"You two sound just like your aunt Carrie!"

"Well, she's right, then. I mean"—Kelly exchanged a look with Martin—"we'll be going to college soon, and we worry about what's going to happen to you when we're gone."

"You do? You worry about me?" I was touched. Blown away, actually. It never occurred to me that my children would worry about me. I worried about them so much, so completely.

I gave and I gave, and yet they wanted to give too. And I rarely let them.

And this is what it means, then, when your children grow up. They worry about you. They know, even if you don't, that there is happiness to be had with other people.

"So, what do you think I should do?" I asked my children— my poised daughter who couldn't believe I could snag a total hottie; my wise son who thought I needed a life.

"Well, that depends. Do you love him?" Kelly gazed at me, unwavering; Martin held his breath. And I knew I wouldn't hurt them, not if I told the truth.

"Yes," I said, surprised by how easy it was to say it. Yet—this was the truth. Finally, beneath all the lies, it came down to this—truth. Paring down everything to an essence—or a moon-beam, filtered through a pine tree. Because no matter how strong I was, no matter how independent, the truth was I'd still felt safe within his arms. And there was no reason to be ashamed of that—that I could share myself, share my love with a wonderful man who wanted me in his life. It didn't lessen me; this time was different. This time, I was strong enough on my own. This time, it could only make me more.

"Yes," I whispered to my children. "I do love him. I do."

"Then tell him." Kelly shook her head at my stupidity.

"That's it? Just tell him?"

"Duh, Mom!" Martin scratched his nose. "Can I go to bed now? I'm kind of beat."

"Me too." Kelly yawned.

"Why, sure. Sure, honey." I raised my face to receive her kiss, his hug—a gentle benediction for the rest of my life, with and without them.

" 'Night."

" 'Night, sweetie. 'Night, Martin!"

" 'Night!" I watched them leave, both of them taller than I remembered. When I thought of them, it was always as shorter than me. And then when I took the time to step back and really study them, see them as a stranger would, I was always struck by how big they were. How angular. On the cusp of the rest of their lives. In their faces I could see more of the adults they would become than I could of the babies they had been. It never failed to move me.

And so we went to sleep, my family and I. Three of us, each in our own room. And despite the size of our house I knew, finally, there was room enough for more. All I had to do was ask.

CHAPTER
22

Tricks and Treats and Spooky Feats!

Come celebrate Halloween at New Cosmos Patriot Park. In light of recent events, the PTA has decided to offer a secure venue for our little ghosts and goblins!

So come early, stay late, and leave plenty of room in your trick-or-treat bag for Patriot Pops!

"You've got to be kidding me," I said.

"What?" Kelly leaned over my shoulder and peered at the flyer Martin had brought home from school.

"Look at this! Look! It's so blatant—they might as well put up a neon sign that says 'Welcome, Super Mom! Come Meet Your Doom!' They know I can't stay away. Kids, sugar, potentially dangerous fencing—it's a Super Mom nightmare!"

"So it's a trap?"

"Oh boy, what a trap." I tossed the flyer into the trash. Then I sat down at the kitchen table.

"So, what are you going to do?" Kelly sat next to me.

"I don't have any choice. I have to go. But this is it. I'm not going to get another chance. If I go I'll be captured, what with the bounty on my head and all. So I have to be prepared. I have to be ready to bring Lex to justice." I reached for a pile of papers—the printed pages of the file I'd taken from Lex's office. Pages and pages of marketing suggestions, descriptions of the miracle of Oralsulin . . . and figures. Indecipherable, foreign. Account numbers, spreadsheets, stock symbols.

"Oy vey," I groaned as I poured myself a vat of coffee and rummaged around in the junk drawer for a calculator. The only one I could find was a plastic Mickey Mouse calculator that came in a box of cereal. It had two functions: add and subtract.

"Let me help," said my daughter, the math whiz. "Let me see what I can come up with." And she reached inside her backpack and pulled out a calculator the size of a small computer. I burst into tears and raised her allowance on the spot.

Meanwhile, my trusty sidekick took it upon himself to do a little work on some of my equipment.

"You really need a new set of wheels, with a turbo engine and fins and an aerodynamic design," Martin said, wiping grease from his hands on one of my good kitchen towels. "But I'm guessing Dad isn't going to raise the child support anytime soon?"

I shook my head.

"Didn't think so. OK. Let me see what I can do. And give me your high heels—I have an idea."

And I stood back and watched as my children—my sidekicks—worked together for the first time in years. All in the name of Super Mom—

(That's me!)

Meanwhile, Carrie kept analyzing me whenever she had a chance.

"All right, so tell me again. You never dreamed as a child?"

"No." I sighed, my legs getting a cramp.

"Yet you do have an unfulfilled wish?"

I snorted. "Pick one."

"Flying," she said.

"Oh, flying!" And I closed my eyes, imagining me—Super Mom—soaring over rooftops, my cape billowing behind me. And the funny thing was, these days I was feeling light enough, free enough, to do it. To fly, free as a bird. It's funny how telling the truth, how pushing away slabs of resentment and fear and lies and guilt, can release you somehow so that you're constantly bobbing up and down. Reaching for the sky.

There was just one thing left—a stone in my pocket. But it was a large one, and it seemed to grow heavier every day. It was the only thing that tethered me to the ground, kept gravel in my shoes, dust in my mouth.

"Just tell him," Kelly urged. So did Carrie. So did Martin.

Just tell him. They were just words. But they weren't, really. I would be handing him my soul, my heart, my hopes and fears and most tender of thoughts. Carl's hands—so strong and capable—would they be open, ready to receive these gifts?

But there was one thing I had to do before I found out. Because I needed someone to catch me, should I stumble and fall while handing over my heart. And if Carl couldn't—Super Mom could.

She was almost ready.

"OK, I think I've got it," Kelly said one day after school. She sat down at the kitchen table, removed a printout from her backpack—folded precisely in quarters—and smoothed it in front of me. "Ta-da!"

"Huh?" I looked at the paper. I turned it right-side up. Then I turned it upside down. I couldn't tell which was which. It was full of numbers and words like "corporate earnings" and "hidden revenue" and more numbers, some of them in black, most of them in red. "What is this?"

"What you need. What you need to bring down your evil empire, Mom!"

"Can you translate for me?"

"God, Mom. Can you even balance your checkbook?" My daughter sighed and flipped her hair.

"Sometimes."

"All right. See this number? And this number here? See? New Cosmos Industries, they didn't make a profit last year. Or the first three quarters of this year. In fact, it appears Lex never put a cent of his own money in the thing."

"Self-made millionaire, my foot!" I snorted. "But so what? Who cares if they didn't make a profit?"

"All right." She began again, speaking slowly. "Let me spell it out for you. You know that campus—it's beautiful. And the theme park—lots and lots of money spent there, right?"

I nodded.

"That's not all. Lex and Patty have a skybox at the football stadium. A luxury penthouse in Gotham City. A condo in Bermuda. Just how do they pay for these things?"

"He's really Batman?"

"Mother! Look—I went down to the county courthouse . . ." She produced another piece of paper—several, actually. Deeds to the skybox, penthouse, condo. "All signed by Edward D. Cobblepot."

"Our mystery moneyman."

"Right! New Cosmos doesn't make any money, so how do they stay in business and employ half the town?"

"Because Moulton Pharmaceuticals pays for everything!"

"That's it. Moulton needs them to stay in business, and they're kicking back to New Cosmos. And to increase Moulton's profits, see, Lex is a pretty big stockholder, and apparently the brains behind the whole thing, so he's cooking the books, coming up with all the marketing ideas, which includes planting the subliminal messages. You said Cobblepot was in Japan? Well, check this out." She handed me a newspaper article.

Yamamoto Industries, creator of the popular video game "American Justice," was sold to American financier Edward D. Cobblepot. The deal was apparently agreed upon last winter at the recommendation of Lex Osborne, founder of New Cosmos Industries, but wasn't announced until American Justice had its initial test marketing in the Midwest. Due to its enormous popularity, Cobblepot has plans to market it throughout the United States this spring.

"So that's it?" I looked at all the charts and numbers and straight lines. "It's all just about cooking the books? No violating any UN treaties? No breaking about a thousand FDA laws? It's just about—books?"

"It's about conflict of interest, and concealing financial ties, and maybe money laundering. Throw in the subliminal messages, and you have something that's pretty—"

"Evil?" I looked at her hopefully.

"Evil!" She smiled, gathered her schoolbooks, and headed upstairs.

"Books," I repeated, gathering up the mess of papers.

The phone rang.

"Hello?"

"Birdie?" It was Patty Osborne; I shoved the papers under the toaster, in case she could see me through the phone.

"Hi, Patty. What's, uh, up?"

"Concerning the Halloween festivities. I have you down to pass out candy. So I need you to be there at six thirty sharp. One must not be late at any cost—"

"Oh, I'm sorry, Patty, but I can't." I wrapped the phone cord around my finger and smiled.

"You—you . . . what?"

"I said I can't."

A long pause. Apparently she was too stunned to speak.

"Patty? Are you OK?"

"Yes, I'm . . . What do you mean, you can't?"

"I can't help you out tomorrow. I have other plans."

"What other plans? What could be more important than your duties as a member of the Hawthorne School District Parent/Teacher Association?"

"Well, to tell the truth, I have a little housecleaning to do." I giggled. "A little mess—oh, all right, a great big giant *self-made* mess—to take care of."

"But, Birdie, one must think of the children—"

"Oh, I am, Patty. Believe me, I am!"

"But . . . but . . ."

And while she was still sputtering, I hung up on her.

CHAPTER 23

Halloween. A night of tricks or treats. I didn't know which one it would be; I hoped the black cats and fake tombstones I passed on my way to New Cosmos Patriot Park weren't any kind of an omen.

I pulled my newly painted minivan into the parking lot. I adjusted my mask, checked my new improved high heels (refurbished with the air-pump soles from Martin's favorite pair of basketball shoes and guaranteed to keep me upright for almost two hours at a time), and applied a fresh coat of lipstick, which made Martin, sitting in the passenger seat dressed as Abe Lincolnator, squirm.

"Do you really need to do that?"

"Yes," I replied. "June Cleaver always had fresh lipstick, even in the midst of a crisis."

"Mom?"

"What?"

"Are you going to be OK?" He looked out his window, his voice husky.

"Sweetie, look at me."

"No."

"Look at me."

He did. Two tracks of tears slid down his dusty cheeks.

"I'm going to be fine. Lex can't hurt me. And the police are really on my side. So don't you worry." I pulled him close, his bony shoulders sticking into my ribs but that was OK. Soon he would be bigger than me, with broad shoulders, too self-contained to cry. But right now he needed to know that his mother would be here for him tomorrow.

I told him I would, but I'm not sure he believed it. I'm not sure I did either.

"I love you, Mom."

"Oh, sweetie!" I buried my face in his neck, so thankful for the gift of him.

"You're not getting any lipstick on me, are you?" His voice was muffled against my shoulder.

"Oh! No . . ." I forced myself to let him go. "Of course not!" I wiped his neck with the edge of my cape. "OK," I said with a shaky smile. "I guess it's time."

"Go, Super Mom!" We touched fists, grabbed our trick-or-treat bags, and got out of the car . . .

Where we were greeted by a small band of Super Moms of assorted shapes and sizes and, apparently—I squinted hard at a tall, broad-shouldered one—genders.

"Trick or treat!" The tall one boomed out in a gruff, bass voice. I took a step toward "her"; she teetered in her size-twelve high heels.

"Stand up straight, Howard!" a tiny Super Mom with glasses barked. "It's just a matter of balance. And adjust your wig."

He did. Although it still sat, like a diseased monkey, somewhat at the back of his bald head.

"What on earth—?" I took a step toward the tiny one. "Carrie? What the—?"

"Surprise!" A tall, slender Super Mom with glossy blond hair stepped forward.

"Kelly? What's going on?"

"Well, we decided you could use a little help tonight. So we decided to dress up like you, as a diversion! Now let's see them try to ambush you!"

"Plus it's fun," squealed Chrissie, smoothing her apron. "I haven't dressed up for Halloween in a couple of years!"

"Fun? These high heels are murder to walk in," Howard grumbled as he held on to the side of a station wagon for dear life.

"I don't—I don't know what to say," I stammered, tears tickling my eyes.

The tiny Super Mom's glasses gleamed in the parking lot lights.

"Uh, Carrie?" I whispered. "Super Mom doesn't wear glasses."

"Well, unless you want me to wander off and be hit by a bumper car," she snapped, "this one does!"

"I just don't know," I began, pinching my right palm so I wouldn't blubber all over the place. "I can't ask you to do this. There's some danger involved, and Super Mom would never put anyone at risk—"

"Shut up already, Super Mom!" Kelly grinned. "We've made up our minds. We're not letting you go in there alone."

"Yeah! Super Mom rocks!" Howard held up a fist.

"Well, thank you. That's all I can say. Thank you from the bottom of my heart. That you all would do this, for me—"

And then I did burst into tears. I turned away and blew my nose on my cape.

"Mom." Martin sidled up to me. "Get a hold of yourself. Superman never cries!"

"I know, I know," I sniffed. "It's just that they're so sweet!"

"Sweet." He shook his head, disgusted.

"OK, OK." I turned to face them with what I hoped was heroic confidence. "Now, just a few rules before we go in. First of all, I don't want anyone to be a hero. Just act normal, have fun, trick-or-treat. They're only interested in me; you guys are just decoys. And if anything happens, don't worry—I'll be there in a jiffy. Second, did everyone remember to bring antibacterial hand wipes? This place is just crawling with germs. Third, don't eat too much candy; you'll get a stomachache. And if anyone does, just let me know. I brought Tums."

Chrissie raised her hand. "Can I, like, arrest anybody?"

"No, Super Mom doesn't have the authority to incarcerate individuals. And, well"—I looked at Howard—"be, um, discreet when going to the bathroom." He blushed. "OK, everyone, I guess . . . just go on in. Spread out, have fun, and don't forget to floss tonight! Now"—I turned to Martin as my valiant band of Super Moms headed to the entrance, Howard hanging on to Carrie for dear life—"do you have the CD?"

He nodded.

"Are you sure you're all right? Are you sure you can do this?"

"Mom!" He looked exasperated beneath his stovepipe hat. "Don't worry. It's under control."

"But I still don't know how you're going to manage to get the sound system—"

"Mom. Trust me. OK?"

I held my breath, looked out across the sea of cars into the twilight. The day was fading; the sky was purple and still. My son was standing before me, called upon to do a man's job.

And for the first time in my life, I believed he could.

"All right, I trust you. After all"—I smiled—"you are my trusty sidekick."

"Yep." Martin patted me on the back and sauntered off toward the entrance, like John Wayne with a trick-or-treat bag. I stayed behind for a minute to collect myself—wipe my tears, calm my nerves, concentrate on what was important. Which was the sight of my family and my friends—the people who believed in me. Suddenly I was impatient for everything to begin. I ran ahead to lead them into the park—Operation Pied Piper, indeed. But before we got to the entrance, I spied a dumpy man with fish lips lurking behind a Mini Cooper that didn't quite cover all of him.

Jimmy Nelson came huffing up to us.

"Wow, look at this! A little group of Super Moms!"

"Do you have film in that?" I pointed to his camera.

He nodded.

"And batteries in the tape recorder?"

"You bet!"

"Good. Just try to stick with me—but don't be too obvious."

"Good luck, Super Mom!"

"Thanks. And make sure you get some candy to take home to your kids." I squeezed his arm. "OK, everybody. Have fun!" And my troops and I entered New Cosmos Patriot Park—only to stop, gaping. Apparently I was a very popular Halloween costume this year.

Before us was an even larger army of Super Moms—fat ones, thin ones, tiny ones tottering in their mothers' high heels. Now, some liberties had been taken with regard to the uniform. A couple of midriffs were bared—something Super Mom normally frowns upon, but right now she was just too choked up to say anything about it. There were some piercings in odd places. One free spirit had written REELECT NIXON! on the back of her cape. And I really didn't want to know what some of them were carrying in their apron pockets. But to me, they were beautiful and brave. Each and every one of them. Even the Goth Super Mom who had dyed her costume black.

"Take that, Lex Osborne!" Howard grinned.

Kelly squeezed my shoulder. "Mom, they love you. They want to be you!" Then she and Chrissie slid right into the sea of Swiffer green that fanned out, capes flapping in the breeze, toward the bright carousel lights and tinkling circus music and tables piled high with special orange-and-black Patriot Pops.

"Be careful," Carrie whispered in my ear. Her glasses, over her Super Mom mask, reflected back the colorful lights of the Ferris wheel.

"Don't worry." I patted her on the top of her head; she didn't swat my hand away. "And you're a good friend."

"Oh, Birdie . . ." Her voice started to wobble.

"Don't. It'll be all right."

She nodded, then marched off into the crowd, followed by Howard, who waved and promptly fell off his high heels.

I turned and started to prowl. In and out, I weaved my way through the crowds of parents and adorable little monsters and goblins and miniature superheroes. Eyes were upon me—suspicious eyes. Some parents pulled their children away when I approached. I never made eye contact, never smiled, never waved. And weaving in and out, all around me, were other Super Moms.

"Super Mom, Super Mom, Super Mom . . ." I heard it above the music, above the cries of "Trick or treat!" My name was on everyone's lips, over and over, like a drumbeat, or a chant. It throbbed in my ears, urging me on, pushing me to finish what I'd started.

Music. Laughter. *Super Mom.* "Can I have candy?" "Can I have popcorn?" *Super Mom.* I followed my name; I turned this way, that way, spinning, soaring—up hills, down streets, running with the wind tickling my cape—Super Mom.

"Super Mom! Super Mom!" Finally I heard it, above all the rest—a cry, a sob. I stood still, closed my eyes, listened, listened—to the wind, to the music, to my heart. To the quivering in my ears, the tautness of my chest, the vibrating of my hand as it lifted of its own accord, pointed, and . . .

I opened my eyes. Kelly was being pulled up a flight of stairs by a heavyset man. How did I know, out of all the possible decoys, that it was Kelly?

How did I know she was my baby when they placed her in my arms, fifteen years ago?

I just did.

"Kelly!" I shouted it, even though I knew she couldn't hear. "I'm coming!" And I pushed my way through the crowd, up a flight of wooden steps, chasing after my daughter. My legs—I couldn't stop them. They propelled me up those stairs faster than I have ever moved in my life.

"Kelly! I'm coming!"

"Super Mom!" I heard her voice echo somewhere above

my head; the steps didn't seem to have an ending. Any minute we'd be in the clouds. The entire structure rumbled and rattled, like we were in an earthquake. I craned my neck and saw that I was climbing a honeycomb of wooden steps, crisscrossed with beams and supporting wooden tracks that climbed and dipped. We were in the underbelly of the Battle of Bunker Hill roller coaster.

"Super Mom!" This yell came from below, where Jimmy Nelson was wheezing and puffing and turning a disturbing shade of green.

"Keep going!" I yelled back. "I can't help you!" I turned around; Kelly and her kidnapper had reached the top of the staircase and were climbing onto a platform. I kept going.

When I reached the platform, I hauled myself up and looked around. It was pretty high—about halfway through the ride— and the wind was fierce. The lights of the amusement park glittered below. It was one of those small operator platforms alongside the tracks. There was a glass booth with some machinery inside, where an attendant could monitor the ride. But the booth appeared to be empty.

"Super Mom!" Kelly was being held by a hulking security guard; she was twisting and squirming in his grip. I recognized him as Lex's buddy from the opening day of the park, when I'd saved the little girl on the bridge.

"Let her go!" I started toward them.

"Stalking innocent children again, are you?" An oily voice stopped me in my tracks. "You thought you were pretty clever, didn't you, Super Mom?" Lex Osborne opened the door to the booth and limped out, no longer on crutches.

"Let the girl go, Lex."

"I'm protecting her from the predatory clutches of Super

Mom. I'm not going to harm her. It's you I want, not one of these poor innocent teenagers you convinced to dress like you. Did you think you would fool me? Me? Of all people?"

"No, Lex." I smiled, so maternally, so sweetly. "Not at all. I have a lot more respect for you than that." I looked out of the corner of my eye; Jimmy had almost reached the landing and was fiddling with his tape recorder. "After all, you were the brains of the operation. Operation Pied Piper. Weren't you?"

"Of course. Do you think Cobblepot could have thought of this on his own?" Lex limped toward me, the wind whipping his white hair so that it looked alive.

"But he had the money."

"Moneymen are stupid men. Stupid, but necessary."

"So why, Lex? Why the subliminal messages? Why not just make your money with Oralsulin, as an investor?"

"Just like a woman." He shook his head. "Always thinking small."

"Just like a man," I retorted. "Always concerned about size."

He glared at me. In the distance I could see roller-coaster cars clattering down a hill; Lex hobbled back inside the booth and pulled some levers. While he was hobbling, I casually backed up to where Jimmy sat, just out of view. I kept my eye on Kelly and her captor. Her gaze was frightened but steady, focused on my every movement. I had the feeling that if I suddenly vanished she would too. But she managed a tiny smile. I smiled back—much more bravely than I felt—then hissed at Jimmy, who was crouching beside the platform.

"Are you getting this?"

"Yes," he gasped.

"OK, just stay with me, no matter what."

"But—"

I straightened up. An empty roller-coaster car slowly rolled to a stop at the platform.

"Get in," Lex barked. The thyroid case bundled Kelly into one of the cars; I gave her a look and she fastened her seat belt.

"What?"

"Just get in. Now." He stepped out of the booth. And that's when I noticed the gun.

"OK." I was amazed to hear my voice, calm and clear. "Whatever you want, Lex." I positioned myself between him and Kelly. "Just don't shoot—" But he grabbed my arm and shoved me into the front car, lowering himself into the seat next to me. As we began to roll, I noticed that Jimmy had managed to heave himself into the very last seat. "So, where are we going?"

"You'll see." Lex stared ahead, a gleeful smile on his face as we ascended a hill—obviously enjoying the ride. I wished that I could too. But it was a little difficult, considering that there was a gun digging into my side, Lex's finger caressing the trigger.

I gulped, but I wasn't so terrified that I neglected to fasten my seat belt.

"Why are you doing this? Can't you let the girl go?" I shouted to Lex over the rumbling of the car as it climbed the wooden tracks.

"Don't worry. I'm not about to kill anybody, not with my reputation. Except, of course, a wanted pervert who was caught luring this poor, innocent child out of the park."

"Who would do such a thing?"

"You would. That's who."

"Ohhhh . . ."

All of a sudden, he started to screech at the top of his lungs—high-pitched, just like a little girl. And we went over the top of the hill.

"Aiieeeeeeee!" We both whooped and hollered; I couldn't help myself. It reminded me of that wild ride with Kevin Stanton—trapped in a situation beyond my control, hurtling toward an unknown destination, a dangerous man at my side. I glanced at Lex as we twisted and dipped, the wind whipping my face, bringing tears to my eyes. His huge white head was a grotesque mask of twisted glee.

We climbed the final hill, pushed back into our seats so that I couldn't see what lay ahead. Finally we went over the edge, screaming at the top of our lungs, hurtling straight down to hell.

But the car slowed down; we weren't in hell after all. We were coasting to a stop at the end of the ride, surrounded by innocent people waiting in line. Lex's henchman dragged Kelly out of the car. I could count every single copper freckle standing out against her pale face. Then Lex hauled me out, putting his arm on my back as if we were the best of friends. If you didn't take into account the cold, hard gun pressed against my spine, hidden by my cape. Jimmy was still sprawled across the bottom of his car, his face fading from green to a neon shade of yellow.

"Now, just keep quiet. Don't say a word and I'll let the girl go. Don't cause a scene here," Lex growled in my ear as he pushed me through the crowd. "I wouldn't want you to embarrass me."

"What's that you said?" I stopped.

Lex waved at the gasping crowd and smiled. "Don't worry folks, don't worry! I have the situation under control! I have captured Super Mom, who was attempting to lure this inno-cent child out of the park. I'm finally bringing this pervert to justice!" His voice dropped to a hiss. "I said don't do anything to embarrass me."

"Embarrass you?" Warning bells went off in my brain; red spots appeared before my eyes. "Embarrass? You?" My nostrils flared; I pawed at the ground like a bull. The white-hot flame of fifteen years' worth of humiliation exploded into a rage that couldn't comprehend the cold steel digging into my flesh. "Nobody says that to me. Not anymore! You want em-barrassment? Do you? Huh? OK, Lex, how about this—?" I whirled around, raised my right hand . . .

But before I could move a finger, the music that had been piping through the loudspeakers came to a scratchy halt. A familiar voice murmured, "Testing, testing. The Super Mom Broadcasting System is on the air!" Another boy's voice jumped in. "It's on, doofus!" Then another voice—warm, male, vaguely scientific—interrupted. "That's enough, boys."

Carl. And Greg, the audio boy genius. Helping Martin. Trust me, he'd said. Oh, I was so glad I had!

And New Cosmos Patriot Park was treated to a little sub-liminal advertising, courtesy of Lex Osborne. Who stood still, his face as white as his hair, as he listened to the voices pour-ing excitedly out of the speakers:

Eat Patriot Pops. Patriot Pops are what you want. Mmmmm. Crispy, sugary. What you crave. Eat Patriot Pops.

"How did you—?" Lex could barely form the words.

"I could hear them, Lex. I heard the voices on the video game. And I heard you talking to Cobblepot on your cell phone about Operation Pied Piper. I know all about Oralsulin—not to mention various financial irregularities at New Cosmos. Me. Super Mom."

"You bitch." His voice was cold, malevolent. He took a step back and raised the gun to my face. "You bitch!"

Kelly screamed; people started scurrying down stairs and behind trash cans. The teenager behind the controls of the coaster fainted dead away.

"That's not a very nice word, Lex." I narrowed my eyes at him. "I think I'll have to wash your mouth out with soap!" Then I fired a quick stream of fluid at the gun, knocking it into a trash can.

"Lars! Cuddles!" Lex screamed. Another hulking hench-man appeared; the one holding Kelly shoved her aside. "Get her!"

"Hello, boys!" I stepped back as the biggest one, a huge blond Viking—Lars, I assumed—approached. He paused to wipe some drool off his chin. Then he lunged at me.

"Oof!" My chin hit the wooden platform and I bit my tongue. Tears sprang to my eyes, but I managed to kick him in his Swedish meatballs with my new, improved Super Mom spiked heels.

"Son uff a beetch!" Lars screamed as he rolled on the floor.

"Wear a cup next time, OK, Lars? And you should know better than to hit a lady. What, were you raised by wolves?"

I heard a low chuckle. I turned and faced Cuddles, who was grinning, showing off a mess of crooked, blackened teeth.

"Don't you floss?" I shook my head and tossed him some dental floss. "That's a shame. Twice-a-year dental appointments, my boy. Remember, be true to your teeth or they'll be false to you!"

Cuddles just stared blankly at the dental floss, spooling it out until he had a nice long rope of it. Which he then tried to tie around my neck.

"Stupid dental floss," I said, choking, tears in my eyes.

I wiggled and gasped and squirmed, the dental floss cutting into my neck, squeezing the breath out of me, while all the while Cuddles laughed in my face until I wasn't sure what would kill me first—the dental floss or his monstrous bad breath. Just before I thought I would pass out, I managed to jab him in the knee with my stiletto. Then I whirled around and flung my trusty cleaning fluid right in his eyes.

"Arrrgh! Arrrgh! It burns! It burns!" He dropped to the floor and covered his eyes.

"Don't rub, it only makes it worse," I told him. Next to Cuddles, Lars kept cupping his groin area and moaning.

"All right." I brushed my hands together. "It's just you and me, Lex. Now, are you going to go quietly?"

"Go where?" He looked oddly pleased, considering that his two henchmen were writhing around in pain at my feet.

"To jail."

"I'm not going anywhere. You, on the other hand—"

Suddenly Police Commissioner Borden and a couple of sergeants ran up some stairs, their guns trained on me.

"All right, Super Mom. Just cooperate and nothing will happen."

"What do you mean?"

"We have a warrant for your arrest. For the abuse of little Jamie Flugal—"

"That total asswipe," I muttered. "Look, I did not harm

that child. Anyway, we have much bigger fish to fry here, Commissioner—don't you hear the voices?" I pointed to a loudspeaker, where the voices were still whispering excitedly about Patriot Pops. "Those are subliminal messages planted in the soundtrack of American Justice!" Borden looked puzzled, glancing back and forth between Lex and me. "Do I have to spell it out for you? This man is responsible for the sickness of hundreds of children!"

Lex smoothed his hair and turned his practiced, oily smile on the police.

"Now, who are you going to believe, Commissioner? This delusional pervert who attacks little children? Or me? A self-made millionaire, employer of hundreds of fine, upstanding Astro Park citizens?"

"No, believe me. You have to believe me." I turned to the sergeants, who lowered their guns and looked at Borden.

"I'm sorry, Super Mom." Borden shook his head sadly. "I really hate to do this, but we have to protect the children."

"That's what I'm trying to do!" I took a step toward him; he looked at me, his big eyes pleading; then he slowly pointed his gun at me.

"I'm sorry, Super Mom. Really I am."

"OK." I sighed, raising my arms. One of the officers advanced, brandishing a pair of handcuffs. "I understand. I didn't want to have to do this, but—" And I knocked all the guns away—one, two, three—with a fierce attack of cleaning fluid. Then I stalked over to them and held them each with my Merciless Gaze. "Now. All three of you. You should be ashamed of yourselves, not believing me. I'm so disappointed in you. The only appropriate punishment I can think of is for you to go to a corner, right now, and think about what you just did. Just think about it. Believe me, this hurts me more than it does you. Now, go! Right now!" My chest started to vibrate, and a mighty roar pushed itself out of my throat: "SUPER TIME OUT!"

The policemen scattered to the corners of the platform like mice. They stood with their noses to the wall. One of them started to sniffle.

"Now"—I stalked over to Lex, who was bristling with rage—"I need you to confess. There's someone who's eager to take your story. Jimmy! Come here!"

Jimmy Nelson heaved himself out of the roller coaster, his face almost back to its normal pasty color. When he surveyed the carnage—Lars and Cuddles writhing on the ground, the three policemen in the corners, Lex quivering yet speechless in front of me—he twisted his fish lips into a huge grin.

"Aww. Way to go, Super Mom! Whatta broad!"

"Just make sure the microphone is on."

He nodded.

I turned to Lex. "Now, are you going to confess the easy way? Or do I have to wash your mouth out with soap?" I reached into my apron and pulled out my new Super Mom Antibacterial Truth-Telling Soap.

"I confess nothing!" Lex finally was able to scream.

"All right, then." I lunged at him, eager to grab hold of that white hair and shove a bar of soap into his mouth. But he screamed again—high-pitched, just like on the roller coaster—and jumped away, across the roller-coaster tracks to the other side of the car. I leaped across the tracks and chased him around the car. We kept running, around and around like we were playing some children's game—

Then all of a sudden the voices stopped and music came back on over the loudspeakers. Circus music, children's music—I recognized the tune immediately. It was the song I'd sung to my babies.

He flies through the air, with the greatest of ease. . . .

"No!" I shouted, frozen by a terrible memory. This had happened before—something bad had happened. . . .

And I felt myself getting weaker and weaker with each note of the song. My hand trembled as everything around me turned gray and fuzzy. Lex peered over at me with a puzzled look in his eyes—colorless now to me . . .

I sank to my knees, weighed down by the past—by my memories. Martin at three, crying in his little toddler bed because "the sun went out." Kelly at six, determined to hold my hand all the way to school even though hers was sticky with peanut butter. Martin and Kelly on Christmas morning, asleep under the tree just like the precious gifts they were.

Martin and Kelly: young, tender, sweet, lisping, missing teeth, straggly hair—Mommy, Mommy, Mommy, I love you, I need you, where are you, come get me, Mommy, Mommy, Mommy . . .

I fell to the roller-coaster tracks and gazed up at Lex, at Jimmy, at the gathering crowd whose faces remained a blur. I felt the night with all its crazy colored lights spin around me, and it was just like the first day—the day when I had my Horrible Swiffer Accident and I passed out in front of the toilet. I remembered the daisies on the wallpaper, dancing around and around, singing this song. I even smelled the same fumes: orange and bleach and ammonia and Swiffer. I must have been leaking somewhere—everywhere—fluid and strength oozing out of my every pore.

I tried to move but was pinned to the ground by some-thing I couldn't see, could only feel: overwhelming sadness that my children would never be that small and soft and per-fect again. I raised my right hand and tried to point it at Lex but it flopped, limp as a noodle, and only a weak splash of fluid dribbled out of it.

"Aha!" I heard Lex say, only it was slow and distorted, as if I were underwater. "So, Super Mom! I see you have a weakness, after all!"

"Something, something Kryptonite," I heard Jimmy mut-ter, tears in his eyes.

I turned my head. Now I could make out faces in the crowd. Two faces in particular—Kelly's and Martin's. Kelly was so beautiful now with her silky hair and calm gray eyes, that level gaze, that wariness. Martin was handsome, awk-ward, his hair flopping over so you could hardly see his eyes, but you could see the uncertainty on his face, the questions he brought with him wherever he went: Do I belong here? Am I wanted? What's expected of me?

My children. My beautiful children . . .

The daring young man on the flying trapeze . . .

Lex started to turn in slow motion. His lips moved, but I couldn't hear what he said. Beneath my head the wooden track rumbled. I heard Jimmy roar, "Nooooo . . ." as he was shoved out of the way by Lex.

And then I recognized other faces in the crowd: Chrissie. Susie Faber. Brian Ferguson. All these children—all these in-nocent children—sick, forever, because of this man.

"Remember the children . . . ," I whispered, and I rolled over and pushed myself up with my hands—which were shaking so much that I collapsed again. The rumbling, the vibrating beneath my head was getting louder, louder . . . People were running over to me, but I looked up and saw that it would be too late. The next roller coaster, full of children, was speeding down the last hill right toward me. It started to slow as it approached the platform, but it wasn't enough; it couldn't stop. I rolled off the track just in time to grasp the fact that it was going to smash into the end of the empty car still on the platform.

"Super Mom! You bitch!" Lex was screaming, stomping around, purple with rage. "You're through! Through! No one can touch me! No one can touch Lex Osborne! I own this town—do you hear me? Screw the children! The precious, precious children!"

And something hot burned in my veins, bucked up my jellied spine, filled my ears with such righteous anger that I could no longer hear that tinny tune. I pulled my gaze away from the past and fastened it firmly on the future. Kelly and Martin were beautiful teenagers. They had been beautiful babies. They would be beautiful adults.

And I had more to do now than just chase my memories down a sidewalk pitted with sadness and loss. I had bad guys to fight, children to protect.

I was Super Mom.

"NOOO!" My Super Mom Sense vibrated, filled my chest, pushed the mighty roar out of my throat and I followed it, springing to my feet, pointing at the oncoming roller coaster. And with a rolling, tickling sensation, fluid came surging out of both my hands, joining into one enormous stream with enough force to stop a roller coaster full of innocent children inches before it slammed into the parked cars. Then, stronger, more powerful than ever, I turned to Lex.

"This is for Chrissie," I said as I grabbed him by the ear. "And this is for Susie." I popped the soap into his mouth. "And for Brian." I shoved it in and out. "Sarah, Kevin, Scott!" I yanked the soap out. Lex spluttered, gagged, choked. I hauled him across the platform. "Are you taking pictures of this?" I asked a stunned Jimmy, then dragged Lex to Police Commissioner Borden's corner.

"Now. Tell him. Everything."

"I—I—we—we—" And he did. He spit and snarled and cried and told it all. About the subliminal messages, the Patriot Pops, the Oralsulin, the kickbacks from Moulton Pharmaceuticals. When he was done, he collapsed onto the floor, a frothing, foaming, quivering mass of self-made maliciousness.

Police Commissioner Borden remained with his nose in the corner.

"You can come out now," I gently told him. He hung his head.

"Oh, Super Mom, I'm sorry—" Then he snapped out of it and reached for his handcuffs, grabbing Lex by his elegant wrists.

"Mo— Super Mom!" Kelly came running up to me, followed by Carrie, Howard, and Chrissie. I turned to face them with my legs apart, my hands on my hips. And that's when I saw Martin step out of the crowd—followed by a scowling Greg and a grave Carl. Our eyes met, and I took a step toward him. But then I felt a tug on my skirt. I looked down. A little girl with red hair grinned up at me, her two front teeth missing.

"Thuper Mom! Thuper Mom!" she lisped. "You dropped thith!" She held up my dish towel cape, the fringe all torn; I felt my shoulders and pulled away a clothespin that was hanging by a flapping piece of fabric.

"Thank you." I bent down to take it from her.

"You know what?"

"What?"

"I want to be jutht like you when I grow up!"

"You do?" She nodded. "Well, then, I think you should have it." I pinned the cape to her and her eyes grew enormous.

"Don't you need it?" she whispered.

"I think I know where I can get another." I smiled and looked over at Carl.

But he was gone.

"Speech! Speech!" Howard kicked off his high heels and tossed his wig in the air.

"Speech! Speech!" Carrie, Chrissie, Martin and Kelly echoed.

"I . . . uh . . . that is, well, thanks . . ." I looked up at the sky, as only something that vast and changeable could contain the words I needed—the words that could possibly express what I was feeling right then. But the stars twinkled knowingly; the words did not exist. So I had to make do with the usual superhero stuff. "I, um, pledge to the citizens of Astro Park that I will keep every child safe, every park bench clean, every person who harbors evil in his heart toward children"—I kicked at Lex on the ground—"behind bars. Now, go have fun, you guys! And when you get home, brush your teeth, clean your rooms, and listen to your mothers!" I saluted jauntily. Then I bandaged a few scrapes and signed some autographs.

"Look this way!" Jimmy called out, raising his camera. I

turned, put my stilettoed foot on top of Lex's belly and smoothed my hair. "Say—say—"

"Cleanup on Aisle Four!" Martin called out.

I grinned.

Flash!

CHAPTER
24

Fortunately for Super Mom, the citizens of Astro Park were so grateful that she managed to get Moulton Pharmaceuticals to provide their children with free Oralsulin for life that they almost forgave her for putting half the town out of work. After Lex was thrown in jail, New Cosmos closed and Patty and Harry sold the house and moved out of state. Which left an opening for PTA president that Carrie was more than happy to fill.

Cobblepot, however, disappeared into the mountains of Japan. The rumor was he joined a Buddhist monastery, leaving poor Lolly to a lifetime of frozen dinners and boxes which would remain forever unpacked.

But most fortunately for Super Mom, all charges against her were dropped. It turned out that Jamie Flugal, the Total Asswipe, was diabetic too. His parents were so thrilled about the free Oralsulin that they decided maybe their son hadn't exactly told the truth, after all. And suddenly everyone else started changing their minds about the events of that afternoon in the schoolyard.

And when Martin came home late from school one day, his jacket collar ripped, I took a page from my daughter's book and didn't say a word.

But when he came home the next day in the same shape, only sporting a big grin and walking rather jauntily, I couldn't keep quiet.

"Well?"

"Well?" He pushed the hair out of his eyes to reveal a big shiner.

"Martin!"

"Don't worry," he said, still grinning. "Jamie Flugal looks even worse than me."

"Well, good," I said, grinning too. Because even a sick kid can be a total asswipe.

CHAPTER 25

WORLD EXCLUSIVE! SUPER MOM BRINGS DOWN EVIL EMPIRE! *By Jimmy Nelson, correspondent.*

"Yuck! I hate this picture. My stomach is sticking out a little . . . and look, I think I'm getting a double chin!"

"Oh, Mom." Kelly sighed. "You sound just like Grandma."

"Wash your mouth out, young lady!"

"Make me."

"I could, you know."

"Yes." She smiled. "I know."

She got up to put a glass away and another newspaper— the *Astro Daily World*, folded back to page three—fell to the floor. She blushed as I picked it up and read the two-inch classified ad.

To the parents and children of Mrs. Flynn's second-grade class of 1998, from Doctor Dan Lee, Dermatologist. I apologize for the trauma I may have caused you by inadvertently giving my wife at the time the incorrect videotape to take to Career Day. It was not her fault the class saw a small snippet of a mature videotape featuring me and my current wife, which was tastefully done at all costs. I also apologize to my ex-wife for the distress this may have caused, and I would like to stress that she was not to blame for the mix-up.

"Well," I said. Then I studied Kelly, who was chewing on a fingernail. "Are you OK, honey?"

She nodded. "Yeah, he talked to me about it. Why did you cover for him, all this time?"

"Because I was an idiot," I said simply. "OK? We're both to blame for what happened—not just one of us, but both of us. It took me too long to understand that."

"Dad, Harry . . . men." Kelly clicked her tongue. "I'm never getting married."

"Don't say that, sweetie. Don't ever say that. There are good men out there . . ." Then I looked at my hands and sighed.

"Mom. Just tell him. You know you want to."

I smiled and tucked her hair behind her ear. And then I let her make me lunch.

"I fixed your heel," Martin said, coming into the kitchen with my shoe in one hand and a tube of Super Glue in the other. "This should hold up."

"The air-pump soles were genius, you know," I told him. He grinned.

Just then we heard a thump at the door. Kelly looked out the kitchen window.

"What's that? I just saw this flash of red outside. . . ."

Martin and I looked at each other, then raced to the door.

"It's here! It's here!" I picked up the envelope edged in gold—*JLA* on the seal.

"What is it?" Kelly peered over my shoulder.

"Let me read it, let me!" Martin jumped up and down.

"OK." I smiled and brushed back his floppy hair. "Trusty sidekick."

" 'Congratulations,' " he read. " 'We are pleased to inform you that you have passed all requirements for membership in the JLA. By bringing down the evil empire of New Cosmos Industries and exposing the dangerous plot to sicken the children of Astro Park, you have proven yourself to be a true superhero indeed—' Mom! You did it!"

"I did, didn't I?" I sat down and closed my eyes. I was used to feeling proud about the children. But not about myself. It was strange and I felt a little bit guilty, as if pride were a precious commodity you had to measure out in small doses. And like any good mother, I was used to sacrificing my own portion for my children.

But for once I allowed myself my full share. And it filled me up, nourished me, gave my skin a healthy glow.

" 'You and your family are invited to attend a special presentation at Club DC, where you'll have the opportunity to purchase one week at our lovely vacation property in the Caribbean, at a special one-time-only low price—' "

"Is this a time-share presentation?" Kelly frowned.

"No, honey, no. I'm a bona fide superhero now. A member of the Justice League of America. Right, Martin?"

He nodded. "Ooh—wait till you hear this next part! 'And we have determined who your superhero mentor will be. After much consideration, we have decided to pair you up with one of our most beloved superheroes, a superhero who needs no introduction to you, I'm sure. It is our pleasure to announce that your mentor for the next year will be none other than . . .

" 'Wonder Woman.' Wonder Woman?! *Wonder Woman!*" Martin fell down on the floor and started shaking all over. Kelly and I just stared at him, astonished. "Wonder Woman! My mom is going to be friends with Wonder Woman! Do you think she'll come over for dinner? How about birthdays? Maybe she'll start dropping in now and then, you know, just to talk about work and stuff? Maybe she'll go on vacation with us, do you think? Maybe she'll—"

"God, Martin. Get a grip." Kelly wrinkled her freckled nose and stepped regally over her twitching brother.

"Well." I reached down and hauled him to his feet. "Whatever happens, I'm sure she'll be a very nice person. Wonder Woman. Wow." I giggled.

"I just can't wait to meet her!"

"Mother, we have to go now!" Kelly called up the stairs.

"Now?"

"Now! We have a very tight schedule!"

"All right." I sighed. I gave my eyelashes one last curl, then studied myself in the mirror.

Every morning I looked at my reflection expecting to see a superhero. But I didn't. I just saw me, with the same pale face and big brown eyes, brown hair, brown clothes. Birdie—a little wren. A little brown wren. Not a superhero. Just a woman.

Yet sometimes when I came home after a night of fighting crime, I could walk by the mirror and be surprised at who I saw. Someone with sparkling eyes, a determined face, cheeks flushed with the thrill of accomplishment. An Amazon who could fight all the battles that came her way, who could create order out of chaos, make heroic sacrifices for those who only ignored her and took her for granted . . .

In other words, a mom. A super mom.

"Mother!" Kelly hollered. "We have got to go!"

"All right, all right." I smiled hopefully at my reflection. Then I ran downstairs.

"Are you ready to do this?" Kelly brushed my collar and straightened my necklace.

"No." I reached out and stroked her cheek, touched by her concern.

"Tough beans," Martin said.

"You have to do this, Mother."

"I do?"

My wise daughter nodded.

"OK," I squeaked. "Do I look OK?"

"Yes, Mom, you do. You really do."

"Is it going to get all mushy?" Martin slumped down into his army jacket.

"I hope so." I smiled at him. What a brave guy he really was. Why didn't I know that before?

"Well, then, to the Mom Mobile." He tossed me the keys, and we all ran out to my little dented minivan and drove away. Or rather, we drove to . . .

A certain scientist's split-level house.

"OK." I took a big breath when I pulled up. "OK." But I didn't move.

"Mom, you're not going to chicken out, are you?"

"No, no. No, I'm not." But I gripped the steering wheel so tightly, I accidentally shot some cleaning fluid out of my left hand; I still wasn't used to being ambidextrous. "Oops."

"C'mon, Mom." Kelly reached over and pried my fingers, one by one, off the wheel. Then she gave me a gentle shove out the door. "Here." She thrust the newspaper into my hand and pushed me up the sidewalk. "We'll hide over there!" And she joined Martin behind a big evergreen bush.

I rang the doorbell. Then I started to leave.

"See, he's not home and—"

"Birdie?"

I froze, then slowly turned back around. There was Carl standing in his doorway with that stupid—beautiful—Rocky and Bullwinkle sweatshirt on, the one he wore the first time at the park. He looked down at me, blinked, then smiled.

"It's not every day I get a visit from a real live superhero. Or should I say—a Super Mom?"

"Both." I blushed and looked at the ground. I was still getting used to this fame business, this heroine stuff. It was a hard mantle to adjust to—especially when you were only five feet three inches and used to being called cute.

"I always knew you could do it." His voice was so warm and kind—it gave me hope. It gave me the courage to look into his eyes once more—to dare to take that first step across the tightrope, that first step back to us.

"I—I— Here." I shoved this week's copy of the *National Enquirer* at him. "Read this."

" 'Mild-mannered Grocery Clerk in Love, by Jimmy Nelson—' " Carl looked up, that adorable pucker appearing above his eyes, those deep dimples bracketing his mouth. I nodded, unable to take my eyes away from his face.

" 'Birdie Lee, of Astro Park, Kansas, would like to tell everybody she's ever met' "—he started to grin—" 'that she has fallen in love with Carl Sayers, fellow PTA parent, scientist, and all-around good guy. "There's no need to hide the truth anymore," the tiny grocery clerk said. "I love this man and I can only hope that he loves me in return. And if he doesn't, then I will sleep outside on his porch every night until he finally realizes we were meant for each other."

" 'Stalker, or lovesick heroine? Could this mild-mannered

grocery clerk and mother of two turn into an obsessed stalker with nefarious intentions? Stay tuned to find out!' "

"Well," I said, blushing again. "It is the *National Enquirer*."

"Yes, it is." Carl folded the paper and cleared his throat. "Birdie?"

"Yes?" Now I was afraid to look into his eyes—all my courage left me, just drained out of the bottom of my feet and left me standing before him, unable to move.

"Birdie." I felt a hand upon my chin, lifting it up—lifting me up—taking me by the arm, enfolding me, bringing me . . .

Home.

"Oh, Birdie," Carl murmured as he swept me up in his arms, nuzzled my hair, my cheek, my throat.

"Oh, Carl," I murmured back as my lips found his and we both drank from each other. I grabbed his neck and held on for dear life as the two of us were swept back into our own magical world—and it was right here, in his doorway. And in his living room. My living room. The street in front of his house. The parking lot at Marvel Food and Fine Beverages. It was anywhere, and everywhere. Just as long as we were together, we would create our own moon glow and bring it with us wherever we went, and it would make us both stronger. I understood that now.

"Do you forgive me?" I rubbed my face against his shirt, drinking in his smell—today a little more vanilla than wood smoke.

"Of course. There's nothing to forgive."

"Dad?" We turned and faced Greg, moving as one.

"Mom?" Still together, we spun back around to Kelly and Martin.

Kelly clapped her hands, her eyes glowing. "Oh, you two are so cute!"

Martin and Greg rolled their eyes and glowered at each other.

"Mom! It's happening!" Martin tugged at my shirt.

"Oh!" And I took my love by the hand and led him out to his front yard.

"Look," Greg said, pointing.

"Up in the sky!" Martin shouted.

"It's a bird," said Kelly. "It's a plane! It's—"

"No way." Carl looked at me, his eyes wide and eager as a little boy's. "No way! It can't be!"

"It is!" I crooked my arm through his and looked up at the sky . . .

Where the words BIRDIE LOVES CARL were being written, faster than a speeding bullet, in white plumes.

"How did you—how did you—"

"It's a perk. Exclusive to members of the Justice League of America." I smiled a little smugly. "He also does birthday parties."

All of a sudden a streak of red-yellow-and-blue flew over us, a jaunty hand raised in salute.

"Thanks, Superman!" I called out.

"No problem, Super Mom!" His words echoed as he flew away, leaping tall buildings in a single bound.

Cars were stopping in the street, with people getting out and looking up at the sky at our message, our declaration—our love.

"All right!" a voice called out.

"Let's hear it for Carl and Birdie," somebody else hooted.

"Let's hear it for Super Mom," Carl whispered in my ear.

Soon all sorts of cars were driving by, honking their approval. Carl and I just stood there holding hands and grinning like idiots while Kelly swooned around us, clapping her hands, and Martin and Greg scowled on opposite ends of the porch.

And I knew, finally, what it was to dream. For it was a dream, wasn't it? Wasn't a dream just something you longed for even when you didn't know it, even when someone else had to point it out to you? Whether or not you were asleep didn't matter. The best dreams, I thought, watching Superman streak across the cloudless sky and feeling Carl's arm loose but steady around my waist, were the ones you wished for with your eyes wide open.

That way you could see how easy it was to make them come true.

ACKNOWLEDGMENTS

Like any superhero, I can't do everything on my own; I have my own personal Justice League of America who helped me use my superpowers to their fullest:

Heartfelt thanks go to Laura Langlie, whose respect and passion for writers and writing, and whose belief in me, got me through the tough times; to Laurie Chittenden for seeing the possibility and turning it into reality; and to Erika Kahn for all her patience and help. I also want to thank Mike Miller, brother and walking encyclopedia of all things superhero; my brother and sister-in-law Mark and Stephanie Miller for their enthusiasm and support; my mother, Pat Miller, for introducing me to books, and to my father, Norman Miller, for teaching me the value of hard work. Thanks to Joyce Greening for bringing Super Mom's costume to life. I am blessed to know many authors whose support has been invaluable, but special thanks go to David Kedson for friendship and support above and beyond the call of duty, and especially to Nicole Hayes—best critique partner, and best friend, an author could ever have. And a special "OK, Miss Smarty Pants, you were right" to Lori Bales, who knew I was a writer before I did.

And last but never least, Dennis Hauser, Alec Hauser, and Ben Hauser: Who needs a butler when I've got you guys around?

Super Mom's work is never done. Astor Park's Mayor Linseed reveals his plans to build a new ballpark and sports complex to bring money and attention to the town; but when the park's construction progresses, a potentially deadly gas pocket is discovered beneath it. Despite the danger, the corrupt mayor continues with the construction project, putting at risk the innocent lives of Astro Park's Little Leaguers and their winning-obsessed parents. Who else but Super Mom can save the day—and teach her town a lesson or two about the dangerously competitive nature of youth sports—all while juggling her two teenage children (one of whom is learning to drive—*gasp!*), keeping her jealous ex-husband at bay, and planning a wedding to her very own Super Man, while they figure out how to merge two households into one?

What happens when a normal, PTA-fearing mother of two teenagers suddenly finds herself thrust into a new career at the tender age of forty-one?

And what if that career happens to involve an entirely new wardrobe, including high heels (which she hasn't worn in decades) and underwire bras (ditto)?

Furthermore, what if the job description includes keeping the world safe for democracy and engaging in hand-to-hand combat with really evil villains with unusual names?

Well, apparently she starts hearing voices.

At least, that's what happened to me, after a full six months on the job as the newest kid on the superhero block, that maternal dynamo known as—

Super Mom. (That's me.)

I'd just come home from yet another busy day of fighting crime. I stumbled up to the back door tired, cranky because I'd forgotten my key, but then realized that it wasn't necessary because the extra set was dangling from the doorknob, practically sending out an engraved invitation to any interested evil villains to c'mon in and take their best shot at me. I sighed, pulled the keys out of the doorknob and pushed the door open with my shoulder, because it's old and it sticks.

"Who left the keys in the back door?" I called, stumbling over the pile of discarded tennis shoes, flip-flops, snow boots and chunky platform wedges just inside the door, none of which was mine. I flipped on the kitchen light, only to shield my eyes from the devastation—the open cabinets, dirty dishes and globs of peanut butter—that greeted me. "Well, I have had it," I muttered, tightening my Apron of Anticipation around my waist, preparing myself for a final, epic battle between good and evil.

(I'm good, for those keeping score.)

"Martin," I called, my hands on my hips. "Pick up your shoes! Kelly, get that backpack out of the way! Has it occurred to anyone around here to close a cabinet door lately? And what have I told you about turning out these lights? Money doesn't grow on trees, you know!"

I was met by a menacing silence that set my Super Mom sense on high alert; I whirled around, tense, ready for the onslaught of an enemy more terrifying than any villain imagined—*Teenagers.*

(They're evil, in case you're still keeping score.)

"Mom, I'll just have to put them on again tomorrow, so what's the use? Jeez!"

"Mother, please! I'll get it later when I do my homework! Have you tried lifting that thing, anyway? Do you want me to put my back out by bringing it all the way up to my room?"

I tugged on the offending backpack, crammed full of high school textbooks; even with my superpowers, I couldn't lift it. So I kicked it out of the way and sighed dramatically, just in

case anyone was paying attention to me. Then I trudged upstairs, untying my Apron of Anticipation, shaking out the dirt
and cookie crumbs that had settled into the pockets—and
bumped into two huge piles of laundry in the hallway. Stepping around them, I tripped over an empty soda can somebody had left in the middle of the hall—only to discover that
it wasn't really empty.

My chest started to vibrate. I clenched my fists, reared my
head back and felt my mouth almost split my face in two.

"ALL RIGHT! THAT'S IT! I HAVE HAD IT. I CANNOT
LIVE IN A PIGSTY ANYMORE. NO ALLOWANCE THIS
WEEK. DO YOU HEAR ME? NO ALLOWANCE!"

My Mighty Roar thundered through the house; mirrors
shook, dishes rattled and I cringed, just waiting. Sure enough,
I heard a huge crash accompanied by the tinkling of shattered glass.

"Mom, that's the second picture this week!" My children
confronted me at the foot of the stairs, their arms folded over
their chests, twin pillars of martyrdom.

"Can't you learn to control yourself?" Kelly arched one
golden eyebrow.

"Now who's going to clean it up?" Martin shook his head.

"Sorry," I mumbled. "Sorry. It just—came out." I took a
deep breath, worked up some quick tears and pulled another
weapon out of my arsenal. *Super Guilt Trip.*

"It's just that I've been a little busy today, fighting crime
and all," I whispered, wiping my eyes with the corner of my
Apron. "I'm sorry if I seem a little cranky—but I did stay up
late last night doing all this laundry. But never mind." I sighed
and sat down on the top step, showing off the cuts and bruises
on my hands, hitching my costume up to reveal a giant gash

on my knee from an earlier battle. (Me versus the Ice Cream Man from Hell, who was notorious for driving away with little kids' change and not giving them their Push-ups. I won. Just in case—you know, the score thing.)

"I'll find the time to put it away for you," I said with a groan. "I'll just have to get up earlier tomorrow, go without my own breakfast, maybe let an evildoer or two slip through the cracks—but that's fine. I don't mind. That's what mothers do, you know. . . ."

"Oh, please." Martin grinned in that patronizing way he inherited from his father; Kelly shook her head.

"Come here, young lady." I sat up straight, my Super Mom Sense—which alerted me to the first sign of a child in trouble—tingling the back of my neck. "What on earth have you done to yourself?" I grabbed a hunk of her glossy blond hair—which was shot through with bright pink streaks—and yanked on it.

"Ow! Oh, that." She shrugged. "Vienna thought it would look cool, so she did it for me after school. It's no big thing, Mother, so stop looking at me like I pierced my tongue."

"Vienna? Tell me, what kind of person names their daughter after a city? And if Vienna thought it would look so cool, why didn't she put one in her own hair?"

"She did. It's purple."

"Oh."

"I'm hungry," Martin interrupted. "There's nothing to eat. When's the last time you went to the grocery store?"

"Well, excuse me. I was a little busy saving the world. But there's plenty to eat. I think I counted fourteen boxes of cereal."

"There's nothing good."

"Why don't we go out to Wally's Pizza Station? We haven't been there in ages. Remember how much you love the little train that brings the pizza to the tables?" I perked up, feeling the burden of being a superhero and a mother of teenagers slide off my shoulders; we always have a good time at Wally's Pizza Station. Plus you get free breadsticks.

"Mother, really. I wouldn't be caught dead in that place." Kelly twisted a pink strand of hair around her finger and admired it.

"It's a little lame," Martin agreed. "Can't we just order in?"

"I guess . . ."

"Forget about me. I'm going to Vienna's to study. She's picking me up in a minute."

"She can drive?"

"Yes, and she's a safe driver, so don't worry."

"Kelly, I'm not so sure. I hardly know her and I've not met her parents and—"

My daughter narrowed her gray eyes at me, put her hands on her hips and hit me with her best shot, simply by asking a question. The Question. The Question that punches every parent in the gut no matter how many times it's asked—and answered: *"Don't you trust me?"*

And the thing is, I do. So far. But sometimes it seems that by saying so, I'm giving her permission to run off and do some terrible, unspeakable thing. Like knock off a couple of liquor stores with a sawed-off shotgun.

"I . . . well, of course I do . . ." I stammered, helpless, my superpowers failing me.

"Thanks, Mom!" She granted me a quick kiss on the cheek. Then she ran off to unearth the perfect pair of chunky wedge shoes from the pile downstairs.

I studied Martin, who, being the younger sibling, knows far too much. If he wasn't my son, I might have to kill him. "What are you looking at?"

"Nothing." He grinned. "Don't forget to order the pizza—pepperoni."

"Right." I sighed as he retreated to his lair to do whatever it is he does when I'm not around. Then I surveyed the piles of laundry surrounding me: faded underwear and mismatched socks and bras held together with safety pins. I plucked out a pair of sweatpants, T-shirt, comfy bra (meaning no underwire) and retreated to my own lair to change clothes and wonder what Wonder Woman was doing tonight. Probably getting a deep-tissue massage from some man slave.

As for me, I trudged downstairs, grabbed a broom and dustpan and swept up the glass from the broken picture frame, then called for the pizza delivery. I made quick work of the kitchen, taking full advantage of my ability to clean with the power of ten thousand Swiffers, which was by far the most practical of the superpowers I had acquired since suffering my Horrible Swiffer Accident last fall. (*Swiffer, by the way, is a remarkable cleaning product that I heartily endorse, and which was not responsible for my Horrible Swiffer Accident, as I had violated the warranty by negligently pouring dangerous combinations of household cleaners in the reservoir and inhaling their fumes due to improper ventilation.)

When I was done with the dustpan, I put it away in the cabinet under the sink. But as I did so, I knocked something over—I heard a metallic thunk—so I knelt down, reached

---

*Just a little legal mumbo jumbo that Proctor and Gamble "suggested" I use from now on.

past the five dozen paper bags, neatly folded, that I keep in there for no apparent reason other than genetics (there are five dozen identical bags underneath my mother's kitchen sink) and grabbed the knocked-over can. I pulled it out, saw that it was a very old can of shower cleaner, chuckled a bit at the idea of me, Super Mom, using a plain old commercial household cleanser, and was about to toss it in the trash when I heard a little "chirrup."

I stopped, looked around me, shook my head, then started toward the trash again.

"Purrupp," chirped something. Something *adorable*, because it was the cutest, brightest little sound you've ever heard.

"Did somebody bring a puppy home?" I called. Neither of my children answered. I bit my lip, opened the cabinet where the trash can was stored and dropped the can—

Only to hear a slightly anguished "ooohhggooogoooo . . ." as it fell into the trash can, down, down, down . . .

And that's when I yelped.

"God, Mother, get a grip," my daughter said as she regally made her way across the kitchen and picked up her backpack with ease. "Are you starting to talk to yourself now?"

"No, but . . . I swear . . ." I looked into the trash. The can of shower cleaner—rusty along the edges, the label faded so that the Scrubbing Bubbles' eyes weren't quite so brightly black—lay nestled among Pop-Tart wrappers and yesterday's paper. "That *can* talked to *me*. . . ."

"Mother. Honestly. You are so losing it." But Kelly stopped to give me a hug before she ran out the door to the tune of one car honking.

"Kelly, when will you be home?" I ran to the door and called after her retreating form, just a gray shadow in the dusk.

"Ten!"

"Because I want you home by ten—oh! Well, then, make sure you are. Home by ten." Then I waved pathetically at my teenage daughter as she got in a car driven by a girl I hardly knew, who happened to be named after the capital of Austria. And if recent history has taught us anything, it's that a girl named after a foreign city is going to be trouble. I told myself that it's not my daughter I don't trust. It's everyone else in the world.

I watched the car back out of the driveway. I couldn't tell if Kelly had buckled her seat belt. I also couldn't tell if Vienna was smoking a cigarette. I definitely couldn't tell if there were any open containers of alcohol or lusty teenage boys stashed in the backseat, and because I couldn't tell, I could only begin to imagine, which is never a good thing to do on an empty stomach, a superhero outfit within easy reach.

I wrestled with my conscience for a full twenty seconds. Then I threw some money down on the table for the pizza guy, ran upstairs, pulled on my costume again and hit the streets in my brand-new Mom Mobile (complete with Super Paint Color Changing Panels, to protect my identity).

I may have even snickered with evil maternal glee as I kept a discreet distance behind the VW Beetle that was speeding my daughter away to points unknown. I definitely forgot how tired I was, how hungry, how my high-heeled pumps pinched my feet. I even forgot about the talking can of shower cleaner.

Because the truth is, a Super Mom's job is never done, especially when her own children are involved.